Cleaver
Square

Daniel Campbell

Sean Campbell

Chapter 1: Hackney Marshes

David Morton was not a night owl. He firmly believed that nothing good ever happened between midnight and ten o'clock, and so the arrogant buzzing of his mobile phone shortly before quarter past eight elicited a sleepy groan. He squinted at the screen as its artificial light illuminated his haggard face. It was work. With a sprightliness belying his age, he threw off his half of the cover and leapt to his feet. A lesser man might have questioned why, at fifty-two years of age, he was still willing to jump at a moment's notice. It was not like he had anything to prove any more.

Morton paused to glance down at his long-suffering wife then prodded her gently awake.

'Sarah! Sarah, I've got to go. Can you reschedule our morning tennis game?'

A hand emerged from underneath the marital duvet, gesticulated rudely then withdrew back underneath the warm cover.

David took his wife's dismissive wave as a yes. A crooked smile crept onto his face as he relished the fact that he would not have to spend his Saturday morning playing nice with the in-laws. Being on call did have some perks.

He dressed quietly, and then crept downstairs. Hunger surged through his stomach, and it took considerable effort to ignore the siren calls of the fridge. While he was the Senior Investigating Officer, he still answered to the Superintendent and the boss frowned on any delays getting to a crime scene. Morton blinked to clear the last bit of sleepy-dust from his eyes, and now that they were fully focussed, reread the text message from dispatch, *"Body found encased in ice. Hackney Marshes. Near Kingfisher Wood. Bring wellington boots."*

***

It was almost nine when Detective Chief Inspector David Morton parked up on the north side of Homerton Road. A handful of cars passed him by, travelling much slower than the forty-mile-per-hour limit to avoid careering off the icy road.

There were few pedestrians out and about, but the one man Morton did see studiously avoided eye contact, his head bowed as he passed. Morton reluctantly stepped out of his climate-controlled car, then slammed the door shut as his breath escaped in a cloud of water vapour. An over-the-shoulder beep confirmed that the car was immobilized. A brand new BMW 5 series wouldn't last long if left unlocked, and Morton still had three years left to go on the hire-purchase deal.

He set off towards Kingfisher Wood, his posture hunched as he strained against the wind. A mist had descended on the Marshes, reducing visibility to less than twenty feet. He could see only the ghostly outline of willow trees looming in the distance. Morton navigated towards Kingfisher Wood by keeping the rushing sounds of the Old River Lea firmly on his right.

After ten minutes of huffing and puffing, the crime scene tape emerged from the mist just past the East Marsh Bridge. Morton quickly ducked under the familiar blue and white tape and trudged towards the south end of Kingfisher Wood. He presumed the area had once been populated by swathes of kingfishers, but Hackney had long ago become too built up to sustain many of the jewel-like birds. These days, the open space was mostly used for sports and recreation rather than conservation.

'Chief! Over here!' Detective Inspector Bertram Ayala would have been virtually invisible in the darkness if it were not for the hastily erected floodlights. In contrast to Morton's hastily assumed attire, Ayala was immaculately turned out in a pinstripe suit which made the blue slip-on evidence booties covering his loafers look all the more ridiculous. Morton smirked at the contrast.

'Morning, Ayala.' Morton resisted the urge to wind up the junior officer by using his much-loathed given name. 'What've we got?'

'Partial decomposition. Shallow burial. We've uncovered part of the body. It's face down. Getting it out of the ground is going to take a while as it's mostly frozen,' Ayala said.

'That's January for you. Get a heater going, and stick up a tent. We don't want any looky-loos getting a peek.'

'Yes sir!' Ayala spun on his bootie-clad heel, and disappeared into the darkness.

While the body was still on ice, there was precious little Morton could do. He had thirty-two staff at his disposal. Every one of them would have been roused by the same text alert he'd received almost an hour previously, but it would probably be at least another hour before he had the whole team on-site. A full search of the woods could only be conducted once everyone had arrived.

A peek at the prostrate body didn't reveal much, as muddy ice obscured Morton's view. Through the mud and grass, Morton could see several body parts. Heels, a single slender arm and a rounded skull protruded, a distance of only around five feet between heels and skull. Without context, that wasn't conclusive as the body parts could be scattered, but it looked likely that the victim might be on the shorter side.

'Morning, handsome,' a lilting Welsh voice called out from behind Morton as he stared at the ground. Morton turned to see his second-in-command emerge from the mist holding a cardboard tray full of coffees. The nearest one had an 'M' for Morton pencilled onto the cardboard sleeve.

'Ah, thank you, Tina,' Morton said. He took a sip, then immediately regretted it. The coffee was vile, the kind found in cheap vending machines. It had probably come from the twenty-four hour petrol station around the corner. At least it was hot.

'Short victim. Reckon it's a woman?' Tina asked.

Morton nodded appreciatively. 'Could well be. The body is short enough, but women are rarely murder victims.'

Tina bent down to examine the corpse, being careful not to disturb the remains.

'Who found the body?'

'That guy.' Tina straightened up, then pointed through the fog. Morton followed her gaze to a bespectacled man wearing sodden wet clothes. He was barely visible despite being less than fifteen feet away. A uniformed officer stood by his side.

Morton approached, and began to evaluate his witness. The man wore torn denim jeans and a rugged wool jumper that gave him a dirty, dishevelled look. In his left hand he held a metal detector, with a grip so tight that his knuckles had turned white.

Morton didn't rate him as a potential witness in the courtroom. He had a weak chin, watery eyes and an untrustworthy demeanour. Morton introduced himself, and shook the man's hand. The weak handshake Morton received confirmed his suspicions.

'Sir, what's your name?'

Tina watched from the side as Morton began the interview. She had a notepad in hand, ready to scribble down anything pertinent. Morton didn't bother; his talent for remembering the smallest detail was legendary among the force. His memory wasn't quite eidetic, but with a visual memory retention rate approaching 90 per cent he never forgot anything important.

'R-R-Robert Lyons.' His teeth chattered in the fierce cold as he spoke, forcing Morton to lean in close to understand him. Lyons was shivering fiercely, so Morton emptied the inside pocket of his overcoat before draping it around the man. He clipped his police-issue BlackBerry to a belt loop, and tucked his half-hunter pocket watch into his trousers before turning his attention back to Lyons.

'What were you doing in the woods, Mr Lyons?' Morton continued once Lyons enshrouded himself within the tent-like overcoat.

'Trying to f-f-find metal in the ground. We do it every Saturday.' Lyon's statement would have seemed pointless without context, so Morton asked him to elaborate for the record.

'The North London Diggers Association. We go out in public land with these,' Robert indicated the cumbersome Garrett metal detector, 'and see what we can find. Usually, it's just the odd coin or drinks can.'

'But not today?'

'No. Well, I was walking through the woods...' Lyons began.

'Where from?' Morton interrupted Mr Lyons before he could start to ramble. If a witness built up a head of steam, it could be hard to get them to stop, and Morton needed the specifics.

'The m-m-market.' Robert gestured through the woods to the east. New Spitalfields Market was just the other side of the river.

'And where were you going?'

'I was heading that way.' Robert gestured roughly due west. 'I found a couple of quid in the East Marsh, and then worked my way up through Kingfisher Wood. We're due to meet up back at the car park in about an hour, the one with the recycling bins. We get rid of all the scrap when we're done for the day so we don't end up digging it up again the next week.'

'But today was different?' Morton prompted.

'Yes. I hadn't been out long when the machine started beeping. I dug down a little, and the beeping continued. It took a while until I hit *it*,' he over-pronounced the last word, reluctant to describe the corpse.

'How did you find the body?'

'Just kept digging. It was about two feet down. When the detector went off, and I still hadn't found anything just under the surface I guessed it wasn't something small like the coins I typically find...' Robert cast a skeletal hand towards the body.

'But bodies don't set off detectors. What was it you found?'

Robert turned away, his face briefly sporting a sheepish expression. Morton held his gaze, letting the awkward silence do his interrogation for him. Moments later, Robert turned back to the detective but refused to meet his gaze. Instead, he kept his eyes firmly cast downwards as he thrust his hand into his bag, drawing out a chunky gold watch. Morton turned towards the uniformed officer and summoned an evidence bag with a snap of his fingers. He turned the bag inside out as a makeshift glove and reached for the watch.

'No! It's mine. I call Treasure Trove,' Robert snatched the watch away, twisting his body to shield the watch, in a vain attempt to invoke a legal right that was essentially "finders, keepers".

'Nope, it's evidence in a murder investigation. Besides, that watch isn't old enough to qualify as treasure trove. Hand it over.' Morton held out the bag expectantly.

With a hint of hesitation Robert placed the watch in the palm of Morton's bagged hand. Morton inverted the bag, enveloping the watch in protective plastic. He then pulled the bag's adhesive tag to seal it and handed it to his second-in-command.

'Tina, make sure this stays with the body. Get a uniform to pick up Mr Lyons so he can make a formal statement back at the station.'

There was no cause to believe Robert knew anything more, but Morton wanted his details on record in case he needed to re-interview Robert in light of later evidence.

***

If he could help it, Morton preferred not to assume a dictatorial style with his staff. In his days as a junior officer, he'd been barked at frequently and had soon come to the conclusion that you caught more flies with honey than with vinegar. The Senior Investigating Officer had a number of perks, not the least of which was the freedom to run his cases as he saw fit. To his credit, Morton had an above-par conviction rate, which meant that he was given a lot of latitude. But murder investigations have to be a "by the book" affair. Morton peered through the mists as the team assembled. The mist was starting to clear, but his team still had to huddle in close to him. As well as his team, Morton was joined by staff from the canine unit and forensic services, so he had a sizeable audience to brief.

Morton upturned an empty kit box to make an improvised stand, and began his briefing.

'I want our area search completed first. We need to cover the whole of the Marshes.' A chorus of groans came from the assembled officers. With over three hundred and thirty-six acres to cover, it would be a considerable task. The composition of the Marshes would further complicate matters. An abundance of clay topsoil gave the Marshes their name, which meant that even a light drizzle might wash away pertinent evidence. The sky loomed a dirty grey overhead, threatening a much heavier downpour. They would need to work exceptionally quickly.

'We're taking no chances here, people. The open land shouldn't take too long, so focus your attention on the scrubland and the trees. If you get tired, take a break. We can't afford to miss anything. The press are going to be all over this, and SO2 had better come out of this looking whiter than white. We'll start with the area immediately by the body, and then expand the grid horizontally and vertically. Photographers will lead at the front, while Canine Squad will stay one step behind.'

The search order would be crucial. Photographs would help establish the scene prior to any disturbance, giving Morton a safety net. It would be impossible to secure such a large area for long, especially with opportunities for entry and egress along the river. Keeping digital records would let him revisit the scene in the same state as it was on the day of the search. Likewise, having cadaver dogs on hand should prevent any body parts going missing. As a secondary benefit the sheer size of the dogs would keep the public at bay. Crowds had already begun to amass near the eastern perimeter. Before the briefing, Morton had taken a few surreptitious photographs of the crowd using his mobile phone. Identifying a suspect or even a witness from such photographs was rare, but not unheard of.

'This will be a standard large-area grid search.' This pronouncement elicited another groan. Morton could have allowed them to perform a more basic search where the group would walk in one direction, then turn and come back along the next section. The grid method meant going in one direction and then turning and going forward again. It meant that every inch of ground got covered twice, but would take twice as long.

'Anything we find gets logged with GPS co-ordinates. Get the lot to Detective Vaughn, as she'll be inventorying all evidence today. The whole lot will go on the evidence map, so photograph everything in situ then log it in the evidence register.' The team should know the drill, but the churn of junior officers necessitated giving the whole spiel. Some of the old hands had heard Morton's briefing speech dozens of times before. Detective Inspector Ayala. Your team will begin the canvass. Start with the crowd, and zero in on anyone uncooperative. Don't forget to interview the rest of the North London Diggers Association.'

A few junior officers laughed at the name, then blushed when Morton glared in their direction. While the officers attempted to display contrition, Morton fought to keep his own laughter in check. Ayala recognised his boss's irrepressible urge to tease the new officers, having been the subject of Morton's humour, and winked.

It would be down to Ayala to identify any potential suspects so they could be located later on for re-interview. At this stage the interviews would be used only to garner initial leads rather than to record detailed information.

The initial canvass was a delicate balancing act; the public had to be given the most basic information in order to question them, and to identify follow-up questions, but it would be inappropriate to release too much information too soon. Joggers, dog walkers and early-morning exercise groups often used the Marshes. With a squad of thirty-two, and just twelve working the canvass, it would be impossible to stop everyone attempting to go in or out; in fact, they'd need a team of thousands to secure the whole perimeter. Ayala would have to work with what he had.

'Sergeant...' Morton frowned as he tried to recall the name of the short, balding officer opposite him, one of his newest team members.

'Turing, sir,' the man volunteered.

'Sergeant Turing, you've got babysitting duty. Assist the Forensics Department any way you can, and make sure you log the chain of custody for every sample they take. Once you're done, report back to Detective Vaughn.' Although not part of Special Operations 2, it would be down to the Met's Forensics Department to lift fingerprints and process all trace evidence.

'With this much organic material, you might not find much. This is a standard locate and lift, so focus in on the obvious inorganics.' Forensics would focus in on lampposts, bridges and bins but Morton didn't expect them to yield anything. It was a relatively high-traffic area so many prints would be smudged, and until the body was excavated, they wouldn't know how long it had been since the murderer had been on the scene.

'Get to it, people!'

Chapter 2: Charlie

Charlie Matthews sat in the back seat of his social worker's Mercedes, and fiddled with the buttons on his overcoat. He wouldn't have had to wear the coat, but the car's heater was broken and so they'd been forced to drive with the windows open to prevent their breath clouding up the windscreen. Apart from that minor fault, Charlie thought the car was the nicest he'd even been in.

It wasn't a long trip, but congestion had hampered their journey, an inevitable consequence of driving in central London. There was no satellite navigation system calling out directions, so Charlie had no way of benchmarking how far there was left to go. It appeared his driver knew London well enough not to need directions.

As they drove, bubblegum pop blared from the sound system, mitigating the otherwise awkward silence. Charlie's head bobbed along to the rhythm, and he was glad he didn't have to talk to the older man. Charlie had never been much of a talker. Social workers tried hard, but there was only so much they had in common with their young charges, and Charlie was no ordinary child.

'Are we nearly there?' Charlie's tongue almost tripped over the words.

Glacial blue eyes pierced the mirror, searching out the boy. Charlie recoiled as their gazes met, ice running through his veins. Hank had a pleasant, handsome face with high cheekbones and pearly white teeth, but something about him made Charlie's stomach churn.

'We'll be there soon, Charlie,' Hank's deep voice surged over the radio and resonated in the confines of the car. The warmth of his dulcet tones contrasted sharply with his angular features.

Charlie nodded hesitantly. There was nothing else to say. His second family in as many months. This time, he promised himself, he wouldn't let himself care. If he never unpacked his bag then he couldn't be abandoned. It's only a temporary home, he told himself.

Just like last one had been.

***

Morton had abandoned the junior detectives to finish the initial search in favour of a bacon sandwich in the warmth of his car. In between mouthfuls, he thumbed the push-to-talk button on his radio and hailed Tina.

'How's it looking, Detective Inspector Vaughn?' Morton's voice crackled over the encrypted radio.

'I've got a wallet, three plasters and a single trainer. Nothing to suggest a connection between those and our victim. We've still got a huge amount of ground to cover. The rain isn't helping. Any chance the departmental budget could stretch to a round of decent coffees and a bite to eat? There's a bakery around the corner.'

'There's no chance of you getting that expense claim through. Send Ayala out for a round of drinks, and I'll reimburse you when he gets back.' Morton would be out of pocket, but it was a cheap price to pay for the morale boost it would engender, and it would repay Tina for the early morning coffee round.

'Sure,' Tina's tone lifted, the smile in her voice self-evident.

'The search team have got another dozen acres to cover, so we'll aim to break for the day when it gets dark at around four o'clock. We'll have uniforms secure the area immediately around the crime scene, and resume at dawn tomorrow.'

'What time is sunrise?' Tina asked.

'08:05. See you in half an hour, and make sure Ayala doesn't forget my sweetener.'

Morton sighed inwardly. Ayala was bound to forget again.

***

With a flick of his wrist, Hank Williams killed the motor, and then adjusted his rear-view mirror to survey the boy in the backseat.

'Charlie, we're here.'

Charlie stepped out into Cleaver Square for the first time. From the green in the centre, it was impossible to see the main road that they'd just pulled in from, which gave the square an isolated feel. There were grandiose townhouses running up and down both sides of the green, but Charlie's destination, Number 36B, was a handsome house even when judged against its neighbours.

'Come on, Charlie, don't be shy.' Hank unloaded Charlie's meagre possessions from the boot. All Charlie had in the world was a simple leather case and a rucksack, both of which Hank carried easily in one oversized hand. Charlie continued to stare at the house, wondering if there would be other children with him.

Without a second warning, Hank scooped Charlie up over his shoulder in a fireman's lift, and bundled him out of the car. A dozen giant strides later, Hank set Charlie down on the doorstep, and knocked on the heavy oak door with his bare knuckles three times in quick succession. Footsteps echoed inside the house, and before Charlie could count to ten he heard a series of locks clicking as they were unlocked. He froze as the door swung inwards, a deer in headlights. A larger-than-life woman appeared in the doorway. She was much taller than Charlie, and wider still. Charlie's first impression was that of a stern matron.

'Hello. I'm Mrs Lattimer, and you must be Charlie.' Mrs Lattimer ran a hand over her plaited hair as she spoke. She was smiling, but it was a superficial kind of smile that didn't reach her beady black eyes.

'Hello,' Charlie squeaked.

'Mrs Lattimer, I'm Hank Williams. I don't think we've met before. I've got the usual paperwork for you to sign; may I step inside please?'

'By all means. Let's sort this paperwork out, and then I'll give Charlie the grand tour.' She spoke with an affected middle-class accent, but the way she failed to enunciate the letter t was classic cockney.

Mrs Lattimer led the pair down a narrow corridor. The walls were covered in embroidered wallpaper which gave the passage a tactile feel, but the pink floral decor was more reminiscent of an old-fashioned tea shop than a family home. The first door they passed was slightly ajar, and Charlie could smell smoke inside as if someone was sat in front of an old-fashioned wood fire. He paused to snatch a glance inside, where a man of about Mrs Lattimer's age sat in a wing-backed leather chair reading a newspaper.

They carried on further, past a spiral staircase, and Charlie began to realise just how big the house was. The steps led down as well as up. Number 36B had a basement. As they finally reached the back of the house the pink wallpaper gave way to a plain coat of blue paint, and Charlie found himself in a Victorian style walk-through larder where enormous packages of rice, pasta and other staples lined the shelves.

Seeing Charlie stare around the larder, Mrs Lattimer chirped up, 'You can never be too careful, dear. You'll never know what you might need. Just last November, we got snowed in for the better part of a month.'

At the back of the larder, partially hidden behind a mishmash of storage boxes, a doorway led through to a large country-style kitchen complete with AGA stove and a huge oak dining table that could easily seat a dozen people. What really drew Charlie's attention wasn't the room itself, but the way the floor appeared to disappear at the back with only a handrail visible. Out of curiosity, Charlie tiptoed towards the rail. The glass roof carried on several feet further, but the kitchen floor did not.

There was one more door to go through at the back of the larder.

'Mrs Lattimer...' Charlie pointed at the empty space.

'Oh, don't worry, dear, it's a light well. Without it, the basement would be dark and full of mould.'

Charlie gripped the guardrail tightly, locking his thumb around the bar for safety, and then carefully leant over the railing. He peered down at a glass and PVC roof set at ground level so that rain ran off into a gutter. Beneath the glass, he could see a number of toys, and a top-heavy bookshelf loaded with leather bound books as well as the occasional knick-knack.

Charlie was wondering who the toys belonged to when Hank's baritone voice brought him back to the conversation, 'Thank you, Mrs Lattimer, we're all done. Goodbye, Charlie!'

Hank snatched up the signed papers, and retreated. It was clear he was intending to let himself out. His footsteps faded out of earshot, and Charlie heard the heavy front door shut with a thud.

Mrs Lattimer's tone changed immediately, 'Listen up, you little toe rag. This is my house, and you live by my rules. No running. No swearing. No shouting. You cause me any trouble, I'll hand you straight back to Children's Services.

'Chores are to be done daily. Each morning you'll get up at six. Mr Lattimer and I rise at seven thirty. I expect breakfast to be on the table by then, and the house to be spotless. I will not be driving you to school, so you'll need to be gone by eight. Do you understand me?'

Charlie edged towards the kitchen doorway. His instincts said to run, but he had nowhere to run to.

'Do you understand?' she repeated, leaning over him.

Without uttering a word, Charlie nodded meekly.

Chapter 3: Dissection

A lingering sweetness hit Morton the moment he stepped out of the elevator, and onto the floor that housed the morgue. It was part of the New Scotland Yard complex but felt a million miles away from the hustle and bustle of the workspace Morton used every day. It was so quiet that Morton could hear every footstep he took echoing on the laminate floor.

As Morton headed for Autopsy Room #3 he passed simple paintings hung on the fastidiously clean walls. They were obviously intended to lighten the mood, but to Morton's eyes the primary colours seemed almost mocking, as if the dead had no right to the dignity of a sombre death. When Morton reached the shuttered steel double doors, built to comfortably accommodate the width of a gurney, he could see the coroner inside. Dr Larry Chiswick seemed almost vampiric in appearance. Even in sunshine he looked pallid, as if he might be joining his charges any day, but in the harsh fluorescent lighting of the morgue the effect was exaggerated.

Without knocking, Morton opened the left-hand side of the door and stepped foot into Dr Chiswick's domain.

The room was devoid of the cheerful pictures in the corridor. Instead, the coroner's tools were arrayed over every visible surface. Racks and shelves housed saws, brushes and all manner of tools. There were no seats, so Morton had to clear a patch of workbench before he parked himself on it.

Morton tapped his fingers on the bench as he waited for the coroner to notice his presence. Larry was infamous for making detectives wait. Morton shrugged; the body wasn't going anywhere. As he waited, his gaze fixed upon the sheet covering the body he was there to see. It had been removed from the body bag and cleaned up by the diener. Scraps of clothing had been bagged, ready to be sent for particulate analysis. Vials, which appeared at first glance to be empty, were arranged in neat columns nearby. Straining to see from the other side of the room, Morton read the small labels which identified various trace particles found on the body. Samples had been taken from underneath the victim's fingernails, between his toes and from his hair.

After a few minutes of Dr Chiswick's pointedly ignoring his visitor, Morton rose from the workbench and strode towards the body. In one clean motion, Morton teased the sheet downwards towards the sternum, revealing the upper half of the corpse. At the opposite end, feet poked out from under the sheet. The toe tag read Joe Bloggs #0113/103, denoting an anonymous corpse. The torso was virtually gone. Slivers of grey-white skin were pulled taut across what remained of the skull, but vast chunks of flesh were missing.

'The body is male, almost certainly Caucasian. Approximately five foot two, but that's subject to the usual margin of error,' Doctor Larry Chiswick broke the silence, forced to interact with his guest. Morton moved to offer a handshake, but the coroner shook his head. The slightest touch would necessitate cleaning his hands again to avoid contaminating the evidence.

'Epiphyses are not yet closed, and there are only minimal signs of accelerated bone maturation. I'd say he was twelve or thirteen years old. Possibly a little younger.'

'It's a kid?' David struggled to choke out the words as bile rose up in his throat.

'Yes, which makes this odd.' Larry held up the plastic evidence bag Morton had collected from Robert Lyons.

The bag held the gentlemen's watch which Lyons had removed from the body. The coroner had cleaned it up, and Morton could now see that it was gold, with a black face. Morton took the bag, and held it up to the light for a closer look.

'Keppler Oechslan?' He read aloud the name engraved in gold just inside the rim.

'It's Swiss. A tourbillon design from the early eighties if I'm not very much mistaken. My father had one just like it.'

'High end?'

'Probably worth more than my annual bonus.' They exchanged wry smiles at the in-joke. The department hadn't paid a bonus in years.

'It's not something a pre-teen should be wearing, and rules out robbery right off the bat. Looks like there's something on the back. Can you put that under the microscope for me?' Morton handed the watch back to the coroner. Each autopsy room was equipped with a large digital microscope and attendant monitor.

With a deft movement of his thumb and forefinger, the doctor flattened the evidence bag either side of the watch, negating the need to remove it from the protective plastic. Sliding it under the lens, he flicked the power on, and fiddled with the focus ring. The back plate of the watch sprung to life on the monitor, and snapped into focus.

'E M something something 1 something J 1 9 7 something then a few more digits underneath which are much too small and faded to read even when magnified,' Larry said.

'An acid wash might bring out the detail – get it over to forensics. They're used to recovering serial numbers from guns so this should be dead easy. You got anything else for me, Larry?'

'I'll send particulates for trace, and I've already logged the victim's fingerprints in the database. I couldn't get a complete set, but it should be enough to find a match if there's one to be found. I also found entomological evidence, but that's got to be sent for an outside consultation, and that'll have to come out of your budget.'

Morton grimaced. He'd have to sweet-talk the Superintendent for the money. He'd cross that bridge if the fingerprints and trace analysis came up blank.

'Pooling suggests this was a body dump. Blood settled on the left-hand side of the body, so he was lying on his side shortly after death. Crime scene photos indicate he was buried face down.'

'When did he die?'

'I can't be certain of the post-mortem interval. We've had plenty of sub-zero days this winter, and the body won't have decomposed at a consistent rate.'

'Give me a ballpark estimate.'

'I'd hazard a guess at weeks rather than days or months, but the forensic evidence gives us a very wide timeframe. Weather records and the insect activity might help narrow that down.'

'Cause of death?'

'Nothing obvious. No broken bones, no scrapes, nicks or other ante-mortem damage. One minor cut consistent with a spade, post-mortem. There's not much tissue left to work with. What little remains has not been subjected to any physical damage that I can discern. There are no signs of gunshot damage and no nicks to the skeleton, so we can probably rule out a stabbing. The killer could have got lucky, or used a more passive method to kill the kid. Assuming it was a murder.'

'I doubt it was an accident. You said yourself the body was dumped.'

'Stranger things have happened,' said Larry.

Silence hung in the air and Morton arched his left eyebrow in disbelief. Even the possibility of an accident was disingenuous at best and an affront to the victim at worst.

'Is poison a possibility?' said Morton.

'I'll get a sample tested for toxicology, but with so little tissue left I can't give you anything certain. For now, the legal cause of death is undetermined.'

Chapter 4: Bournemouth Bound

For only the second time in his career, Morton found himself reading a magazine while on duty. Like the first time, Morton was waiting for his Community Liaison Officer. He knew all the case details down to the GPS co-ordinates each item of evidence had been collected at, but he still carried a copy of everything in a folder to provide to Tracey McDowell. Sod's Law said that if he'd left it all back at the station then Tracey would have demanded it before she carried out his search.

Since the last police restructure, probably the tenth in as many years, responsibility for the missing children database had been shunted over to the Serious Organised Crime Agency. They were too busy dealing with drugs, gangs and other headline-worthy work, so they farmed it out to another organisation.

Unfortunately, the Child Exploitation and Online Protection Agency ran on their own time. The hands on the cheap school-style plastic clock on the waiting room wall above Morton's head ticked along at a snail's pace.

After what seemed like an eternity of thumbing through fishing articles, and learning only that trout rarely surface to eat, Morton was permitted into McDowell's office. It wasn't as nicely decorated as his own office, nor was her desk adorned with the personal knick-knacks he had accumulated over the years, but for a middle management jobsworth it was pretty impressive.

'Good morning, Mr Morton. Please, take a seat,' said Tracey McDowell. McDowell stood behind her desk with her hands resting on the back of her leather chair. She obviously had no intention of sitting down.

Morton bristled at not being addressed by rank. He was in her office, and she wanted him to know it. Morton ignored her offer of a chair.

'Miss McDowell, let's cut to the chase. I've got a body in the morgue, and I need to identify it. Fingerprints and DNA have yielded nothing. I need to search the missing children database.'

'As you wish. Give me the basic details.'

'Our victim is male. Approximately five feet two inches. White. Early puberty, so he could be anything from ten to thirteen years old.'

'OK. The search won't take too long. Assuming we're searching just London, there are usually only about fifty kids missing at any given time. Do you know how long he's been gone?'

'Weeks. The body was dumped before the recent icy snap, but not much before. Otherwise he'd probably have been found sooner.'

'OK...' McDowell leant over her laptop as she spoke, trying to type without sitting down. In hindsight, she might have realised that it wasn't the best move to make while wearing a low-cut top.

'There are no missing males in London of that age and height.' Tracey turned the screen towards Morton so that he could see for himself.

'Can you try a wider geographical search?' Morton demanded.

'This is just the national database, but yes, I can extend the geographical parameters to include all of the UK. If you want to go international, then you'll need to talk to Interpol.'

'National is fine. He was found in central London. Someone must be missing him.'

This time, the search took a few moments longer. Tracey shook her head. 'Still nothing.'

'What if you widen the search parameters?'

'I've got a twelve-year-old missing in Bradford. White, four foot ten.'

Morton scanned the parameters from the autopsy report. 'Too short.'

'The only other missing child I've got is a fifteen-year-old, five foot two, white. Went missing approx six weeks ago.'

'Sounds plausible. Our Joe Bloggs could be a very late developer. He's definitely short enough. You got a name?'

'Rick Houton. American family, live down in Bournemouth.'

'Road trip.' Morton's crow's feet became pronounced as he suppressed a smile.

***

The Houton family home was a four-hour round trip from Westminster. With the other leads being handled by Detectives Vaughn and Ayala, Morton was free to take a leisurely drive. He could simply have requested a local officer collect a DNA sample and courier it up to London, but this got him out of the office and gave him the opportunity to size up the Houtons as possible suspects.

They lived in a new build on West Overcliff Drive, overlooking the English Channel. It was a pricey area, minutes from the beach. Despite the January weather, a few cars were still parked along the cliff top on the double yellow lines. Morton parked up next to an Aston Martin and felt a sudden rush of schadenfreude as he spotted a black and yellow parking notice affixed to the windscreen.

The garishly named Houton Manor wasn't visible from the road. It was concealed behind an eight-feet-high fence with a security gate. He hit the intercom button next to the gate, and explained the reason for his visit. The gate swung open, allowing him to proceed down a private gravel road towards the house. It wasn't truly a Manor, at least not yet. The house was surrounded by scaffolding, and there was a pile of bricks outside.

An assortment of builder's tools covered by tarpaulin suggested recent activity. The disappearance of their son had not hampered the Houtons' home renovation plans. If one of Morton's boys were missing, he'd be out there searching come hell or high water, not messing about with building work.

Morton glanced at the windows to make sure the Houtons weren't watching, and then pulled a penknife from his pocket to cut a quick sample from the tarpaulin, to test its chemical composition against the sheet the body had been found in. It wouldn't hold up in court, but if it proved to be a viable lead he could simply come back for a legitimate sample.

Matching his and hers 4x4s in baby blue and coral pink were parked in the driveway. The cars were adorned with a pair of vanity plates that made them look even more conspicuous, HOU73N1 and HOU73N2.

A few brisk strides later, Morton rang the doorbell and a chime rang out from inside the house. Morton had neglected to call ahead before ringing at the security gate. Given advance warning, most individuals would take the time to put on a veneer of respectability.

Mrs Houton answered the door. Morton flashed his identification, 'Good afternoon. Mrs Houton, I presume. I'm Detective Chief Inspector David Morton. Please may I come in?'

Mrs Houton silently led the way through to the living room, her buttocks jiggling despite the tight-fitting Lycra. The largest sofa was occupied by her husband, a behemoth of a man wearing a sweat-stained t-shirt, and loose-fitting trousers. The otherwise pristine cream-coloured leather sofa was ruined by the sweaty silhouette of Mr Houton. Morton took an opposing seat, and tried to suppress his gag reflex.

'Mr and Mrs Houton, I realise you'll have been through all the details with your local police several times already but I'd like you to tell me what happened to your son.'

'Rick is our only son.' Mr Houton chewed on a beef jerky as he spoke. With a pudgy hand, he proffered the packet to Morton.

'No, thank you.'

'He can be a bit of a loner. He's at a boarding school in West Sussex from Monday to Friday. We drop him up off at Christchurch Station every Monday morning at six, and pick him up on Friday evening at seven. When we went to pick him up on the twenty-third of November, he wasn't there.'

'Did he leave the school that day?'

'Yes. His peers saw him get on the train a little after school got out.'

'What about CCTV footage?'

'The police tried to track him. He definitely got on the first train, but they lost sight of him after that. They said it was a busy commuter train. It was standing room only, and the cameras are all ceiling mounted, so taller passengers obscured the view. They're still sifting through CCTV from the other stations along the route in case he got dragged off, but not all of them have complete coverage. We know he definitely didn't make it to Christchurch.'

'What's he like as a kid? You said he's a bit of a loner. Has he always been that way?' Morton hinted at the possibility that Rick might have changed recently, which could happen when teenagers became hooked on drugs, and one of the most common reasons for a teenager to become the subject of a missing persons report.

'Yep, never much liked to play nice with the other kids. When he was little, he used to hoard the toys,' Mr Houton said.

Morton resisted the temptation to roll his eyes; the kid sounded charming.

'How are his marks at school?'

'Exemplary. He's doing three languages.' The father huffed proudly.

'Except Physical Education, dear,' Mrs Houton interrupted, 'he takes after you that way.'

Morton realised that it was unlikely Rick Houton was Joe Bloggs Junior. The body belonged to a skinny child, not someone remotely like Mr Houton. Rick had only been missing since November and it seemed unlikely he could have lost that much weight so quickly.

Mr Houton looked like he wanted to say something, but a glare from his wife cut him off.

'OK. Can I ask what you both do for a living?' Morton quickly changed tack at the prospect of a marital argument interrupting his questioning.

'She's a housewife,' Mr Houton shot a dark look at his wife, 'I'm a day trader. Currencies, commodities, bonds. That sort of thing.'

'And where do you work?'

'I work from home. All I need is a laptop.' Mr Houton puffed his chest out proudly.

'Do you have a photo of your son?' There was a distinct absence of family photos in the sitting room. A few frames housed photos of people Morton presumed were distant relatives, while pride of place was given to a large portrait of Mr and Mrs Houton hung on the wall above the mantel. There were no images of Rick on display. Perhaps the Houtons had removed the constant reminders of their missing son.

'We gave our most recent print, one from his school, to the police already.'

'I see. Could you perhaps email me a copy?'

'Sure.'

'Send it over to DCI underscore David dot Morton at met dot police dot uk please. I'm also going to need a DNA sample from you.'

At his words, Mrs Houton tugged at her hair, freeing a solitary strand, 'Will this do?'

Taking the hair, David held it up to the light to check for the presence of a root. Not all hair could be used for DNA analysis. Out of the three stages of hair growth, anagen, catagen and telogen, only anagen hairs have roots, and only the root contains DNA. The specimen Mrs Houton provided had a white root clearly visible at the tip.

'That should do just fine.' David had hoped to obtain DNA from the mother. Using the father's DNA carried the risk of exposing marital indiscretion that would skew the results, and the tests all came out of the departmental budget. This way avoided any chance of a retest being required.

Chapter 5: Nothing Probative?

In any large investigation, one of the senior officers had to take responsibility for collecting all the evidence. That meant that either Tina Vaughn or Bertram Ayala would have to deal with bagging and tagging it, then sifting through it all for relevance. This time, it was Tina's turn.

Every scrap, fibre, rock, bug or hair collected in the vicinity of the Marshes had been dumped into the recently set up Incident Room for Tina to deal with. From what she had found so far, Tina was disappointed. There were no bullets, guns or weapons. Only two items, both found with the body, had been covered in blood. Even the cadaver dogs had come home empty-handed.

Tina suspected that only the mesh net and tarpaulin found wrapped around the body would prove probative. Tina suspected the latter was used to carry the body, but the former was puzzling. Both were found near the dump site, and both tested positive when subjected to a Luminol Chemiluminescence Test, which was a fancy mixture of Luminol powder, hydrogen peroxide and hydroxide. When it was sprayed onto blood, the mixture caused the iron content to produce a blue glow under ultraviolet light. Both the mesh net and the tarpaulin had lit up, but that wasn't conclusive as blood wasn't the only reactant.

Anything containing iron like bleach or even horseradish could set it off. Tina hated Luminol. On her first-ever case, the crime scene had been liberally doused in bleach. Consequently, when she sprayed Luminol the whole place had lit up like a Christmas tree.

The sheer volume of evidence collected struck Tina as overkill. From the contents of the Incident Room, it would be easy to assume that every scrap and fibre in the Marshes had been collected with little regard to what was germane. There was no way every item could be forensically tested; doing that would bankrupt the Met. All of it had been laid out on long tables in the Incident Room.

Every item from the Marshes came into the room inside an evidence bag. It was up to Tina to inspect the evidence, and then reseal it back inside another plastic evidence bag where it would be safe from contamination and labelled by Tina's fair hand. Documentation lay beside each item showing a photograph of the scene plus the evidence log, which was needed to document the chain of custody. Tina had separated the evidence out into several groups: biological evidence on one table, plastic on another. Geological samples nestled on the smallest table in the corner. The primary table held a large tarpaulin mat, one side of which was smeared with blood.

At the back of the room a set of four temporary boards ran along the length of the wall. One, intended to profile suspects, was empty. Furthermost from the door, the smallest board was plastered with key facts: the sketchy details about the victim, and the basics of the crime. The most pertinent document was a copy of the coroner's report. Of course, all documentation was available digitally, but sometimes holding a physical printout just seemed to work better.

The third board featured an A1 map of Hackney Marshes. It showed transport links, power lines and routes of egress in a variety of colours, and had been studded with pins demarking the location of each piece of evidence found.

The body had been dumped in a very public park, seemingly without anyone noticing. In her gut, Tina knew it must have been a night-time body dump. But why hadn't the body been found sooner?

The fourth and final board detailed the evidence that had been found, where it was found and what it could mean to the case.

Tina spoke aloud, holding a Dictaphone aloft to record her thoughts: 'DNA proves the blood on the tarp matches Joe Bloggs Junior.' She scribbled the reference code for the DNA report in her notebook to remind her to reference it in her Evidence Report.

'Garden variety, approximately eight feet by ten feet. It was probably used to transport the victim. The question is: why is blood present? The autopsy showed no signs of obvious trauma.'

***

'Sarcophaga haemorrhoidalis, like other calyptrate flies, go through four life stages: egg, larvae, pupae and adult,' Dr Hafiz spoke slowly. His choice of words was deliberate, even careful. It was a trait Morton often found when dealing with expert witnesses used to appearing in court. From Hafiz's use of technical terms without regard for his audience, Morton surmised that Hafiz felt more at home here, in the University College London lecture theatre in which they now found themselves, than in any courtroom.

'Give me a timeframe, not a lecture on biology.' Already irritated by the sizable chunk of change that had left the departmental budget to pay for Dr Hafiz's expertise, Morton's patience was running out.

'The complete life cycle of a blowfly takes about twenty-three days,' Hafiz drew out his speech as if he was enjoying teasing the detective.

'So, our body was in the Marshes for twenty-three days?'

'I didn't say that. There was a complete absence of adult blowflies.'

'So it's less than the twenty-three days then,' Morton concluded smugly.

'Again, I didn't say that either,' Hafiz admonished his overgrown student. 'Insect activity gives us a timeframe between death and the body's being frozen. If you combine that with the last night the temperature in Kingfisher Wood was above zero degrees, then work backwards, that will give us a timeframe.'

'The body was found on Thursday January the third, and the last day above freezing before then was around Christmas Eve. So if we work backwards, he was killed after December first, but before Christmas.'

'If we assume that he wasn't frozen before being dumped then yes, but a body could have been kept on ice.'

'Lividity did indicate a body dump, so I can't rule that out.'

'Well, I can't help with that, but judging by the average temperature the flies would have developed very slowly. At room temperature, between twenty and twenty-five degrees Celsius, it takes between seven and nine days to go from egg to pupae.' Hafiz held up two glass specimen jars. One held a fly, while an almost invisible egg occupied the smaller of the two.

'And at the temperatures we had in December?'

'Probably closer to twelve, but that is a loose estimate. There are only a small number of early stage pupae. Most of the insects are in their larval stage, with plenty of egg casings. Larvae have between one and three instars. That suggests between ten days and two weeks from death to being subjected to subzero temperatures.'

'Giving us a timeframe between the tenth and fourteenth of December.'

Hafiz smiled, please at how quickly Morton had cottoned on.

'That's about it. Blowflies can fly in any weather, so they're usually the first insect to land on a body. The lack of other entomological evidence can be associated with the inclement weather. We had a pretty balmy weekend at the start of December so I doubt I'm too far out, even accounting for the time it takes for flies to find the body.'

'Thanks, Doctor Hafiz.' Morton shook the man's hand. Perhaps it hadn't been an expensive waste of time after all.

***

'Ah, Mrs Lattimer. Thank you for coming in.' Charlie's form tutor, Mr Neil, had a cheerful Geordie twang that belied the seriousness of their meeting.

The office was barely larger than a cubicle. Mrs Lattimer had been forced to sidle in sideways in order to close the door behind her. A plastic seat, obviously intended for a child, had been provided for her. A flat-pack desk and chair filled out the rest of the room. With two adults present, it wouldn't take long for the minuscule window to steam up. It was a good job that Mrs Lattimer did not appear to be claustrophobic.

'It's not like I had a choice. You know as well as I do that Charlie's in the system. If I don't turn up to crap like this, I don't get paid.'

Mr Neil's face contorted, aghast at Mrs Lattimer's blunt reply.

Composing himself, he continued, 'Be that as it may, Mrs Lattimer, Charlie needs extra help. I've spoken to a number of his teachers. He has trouble with reading and writing, rarely volunteers an answer in class and just doesn't seem to be putting the effort in.'

'Of course 'e is. He's not the sharpest tool in the shed, you know.'

'Mrs Lattimer! Show some compassion. Charlie has excelled in his maths and art classes but a number of his teachers have told me they've had trouble communicating with him. His standard of written English is nothing short of abysmal. I believe he might be suffering from some sort of learning difficulty. With your permission, I'd like to send him to an educational psychologist.'

'He doesn't need no psychologist. What he needs is a bloody English teacher.' Mrs Lattimer knew full well that Mr Neil taught English, as her own son was in his class.

'Mrs Lattimer. You are in loco parentis. Are you going to sign a consent form, or do I need to talk to Children's Services about you?' Mr Neil slid an A4 sheet of paper across the desk, and held out a biro expectantly.

Grudgingly taking the pen, Mrs Lattimer mumbled, 'I'll sign the bloody form. That kid is nothing but trouble.'

Chapter 6: Canvassing Hackney

Blisters were the least of Ayala's problems. He'd been walking for hours, stopping passers-by, and knocking on doors at homes on every side of the Marshes. He didn't have much to go on. A child's body had been found, but they had no idea who the victim was, let alone the killer. He had to give that snippet up to those he was questioning, but without additional details Ayala's questions were totally unfocussed. He was reduced to little better than asking if they had seen anything unusual.

Ayala stood on yet another doorstep and rang the doorbell. Curtains were drawn across the front window, but light bled around the edges. Someone was home. Ayala rang again and a hand thrust aside the curtain to look at him. Ayala held up his badge. His leg muscles tensed, half expecting the man to run for the back door. Instead, the door opened hesitantly. It was kept on the latch.

'Lemme see that more closely,' a disembodied voice demanded.

'Sure,' Ayala held out his badge. A hand snatched it inside quickly. A few seconds later, the door swung open outwards. Ayala stepped back in surprise. Regaining his poise, he expectantly held out his hand, palm up.

'Whaddya want?' The homeowner returned Ayala's badge as he spoke.

'I'm Detective Ayala. A body was found nearby, and I'd like to ask you a few questions.'

'I don't know nothing about no body.'

Ayala ignored the double negative, 'It was a child. You got any kids, Mr...?'

'Blake. And no, I don't. Got a niece though.'

'How old is your niece?' Ayala sought to build rapport.

'She's ten.'

'The kid who died wasn't much older.'

'I'll answer ya questions; I didn't say I wouldn't, but I don't know nuffin' about no bodies.' Blake's tone shifted from angry to indignant.

'How long have you lived around here, Mr Blake?'

'All my life.'

'You heard of any children going missing locally?'

'Nope. Not summat I'd know about though. My friends ain't the child rearing sort, ya see.'

'Do you ever go into the Marshes?'

'Yeh. I jog through it every now 'n' again.'

'How about late last year?'

'Hell no. I like to jog when it's sunny. I ain't freezing my bloody balls off for a bit of exercise.'

'When was the last time you ran?'

'Mebbe October.'

'You sure?'

'Naw, might have been earlier. Been dead icy since then, so wouldn't have been after. Last few weeks, it's been arctic.'

'Did you go into the Marshes in November or December at all?'

'Hang on; I thought you said you're here about some kid? I ain't a grass.'

'What do you mean?'

'The muggings!'

'Mr Blake, I'm not here about any muggings.'

'Bloody typical. Two months of muggings, people too scared to venture out and no bleeding sign of a copper. A kid dies, and you lot swarm all over Hackney.'

'Mr Blake, I'm with Special Operations. I only investigate murder cases.'

'Save it, ya daft twat.'

'No need for insults, Mr Blake. If you want to file a complaint, call the non-emergency line on one zero one.'

Chapter 7: From Bone

It was with mixed feelings that Morton ventured down the long hallway towards the office of Doctor Jess McKay. Jess had proved her worth in previous cases, but when it came time to take the evidence to court her facial reconstructions were always derided by defence lawyers as 'mere mock-ups'. As multiple people could match a reconstruction, it was never going to rise to the criminal standard of beyond reasonable proof. Morton hoped that the reconstruction would open up new investigative leads. Once they found the victim, DNA would do the rest.

Jess's door plaque proclaimed her to be the Met's resident anthropologist, but the mountain of clay that greeted Morton as he entered would have been more at home in an artist's studio. But McKay was something of an artist. She provided what Morton knew to be an inexact science, facial reconstruction. She had been supplied with digital scans of Joe Bloggs' skull in the hope that she could rebuild his face.

It wasn't a magic bullet. Morton's team had already begun searching school and library databases using cranial measurements, and the reconstruction wouldn't suddenly ping a result in some obscure database. Morton snorted. If television crime dramas were true, policing would be so much easier. Facial measurements weren't like DNA. Multiple individuals could share the same size nose or eye placement, and with a city of millions like London that meant a lot of false positives when relying on such generic data.

Jess looked up as Morton entered, her heart-shaped face beset with a smile.

'Hey, Jess. How's it going?'

'Not bad. I've laid down clay strips to build up the face. Thanks for the FORDISC measurements, by the way.' Jess referred to the cranial scan that told her how far apart Joe's features were.

'No problem. Ayala sorted the scan. But for some reason he didn't want to come down and see the results,' Morton said.

Jess's almond eyes flared, then she broke into a grin. 'He still thinks it was his fault, you know. He's absolutely clueless. Are you ever going to tell him?'

'And ruin the only leverage I've got on the man? Nope, the day he finds out what happened, I'll have to get my own coffee.'

'Don't you have an intern to get you coffee? I love mine. When she turns up on time.'

'I'll swap you Ayala if you like.'

'No thanks. Letting Bertram loose on clay would be a disaster. My reconstructions would wind up looking like a kid's papier-mâché homework.'

'How's the progress on my reconstruction?' Morton asked hopefully.

'I'm done rebuilding the face using the data you gave. We know he was white and male. His measurements suggested European so I added anthropologically correct markers to the skull for his forehead, nose, lips and chin, then layered the clay up to those markers. The soft tissue elements are a lot less scientific. I've taken an educated guess and given him brown hair and brown eyes. Want to see the result?'

'Please.'

The reconstruction was stored in Jess' studio. It was a tiny little room behind her desk where she stored all of her tools. She was fiercely private about it. Morton wasn't quite sure why, but for as long as he had known her, Jess had carried the key to the studio around her neck. Morton watched her fumble with her necklace, and then unclasp a tiny key from it. She disappeared into the studio, where Morton could hear her muttering to her intern.

On her return, Jess placed the reconstruction in front of Morton. The hollowed-out skull had been given a new lease of life with plump cheeks and a pair of twinkly glass eyes that stared out at Morton without blinking.

'Jess, that's amazing. He looks so young.'

'He does, doesn't he? Catch him, David. No child deserves an end like this.'

'I will.'

Jess smiled, as if that settled it. She knew Morton would keep his word. 'I'll email across digital scans, front and side photos, and the chain of evidence paperwork,' Jess said.

Morton nodded his thanks, took her left hand and raised it to his lips, then gently kissed it.

'It was good to see you again, Jess.'

***

Martin Neil poked at his dinner half-heartedly as it began to cool.

'You feeling OK?' his wife asked softly.

'I'm fine, thanks, Ingrid.'

'Then there's something wrong with my cooking?'

'No, dear. It's not that. I'm worried about one of my kids. This Charlie, he's been getting glowing praise in Maths and Art, but whenever I speak to him, he's withdrawn. He barely says a word.'

'Maybe he just doesn't like you,' Ingrid teased her husband. 'You are a bit of a dork.'

'Hey! My kids love me. Anyway, it's not that. I don't think so, anyway... Maybe it is that. I just get a weird feeling whenever I talk to him. I know he's with foster parents. That was in his notes that I got when he joined my class. I'd keep an eye on a new kid anyway, but under the circumstances I feel I should be doing more to help him.'

'Is he turning up to class hungry? Are there bags under his eyes?'

'No.'

'Is he covered in bruises?'

'No. But he doesn't have any friends. He just wanders around on his own. I've seen him at break times, sat in the corner of the common room.'

'You can't be his friend, Martin. He's new; it'll take time for him to adjust. If you're worried, have a word with the foster parents.' Ingrid folded her arms as she spoke.

'That witch? She doesn't care about anything other than her pay cheque.'

'Then leave it. There's not much you can do.'

'I guess.' Martin stood, lifted his dinner plate, then swept his half-eaten meal into the bin behind him.

***

'Doctor Jensen, thanks for making it down this late.' Morton strode the length of the Incident Room to greet the younger man.

'No problem, David. What am I looking at?' Doctor Jensen waved an arm at the incident information boards.

'I've got a child victim, about twelve years old. No obvious trauma, no sexual assault.'

'So no weapon marks. Anything probative at the scene?'

'No. We found nothing of note other than a tarpaulin sheet that we think was used for transportation, as well as some netting mixed up with it. The body was pretty badly decomposed though. It seems he was in the ground for at least a few weeks,' Morton said.

'What about trophies? Do we know if the victim is missing anything?'

'The whole skeleton was left behind. Our victim had no personal belongings on him except a watch, but there's no way to know if he usually carried anything else. His clothes were still there. It looked like they degraded in situ. He wasn't wearing anything fancy, just generic cotton and denim.'

'You're not giving me much to go on here.' The doctor smiled wistfully.

'You've done a lot more with a lot less in the past.'

'Ah, flattery gets you everywhere. Any similar crimes on file?'

'Nothing. Thankfully, child murder is relatively rare.'

'Which either means it isn't a serial, it's his first, or we don't know about other victims yet.'

'Cheerful, and you've covered all the bases.'

Jensen paused to stare at the crime scene photographs. 'The how is pertinent. It's clean, almost clinical. No broken bones, no tool marks. The body is decomposed, but it's pristine. The murder wasn't done in a fit of rage. We know it wasn't sexually motivated. This was cold, deliberate. Our killer is likely to be suffering some form of psychopathy.'

'Is he likely to have sought help for that?' Morton asked.

'No. Dumping the body in a public place is arrogant. The killer felt invulnerable. Dumping the body in the Marshes was a power trip. Narcissists don't seek help. But that arrogance could be his downfall. Did the tarpaulin sheet reveal anything?'

'Nope, 100 per cent generic, and it's clean; there are no fibres, fingerprints or other useful trace material. The kid's blood is all over it, but that's it.'

'That means he's cautious, or simply smart. He planned carefully enough to wear gloves, and he used a weapon that didn't leave any forensic markers. David, this is a dangerous perpetrator. He kills ruthlessly, cleanly and without remorse.'

'You keep saying he. Could the killer be a woman?'

'Doubtful, very doubtful. It's a possibility, but women tend to kill by passive means. The toxicology report,' he pointed with his index finger at the board, 'is negative.'

'There's no sign of trauma on the body though. The tissue that was left doesn't seem to have been battered other than by moving and digging it up. That could be called passive. For all we know, he could have been smothered.'

'There's not enough tissue to tell, and you know it. I'll concede we can't rule out a female killer, but it's highly unlikely. History tells us that female child killers rarely act alone. My gut, and my profile report, says male.'

'OK. What about the victim? Why kill a child if not out of anger, or some twisted perversion?'

'Power. He took pleasure in the killing.' Seeing Morton's quizzical expression, Jensen explained further with a slow shake of his head, 'That doesn't mean he was sadistic. He felt a sense of victory during the commission of the crime. He felt superior. It's likely he lacks that sense of fulfilment elsewhere in his life. He could be a blue collar worker, or some sort of day labourer.'

'How old?'

'Mid twenties to late thirties. Unless he's moved from another jurisdiction, he's not been active long. This guy enjoys manipulating the victim, then killing them. He won't stop at one victim. It's likely he took some sort of trophy to help him relive the experience. Keep an eye out for anything the victim might be missing.'

'Always.' Morton wondered why the watch wasn't taken; taking it would have reduced the chance of exposure.

'David, give this all you've got. The kill won't satiate his appetite for long. This guy will be back, again and again. He's a prime candidate for escalation.'

'Meaning?'

'The second you get close enough to threaten his feeling of power, he'll kill again to reassert his dominance.'

***

Charlie quivered under a thin blanket, his stomach aching. The distant rumblings of traffic passing down Kennington Park Road reverberated through the open window. It was a cold night, but Mrs Lattimer had forced the window open from the top, sliding the upper pane down over the lower one. It was too heavy for Charlie to close, and he did not dare risk incurring her wrath anyway.

However, compared to her husband, Mrs Lattimer was a pussycat. Charlie had only seen Mr Roger Lattimer in a rage once, when James Lattimer had tried to sneak out after dark. His calm verbal chastisement of James had seemed reasonable at first. He had not even bothered to rise from his wingback Chippendale. But when James had answered back, his father had struck with a ferocity that left welts on his son's upper legs and back. Only his forearm, lower legs and face had remained unscathed: all the parts of James that were visible in public.

When Charlie heard his door creak, and a line of light was cast across the room, he had feigned sleep.

'Charlie. Wake up,' Roger was almost conversational. He watched the boy's chest rise and fall slowly.

'Charlie. I know you're awake. You're not even snoring.'

Charlie bit his lip. It was now or never. He could come clean, and risk a beating. Or continue to ignore him. He mentally flipped a coin. Heads. Time to come clean. He sat up, rubbing his eyes as if he had just been woken up.

'Mr Lattimer?'

'Good evening, Charlie. My wife tells me you've been struggling in school. In this household, failure comes at a price. Hold out your hand.'

Charlie struggled to hold his arm steady as he held out his right hand.

'Now roll up your sleeve,' Roger said coldly.

Charlie slowly brought his other arm up from under the blanket, and used his left hand to roll up his right sleeve.

Roger Lattimer slowly unbuckled his belt, and then held it by the metal clasp. He wound the loose leather around his fingers until only a foot or so was left dangling, then paused for a moment.

Then he raised his hand, took aim at Charlie's upper arm, and brought it down with a chop that cut through the air. Once. Twice. Three times. Charlie yelped, eyes welling up with tears instantly.

'Next time, it'll be the metal end, boy.'

Chapter 8: Nowhere Fast

Morton reached for his mug of coffee to find that it was stone cold. His watch read 22:00, but it felt much later. He vaguely recalled bidding Tina goodnight about an hour ago.

It wouldn't be too bad if he'd actually achieved something, but poring over particulate analysis was dry work, and he'd learned nothing. It wasn't as if he needed a report to tell him that there were insects, pebbles and rubbish all over the Marshes.

Morton's office door opened, flooding the room with cold air from the corridor. A silhouette appeared in the hallway, wrapped up in a woollen overcoat and wearing his trademark black and gold scarf. Ayala was clearly on his way home.

'Ayala?'

'Evening, boss. Just wanted to drop this in for you.' Ayala held up a brown A4 envelope stuffed with the field report outlining his findings from the initial canvass. 'Didn't expect to find you here this late. How's it going?'

'Not well. No one appears to be missing our victim.' Morton fiddled absentmindedly with his mug.

'Anything from odontology?' Ayala referred to the forensic dentistry that was slowly catching on.

'Dirk, the new guy dealing with teeth, says no known matches. You know how spotty the NHS can be for maintaining digital records. I don't think all dentists bother x-raying kids that young anyway.'

'Could the kid's parents have killed him? That would explain the lack of a missing person report.'

'Or the killer could have taken out the parents as well, and buried them elsewhere. You know of any open cases that might fit?' Morton enquired.

'Not offhand, boss. But I'm not really in the loop with the other Murder Investigation Teams.'

'Worth asking. Even if our hypothesis were correct, the other bodies might not turn up for years. I'll rerun the DNA comparison search just in case, and place a flag on it for notification in the event of a hit. How'd the canvass go?'

'Not much low-hanging fruit to be had, which is no surprise given that all we had to go on was a partially degraded skeleton. That doesn't lend itself to very specific questioning. From what we did ask, no one admitted to knowing anything substantial. Except the usual nutters.' Ayala referred to the crazies, the psychics and those wanting to cut a deal who crawled out of the woodwork whenever the police started digging for information.

'So you learnt nothing.'

'I learnt a little,' Ayala said defensively, 'I found out there's been a spate of muggings in the area. Not surprising for Hackney.'

'Homerton especially is a dive.' Morton cracked a lopsided grin. He used to live there.

'Having spent days walking around it, I'd be inclined to agree. Between the muggings, the recent weather and people staying in over Christmas, it's no surprise the body wasn't found sooner. Not many joggers go cross-country in the middle of an icy winter, and the body was bang in the middle of Kingfisher Wood. Apparently the football pitch nearby gets used once a week, but I doubt our killer dumped the body on a match day.'

'Good work. I hate to say it, but you're going back to the dive tomorrow. This time, you'll take a digital reconstruction of Joe Bloggs' face with you. Our sculptor finished up this afternoon. Scans are in your email inbox.'

'Great,' Ayala said sarcastically.

Morton grinned. Been there, done that.

***

The dining room of Patricia Bonde, David's mother-in-law, was designed to impress the visitor with her taste and sophistication. It was adorned with a very long table covered in silk, and the longest wall hosted a balcony from which the rest of Hammersmith, and the Thames beyond, could be seen.

The maze of red wine glasses, white wine glasses, sherry glasses, and brandy snifters arrayed over the table was thoroughly alien to Morton despite Patricia's best efforts to instil some culture into her only son-in-law. He had spent the evening ignoring his mother-in-law's pointed glare, and simply used the glass closest to him for all beverages.

'Darling, that dress is dee-lightful!' Patricia drawled.

'Oh, totally, babe. It's scrumptious,' another member of the extended family chimed in. Morton never could remember her name. She was his wife's cousin, twice removed. As if anyone knew what that meant.

'David, don't you think Sarah's dress looks amazing?' Patricia prompted.

Morton nodded his assent. There was no point in saying any more. His mother-in-law always cut him off. At the other end of the dining room Sarah's father, Patricia's second husband, give him a wistful smile. At least he'd been smart enough to sit at the other end of the table from the women.

It was at that moment that Morton was saved by his BlackBerry. 'Sorry all, duty calls.'

With a nod, he rose from his seat and made for the balcony. An ironwork chair sat away from the French doors. Morton took the seat, shivered at the cold metal's grasp reaching through his suit, then answered his phone.

'David Morton.'

'Hi, David. This is Tracey McDowell. I've just been emailed the results of the search you asked me to run.'

'And?'

'No matches in any UK database. Sorry.' McDowell sounded almost sympathetic.

'Damn!' Morton cursed. Then, recovering from his frustration, he remembered his manners and added, 'Thanks for letting me know, Tracey.'

He had no desire to immediately return to dinner, so he kept his phone in hand as if still talking, but instead gazed out over the London skyline. As usual it was awash with a sea of lights, but a dark ribbon cut through its heart where the inky darkness of the Thames lay.

Somewhere out there was a child killer. David harboured some hope that the reconstruction would jog a memory or two, but the view reminded him just how big London was. For a few minutes, Morton continued to marvel at the impossibility of finding one man among the millions who called London home. It was only when he began to shiver that he decided to return to the dinner party. The in-laws weren't much company, but they were family and the wing-rib was delicious.

***

Hail pelted Ayala as he dashed from doorway to doorway. Most of the flats in the area were within twenty-storey high-rises built by the council. They afforded some protection from the elements, but Ayala still cursed his misfortune in having to visit them. Few had working lifts.

Ayala's unhappiness was exacerbated by his aching shoulder. He carried a leather bag with a few hundred greyscale copies of the facial reconstruction, but so far most residents had declined to take a copy. In a nicer neighbourhood, he'd have already garnered an army of supporters to nail them to lampposts and plaster them to walls, but the people of Hackney were jaded. Violence, drugs and crime were a part of life for them.

In his left hand, Ayala carried his sole colour copy of the reconstruction, which Tina had laminated for him. He made his way to the next flat and thumped on the door. An elderly gentleman answered wearing only a robe and slippers. He leant heavily on a cane and waited for Ayala to speak.

'Good morning.'

'Good morning,' the old man at the door echoed. His eyes were dull and his expression vacant.

'I'm Detective Inspector Ayala. Do you recognise this child?'

'That could be Billy!' The man became animated, as if a light had been switched on somewhere inside his brain.

'Billy?'

'Yes!' With an awkward twist that seemed to favour his left hip, he yelled back into the flat, 'Agnes! Agnes! This detective knows Billy.'

A woman came into view, and gently touched her husband on the arm.

'Dear, would you go and put the kettle on please? It's cold out and the nice policeman might need a hot drink.'

'Ma'am, I'm fine, honestly.' Despite Ayala's protests, Agnes's husband limped off towards the kitchen.

The woman shook her head, and then whispered to avoid her husband overhearing: 'I'm sorry. We don't know who that is.'

'Your... husband?'

When the woman nodded, Ayala continued: 'He seemed to think this child was called Billy.'

'Billy's been dead for forty years. My husband has Alzheimer's. I'm sorry to have wasted your time, officer.'

'No problem. If you think of anything, please call me.' Ayala handed over one of the greyscale printouts from his bag. Agnes' hands trembled as she took it, her eyes briefly taking in the number for the police incident line printed in bold type across the top of the photocopy.

One flat down and one family's tragedy told, Ayala turned his back on Agnes. His steps were a little heavier as he left. There were hundreds more flats to go.

Chapter 9: Under Fire

'DEAD TEENAGER FOUND IN HACKNEY: POLICE CLUELESS'

Morton surveyed the newspaper over his reading glasses. As usual, the press had jumped to the wrong conclusions. He'd deliberately avoided calling an early press conference for the simple reason there wasn't much to tell yet, and the idea that a child killer could be on the loose would only incite panic.

But someone Ayala had spoken to had provided the tabloids with a copy of the reconstruction photo. It wasn't a great surprise, as Ayala handed out hundreds of them. Unfortunately, the press hadn't stopped at simply reporting the facts, and as Morton reread the article yet again he felt his blood begin to boil.

'A paedophile may be on the loose in Hackney, it was suspected after a child's body turned up encased in ice.[otherwise this is saying he wasn't on the loose before the body was discovered] The body is believed to have been found on the eastern side of Hackney Marshes after the area was closed off to public access by officers from the Metropolitan Police.

'A local resident who wishes to remain anonymous has this to say, 'They dun know who he is. They been 'round the whole estate with a picture asking if we know 'im.

'The composite appears to be a forensic reconstruction, commonly used when the body is too badly damaged to be identified. A sadist may be on the loose. Residents are advised to lock their doors, keep their children close and not venture out after dark.'

'Drivel. Lazy, baseless fear-mongering. The whole article is conjecture at best.'

'I agree, dear,' his wife replied. Sarah knew better than to disagree with her husband's intense dislike of the press.

'What do they mean, 'stay in after dark'? It's January – it's always dark!'

'Writing on a deadline is never going to lead to literary genius. As for the rest of it, you know they sensationalise everything just to sell copy,' Sarah replied, casually flicking her hair in the hope that her husband would notice her new haircut. Fat chance, she thought as she picked up a pair of yellow marigold gloves, pulled them on and turned towards the mountain of plates beside the sink. She sometimes wondered if David would notice if she dyed her hair pink.

Morton fumed silently as he worked on his toast, which was piled high with butter and marmalade. Sarah bit her tongue to avoid making a shrill comment about his cholesterol. He was in a bad mood already, and he wouldn't appreciate being chided.

'I suppose the extra exposure might help identify the body. But I was hoping to have a better grasp of the facts before I called a press conference. I just hope we don't end up with a panic on our hands, or worse, a vigilante.'

Sarah exhaled patiently, and continued to wash up. 'The cat's out of the bag now.'

Morton stroked his chin thoughtfully. 'Perhaps it is, but there is one silver lining. All the time the press is lampooning me as useless, the killer might not be as careful as he should be. This could turn out to be a blessing in disguise.'

***

The moment Mr and Mrs Lattimer had left for their social engagement, the babysitter hurried in her boyfriend and staked out the main sitting room for the evening. A bottle of merlot pilfered from the wine rack in the kitchen sat beside the couple. They had not thought to let it breathe before beginning to drink.

James Lattimer and Charlie had been left to their own devices, which suited all concerned. They were in the basement splayed out on a pair of well-worn beanbags with their eyes glued to a projector screen. Life-size cartoon characters were attempting to bash each other to death courtesy of James' games console.

Charlie erupted with laughter as his character head-butted and slapped his way to victory. For James, who had just suffered his fourth loss in a row, it was less amusing. Enraged, he flung his controller at the wall with all his might. A shower of plastic rained down on the carpet, and a 'Controller Disconnected' error flashed up on the screen.

James stomped towards the door, then spun on one foot and screamed at Charlie, 'I hate you!'

James' footsteps could be heard carrying him up two floors to his bedroom. Once he was alone in the quiet of the basement, Charlie shrugged. Love and hate were just words. He mashed a button, and the game switched to one-player mode. He had no problem playing against the machine. He preferred it that way. The one person Charlie could always count on was himself.

Chapter 10: Dead End

Morton rested his chin on his palm and stared at his desk. While the Incident Room was an invaluable resource with its huge conference table and easy access, he always found that he did his best thinking in his office. It was three floors up and almost always silent.

Most of the room was sparse and utilitarian, but the desk was his own. He'd inherited it from his father, and it now sat adorned with various knick-knacks and mementos. On the left-hand side of the desk Morton had a shell casing from his first case, as well as a clock given to him for thirty years' service. On the right-hand side were the cold case files which Morton kept to remind himself to stay vigilant. He knew he'd take some of those cases to his grave, but it didn't stop him flipping through the evidence every so often.

The biggest knick-knack, which Morton kept front and centre so that he could look at it often, was a digital photo frame. Images of his wedding day faded in and out of existence in a slideshow. Sarah looked so much younger then. Almost three decades had flown by since they had eloped. Of course, they'd had a second ceremony later to avoid the ire of her father. Morton's in-laws still didn't know about the original, and in Morton's mind, real wedding. Every year, Morton took a perverse pleasure in getting all his anniversary cards a month late.

The real ceremony had been a Valentine's Day wedding. A last-minute cancellation had opened up at St James' in Piccadilly, and Morton had roped in a pair of police constables to act as witnesses. With the anniversary mere weeks away, and thirty years being an auspicious milestone, he knew he'd better come up with something impressive. Pearls were just too obvious, flowers too impersonal. Morton bit his lip as he strained to think of the perfect present for Sarah.

For what seemed like the hundredth time that week, the buzz of his BlackBerry vibrated against the oak desk and interrupted his thought process.

'Morton,' he answered.

'Chief, this is Stuart Purcell from Forensics. We tested the sample you obtained from Mrs Houton against Joe Bloggs Junior. No match. Our Joe Bloggs Junior is not Rick Houton.'

Morton exhaled. It was no surprise really. It didn't seem likely that the skinny child found in the Marshes could have been related to the morbidly obese man that Morton had met in Bournemouth.

'How certain are you?'

'Almost 100 per cent.'

'Only almost?'

'There's always the chance a mistake could be made. Sometimes you find what we call chimaeras. These are people who have two sets of DNA, so the sample won't match.'

'How's that happen?' Morton asked. His eyes flicked to the calendar to make sure it wasn't somehow April first already.

'Basically, it's when an egg is fertilised by two sperm, but for some reason doesn't split into twins.'

Morton rolled his eyes. The new kid was a show-off. 'Sounds pretty rare,' he said politely.

'About one in a million.'

'So, you're pretty sure then. Thanks very much.' Morton rang off with a click.

Morton made a snap decision; he'd let local police inform the Houtons that it wasn't their son. He crossed his fingers that the hope it would give them that Rick was alive wouldn't turn out to be false.

***

Ayala tapped his foot restlessly against the synthetic flooring as he waited for the lab tech to pronounce the acid etching complete. The Chief had ordered that the Joe Bloggs watch be stripped down by forensics, and they were in the process of trying to restore the inscription. That meant grinding the back plate down so it became smooth, then applying a mix of hydrochloric acid, copper, chloride, ethyl alcohol and water known as Fry's reagent. The forensics team was more accustomed to using the method to recover serial numbers from guns, but it worked for both ferrous and non-ferrous metals.

A tech had been in several times to check on progress. Working with acid meant wearing down layers of metal. Too little, and the etching wouldn't reappear. Too much, and it was gone for good. Little and often was the order of the day; every fifteen minutes the tech meandered over to brush a minuscule quantity of acid onto the surface, taking his time to ensure an even application.

As a small safeguard, Ayala had set up a webcam pointed at the work surface. Not only would this be ample procedural documentation for any eventual court proceedings, but it would capture the serial number on video if the acid began to damage the etching. Acid was prone to carry on reacting long after any etching reappeared, and the procedure could never be repeated, unlike the many forensic tests that didn't destroy or degrade the sample.

As the tech leant in to check on the sample he turned towards Ayala. 'It's going to be a few hours yet, Detective. You might want to come back later.'

Ayala didn't move. He had his orders, and he had every intention of staying there until he had his answers.

***

The perfect anniversary gift leapt into Morton's mind as he drove home from work. It was so simple that Morton was shocked he hadn't thought of it before. He made a mental note to double-check Sarah's passport was in date when he had half a chance. Their first trip abroad together had been their honeymoon.

With no kids to care for, and no rent to pay as they were living with his parents at the time, they had decided to drive across Europe to Venice in a rented Aston Martin. Their route had seen them jump on a then-fairly-new roll on, roll off ferry from Dover to Calais, then coast on down to drive through the Alps via the Mont Blanc tunnel. From there on out, it had been plain sailing straight across Italy. The drive had knocked four days off either end of the holiday, but they were so wrapped up in each other's company that the pit stops didn't bother them.

Morton's fingers tapped lightly on the steering wheel, and he hummed along to the radio. Not even the legendary traffic jams on the City Road could dent his mood as he dreamed of recreating those two perfect weeks.

It wouldn't be cheap to do it all over again. Hotels along the route would be heaving with couples celebrating St Valentine's Day, but perhaps recreating the trip would help rekindle the old flame. Then it would be worth every penny.

Chapter 11: Watch This

As Morton sat at his desk typing up a draft itinerary for his romantic Valentine's Day getaway, Ayala bounded into his office without so much as a cursory tap on the door.

'Detective, did we swap offices when I wasn't paying attention, or did you just come into my office without knocking?' Morton set his jaw in mock anger, careful to keep his tone playful, but his eyes flashed darkly at the intrusion.

'Sorry, boss,' Ayala replied, 'but I had to give you this.' He triumphantly threw two close-up photographs on the desk. Both showed the watch found with Joe Bloggs Junior.

'E M + J C 18J 1971?' Morton read the recovered inscription from the first photograph aloud.

'Yep. Sounds like a wedding date to me, boss.'

'Nah. It's more likely to be an engagement; they've got different initials for the surname.'

'Could be, boss, but the information from the other photo is the really important thing.'

'UNQAC1979CBMTL. What's the significance?'

'These high-end watches are handmade. Every single piece gets a unique serial number. The manufacturer is bound to know who bought it. We can track it down from there and ID our kid.' Ayala beamed proudly.

'Great work. Get on it then.' Morton leant back in his chair. They were finally getting somewhere.

***

Red ink dominated the page when Charlie had his marked Romeo and Juliet essay returned. English was the last class of the day, and class 8M were packing their bags when the bell rang.

'Not you two – stay behind.' Mr Neil pointed at Charlie and the kid sitting next to him. The two pupils exchanged curious glances, but obediently sat back down on the chairs nearest the door, and watched their classmates escape.

When the rest of the class were gone, Mr Neil gently shut the door then perched on a table in front of the duo.

'Liam. Your work wasn't good enough. I asked for five hundred words minimum. You turned in less than two hundred.'

'Sorry, sir.'

'Do it again. Tonight. I want to see it on my desk first thing in the morning. Is that clear? Otherwise it's detention on Friday.'

'But sir! Friday is the game against Redwood!'

'It doesn't matter. I want to see the football team lift the trophy as much as you do, but I also want you to do your homework properly. No excuses. If you want to play then do the essay tonight. Do I make myself clear?'

'Yes sir.'

'Good. Then off you go. Don't forget to close the door on your way out.'

Once Liam was gone, Mr Neil turned his attention to Charlie's essay.

'This,' he held the essay up in front of him as he spoke, 'is not acceptable. Did you write it yourself?'

Charlie nodded. His hands were resting on the desk, but they were shaking uncontrollably.

'It's the right length, but it's compete nonsense. It looks like you've put it through Google Translate! 'Romeo and Juliet is a play written by Shakespeare, who has two star crossed lovers'. Genders have been mixed up, and don't get me started on your use of tenses.' Mr Neil scowled down at Charlie, personally affronted.

'Look, I know you've got an appointment booked with the school psychologist for next week, so I'm not going to ask you to redo it before then. But I have to ask, do you need any extra help from me, Charlie?'

Charlie shrugged, his shoulders rolling back in their sockets, and his hands upturned in an 'I don't know' gesture.

'I'm putting you in detention this week.'

Charlie looked indignant as Mr Neil pulled out the blue slips used to notify parents that their children would be kept behind.

'Yes, again. I expect a bit more effort from you, Charlie. If you can't do something, then ask for help. That's what I'm here for. We'll redo the whole essay together, so bring your copy of the play.'

Charlie reluctantly took the detention slip, folded it twice and pocketed it.

Mr Neil glanced at the clock. 'It's getting on a bit. You'd better go. I don't want you being late home. But if you need to talk, come find me tomorrow during lunch.'

***

Verifying that the watch was a real, original Keppler Oechslan had been easy. A quick visit to the manufacturer's website allowed Ayala to punch in the serial number that he had recovered. The tricky bit was going from there to the purchaser details. On screen, it only confirmed that the warranty was expired.

A telephone number for Keppler Oechslan proved elusive. The company website provided an online contact form, but trying to find someone Ayala could actually talk to drew a blank.

Ayala was about to email when he had a brainwave. He pulled up the database of UK companies from Companies House and searched for the UK subsidiary of Keppler Oechslan SARL. That gave him the names and addresses of all their directors. From there, it was a short jump to getting their phone numbers. Snatching up the wireless handset from the Incident Room's conference table, Ayala deftly punched in the number of the first director on his list. It was answered after only two rings.

'Hi, is that Terrence Quinn?'

'It is. Who am I speaking to?' Quinn's tone was cautious, wary of nuisance callers.

'This is Detective Inspector Ayala from the Metropolitan Police.'

'How can I verify that?'

Taken aback, Ayala didn't respond.

'Officer, how can I verify who you are?'

'Call the Metropolitan Police switchboard – 020 7230 1212. Ask for Detective Inspector Ayala. That's A-Y-A-L-A. I work in Special Operations.'

'OK.' Without further ado, the line went dead.

Ayala wasn't sure whether to be annoyed or amused. No one had ever questioned his identity on the telephone before, and it didn't occur to him that it might simply be a stalling tactic.

Ayala stared at the phone in front of him and began to hum as he waited. Ten minutes later he was still willing the phone to ring. He resolved to give it five more minutes before he called Quinn back, then pocketed the cordless phone and went to grab a coffee from the vending machine in the hallway.

Seconds before Ayala's arbitrary call-back deadline, his Mozart ringtone reverberated around the cramped office.

'Hello?'

'Hi, Detective Ayala. Sorry for the delay. I'm in a teleconference with my lawyer on the other line. How can I help you?'

'I'm investigating a murder. I need to trace the owner of one of your watches from a serial number.'

The line went quiet. Only an incoherent mumble let Ayala know he was still there. Evidently, Quinn had chosen to relay the request to his lawyer.

The line crackled as Quinn switched back.

'I'm afraid that's not going to happen, Detective. Our customers are very private individuals. Our watches cost a considerable sum, and those with the money to buy them value confidentiality.'

'With all due respect, damn your customers' secrecy!'

'I have nothing more to say on the matter. Goodbye, Detective.'

The line went dead. Ayala cursed.

Chapter 12: Low Credit

Sarah waited until her husband left, gave him five minutes in case he had forgotten something, then triple-bolted the front door. She flipped up her laptop lid, and then fished a slip of paper out of the safe.

The household finances were David's domain, but Sarah was the more computer-literate spouse. She'd checked their credit card statement online the night before while they were both in the sitting room, but had only had a moment to peruse the details. She needed to be sure before she confronted him.

Sarah brought up David's eBanking website. It wasn't a simple password system. The first eight digits from David's credit card had to be entered to log on to the system, and then Sarah punched in their postcode and David's full name, and finally the password Sarah had scribbled on a scrap of paper. David had hated putting it down on paper, but it was too long to remember when they had so many online accounts. For a little bit of extra security he'd written the code back to front.

The page refreshed, and she was in.

'Available credit: £115.28. Current balance owed: £4,884.72.'

Sarah clapped her hands over her mouth in horror. They were five thousand pounds in hock. What the hell had he been buying?

Sarah clicked on the balance to see the most recent transactions. There were six listed, with the newest charge at the top of the screen.

'*£680.32 WorldPay*

'*£1311 Sage Pay*

'*£1922.44   PayPal   *DIAMONDJEWLZ CAMDEN*

'*£850 WESTERN UNION*

'*£120 ORCHIDS DIRECT*

'*£0.96 PayPal * Tubit Games*'

'Flowers and jewellery? I knew that bastard liked to look, but I never thought he'd cheat on me again. I'm going to kill him!'

Tears began to stream from Sarah's eyes, turning her carefully applied make-up into a panda mask. She thumped the sofa in anger, and her laptop fell to the floor with a thud.

'Who is she, David? If it's that trollop at work, I will slap her, even if it is in a police station.'

***

Despite his being a relatively youthful thirty-two, Kiaran O'Connor's office eclipsed that of David Morton in both size and luxury. It was divided into a front and rear section, with two paralegals and a secretary guarding the inner sanctum. As soon as David set foot inside the inner office, he was forced to weave his way around stacks of statute books, case folders and printouts that were arranged haphazardly in teetering piles. They clearly made sense to Kiaran as he shuffled around, taking papers from one pile and adding them to another.

'Kiaran, what we need is a search warrant. We found a watch with the body in the Marshes. Ayala had forensics acid-wash the back plate, which gave us a serial number. Keppler Oechslan know who bought it, and when. This isn't a garden-variety watch; it's practically bespoke, a really high-end model, though it is fairly old now. I need to see their records.'

Kiaran O'Connor stopped sorting paperwork, and looked up; his gaze met Morton's. 'If it's so old, why would they still have records?'

Morton shrugged, 'Authentication? Preventing copycats?'

'That's farfetched, David, and you know it.'

'Kiaran, if they didn't have anything then they'd have simply said so. They actively consulted counsel then refused our request. Why bother using a valuable resource rather than simply saying 'Sorry, we don't have anything' and moving on?'

'OK, do we know where the records are?'

Morton winced, 'We're hoping they've got them at their London subsidiary. Could all be cloud-based, though.'

'Well, that's a great answer, David. Really convincing. The magistrates are going to love it.'

'We've got to try, Kiaran. We're running out of leads here. It's an engraved watch found on a dead child. That's got to be enough to secure a warrant to search corporate records?'

'I'll give it a go.' While Kiaran's tone conveyed doubt, Morton stifled a sigh of relief at getting the prosecutor on board. Without him, there would have been no chance of a warrant.

***

Inside the concrete edifice of Highbury Magistrates Court, Kiaran surveyed the crowds of bustling legal forum. It was the usual crowd: drunks, dealers and thieves, the kind of client that that passed through every week. Among the down-and-out petty criminals, Kiaran could see the occasional hardened criminal waiting to be committed to the Crown Court.

The desolate interior, by no means as shabby as the view from the outside, was entirely functional. Benches were scattered along narrow hallways leading to the courtrooms. The downtrodden loitered in the wings waiting for their cases to be called, while lawyers strutted to work shrouded in their self-importance.

Even seated among the crowd outside Court One, Kiaran's six-foot-three frame, clad in barrister's gown, could not be missed. He cradled his horsehair wig in his hands as he waited for his case to be called. Putting it on too early caused his shaved head to sweat, and it could quickly become itchy.

When his case was called, he rose to his feet then strode briskly into Court One. As it was an ex parte application, the defence table to his right was empty. An usher and two members of the public rounded out the courtroom, but they were behind him, well out of eyeline.

At the end of the room, a crest hung on the wall behind the magistrate with the motto of 'Dieu et Mon Droit' embossed in gold. God and my right, Kiaran mentally translated. He was still baffled as to why the English court system had their motto in French.

Beneath the crest, a solitary justice of the peace sat on a raised dais. Wooden panelling, as well as elevation, physically separated him from the lawyers, court staff and the defendant's dock.

'Your Worship,' Kiaran addressed the bench, 'if it may please the court I would present an application under section eight of the Police and Criminal Evidence Act 1984.'

The lay magistrate waved in assent. He was not a lawyer, and clearly just wanted to get down to the details. An usher stepped forward to take Kiaran's form, marked *'Criminal Procedure APPLICATION FOR SEARCH WARRANT (Criminal Procedure Rules, rule 6.30; section 8, Police and Criminal Evidence Act 1984)'* up to the bench. The form was a simple one, and had been completed by Morton hours earlier but Kiaran had chosen to deliver the application to answer the thorny issue of whether the material was on-site. The magistrate flicked through rapidly, and then looked up expectantly.

'Sir, a child was murdered and the body dumped in Hackney Marsh. On his person was an expensive Swiss watch. Forensic investigation revealed that this watch was etched with a unique serial number which could identify the purchaser and therefore identify the body. The owners of the records have refused access.'

Satisfied that the application had cleared the first hurdle requiring there to be a serious arrestable offence, the magistrate nodded. 'Where are the records? Are they printed records or digital?'

Kiaran paused. The questions put them on rocky ground as he needed to show that material records were kept on the premises of Keppler Oechslan.

'Sir, the manufacturer is Keppler Oechslan, and the address is as detailed in the form supplied to the court. We're unsure of the medium at this time.'

'Then you don't really know if the records are on-site at all.'

'Not definitively, no,' Kiaran admitted, 'but they only have one registered address in the country. It's highly probable that the material is on-site, or access to it can be had on-site.'

The magistrate waggled a gnarly finger at Kiaran. 'That sounds awfully close to a fishing expedition, Mr O'Connor.'

'Your Honour, this is a murder investigation. We're talking about forty-year-old purchase records for wrist wear here, not an intrusion into a private home or medical records.'

The magistrate paused for a moment then capitulated, 'I'll allow it. I trust there are no concerns about privileged material?'

'Sir, these are simple purchase records. Nothing unusual about them.'

'And you think this will yield relevant evidence?'

'Unequivocally,' Kiaran said more firmly than he believed.

The magistrate made a snap decision. He only had a few minutes to deal with each case. 'Application granted.'

Kiaran nodded his thanks, and then stood stock-still in the courtroom as he waited for either the magistrate to exit, or another lawyer to enter. Thanks to an antiquated custom known as dressing the court, Kiaran was prohibited from leaving the judge alone in the courtroom. Kiaran cursed Morton as he watched the hands on his watch tick by. When the magistrate finally rose, Kiaran pulled off his wig and sprinted for the robing room. He was due on the other side of London, and would have to run for the tube.

Chapter 13: Warehouse

Argall Way was about half a mile north of where the body had been found. Keppler Oechslan's UK subsidiary was being run from a pair of old warehouses. It used to be a prosperous area when the nearby canal had been used to ferry goods around, but the M25 circular had pulled most of the industrial units further out of London.

'Doesn't look like a high-end watch manufacturer to me, Chief.' Ayala eyed up a broken window in an adjacent building.

'It's a rough area. But with London rent the way it is, it must make financial sense being out here,' Morton answered.

'I guess the rough look hides the value of the goods they're moving too. I'd have gone for a little boutique in Hatton Garden personally.'

'You can't move volume without a warehouse, and this place is enormous. It looks like the front door is just for the site office. Let's go ahead of the others and serve this warrant.' Morton indicated for the search team to wait by the kerb until summoned by radio.

Automatic doors slid open as Morton approached the building, opening out into a cramped office area filled with four desks, one in each corner. The desk nearest the door was empty. A brunette in her twenties twirled the cord of her desk phone around a finger as she chatted with a customer, while another clerk with hot pink nail varnish that matched her hair shuffled papers.

At the last desk a middle-aged man with a burgeoning waistline eyed them from behind his laptop. He wore a double-breasted suit with a wide navy pin, and looked the epitome of middle management. In the bank of steel cabinets behind the businessman, Morton could see a hazy reflection of laptop screen which displayed a game of solitaire.

'Terrence Quinn?' Morton hazarded a guess.

'No, sorry. Mr Quinn isn't in today.'

'What's your name?'

'Gregory Dillon. I'm the warehouse manager.'

'Well, Greg, this is a warrant to search your premises for records pertaining to the sale of a watch with the registration code UNQAC1979CBMTL.' Morton surveyed Greg intently, watching for any reaction.

'1979? We haven't digitised that far back yet.' Greg glanced over at one of the girls on the other desk, who was now off the phone and listening intently to the conversation. 'Have we, Tracey?'

'No sir.'

'But you do have the records?' Morton queried, his gaze never leaving Greg.

'Well yeah, but...'

'But what?'

'We sell a lot of watches. And our records from back then aren't exactly organised.'

'Show us.'

Greg led Morton and Ayala through a key-coded door. 8678. Morton made a mental note, just in case. Behind the door a long corridor appeared to run the length of the warehouse. Low-wattage bulbs hung bare in the ceiling, serving up dull illumination. Keppler Oechslan had not yet made the move to the newer energy-saving bulbs.

As they traversed the corridor, the trio passed a number of doors. Those on the left were windowed, with a view over the warehouse floor. Boxes were piled neatly on thin metal frames. Plastic wrapping materials posed a trip hazard to anyone brave enough to venture in, with thick plastic strapping in abundance near the loading bay. Staff in fluorescent jackets could be seen unpacking crates, packing boxes and driving forklift trucks. Greg wasn't kidding when he said they sold a lot of watches.

At the end of the corridor, they came to a thick metal door with no windows. Greg fiddled with a tiny iron key and then the door swung inwards with a loud creak, as if no one had been in the records room for a long time.

'Gents, this is the records room.' Greg sported a nasty grin as he stood aside to let the detectives past.

'Oh crap.' Ayala dragged out the first syllable, the sound coming out much like a dog whimpering.

Beyond the doorway, there were stacks of crates piled high, and loose paper was scattered everywhere. Under the deluge, Morton could just about make out the remnants of office furniture.

Morton frowned. According to Ayala the serial number had been verified by Keppler Oechslan's website, so it didn't make sense for them to have only paper records. He asked Greg about it.

'Our system recognized the format. That's all. We've been using fourteen-digit serials for years.'

'Then how did it know the warranty had expired if it didn't check against a database?'

'The year of manufacture is in the middle of the serial. The computer checks that, and then compares it to the current date. We round up, so it gives some customers a few extra months. It's better than adding a full date to the code.'

'Right. Thanks. We'll take it from here.'

Greg left them alone with the morass of dusty paperwork, and Ayala's shoulders sagged as if he knew what was coming next.

'Ayala, go get the lads in. You'll be here all night.'

'I'll be here all night? Where are you going?'

'I'm taking my wife out for dinner.' Morton smiled sadistically; being in charge did have its perks.

***

Sarah alternated between sipping wine, a glass of rioja, and watching her husband for any sign of duplicity.

'So now Ayala's got to sort through thousands of old documents. Some are yellowed and faded. It reminds me of the time that old DCI Crombie had me out looking for those stolen wigs and told me to comb the area. It took me months to get the joke.' Morton paused, expecting at least a polite chuckle from his wife. When none was forthcoming, he realised something was up.

'What's wrong? You usually love my jokes.'

'You know damn well what's wrong.' She kept her voice low. There were other couples dining only a few feet away, and she didn't want to cause a scene. Yet.

Morton frowned, 'What are you talking about?'

'Don't play coy with me.' Her voice had become shrill, and the nearest table began to stare.

'Sarah, I really have no idea what you're talking about, but keep it down. We're causing a scene here.'

'I found them,' she hissed.

'The brochures?' Morton asked.

'No, the charges on the credit card. Five thousand pounds, David! Who the hell is she?'

'Where is this coming from? I haven't touched the credit card!'

Silently, Sarah delved into her handbag, then thrust a printout of the credit card statement at David.

His eyes widened as he read the document, then contracted with suspicion.

'It's got to be a mistake. I haven't authorised any of these charges, except for Orchids Direct. I ordered those for you for Valentine's Day next month.'

Sarah's expression softened, 'So, you're not cheating on me?' Her tone was hurt, but hopeful. Maybe it was all one big understanding.

'Sarah, I love you. Apart from that one time...' Morton trailed off. He looked at Sarah, with puppy dog eyes.

It worked. Fighting back the tears, Sarah sobbed, 'Can we go home, David?'

'Of course we can.' Morton signalled a nearby waiter for the bill.

The waiter looked bemused. Few diners had only an appetizer and one drink each. He left to fetch the bill all the same. When it arrived, Morton glanced at the bill then handed over his Amex, which was promptly inserted into a wireless chip and PIN machine. He punched in his PIN.

'Card Declined.'

Annoyed, Morton handed the machine back to the waiter. 'Sorry, I think I must have hit a wrong number. Can you clear the transaction?'

The waiter dithered. He could see that the transaction had gone further than a simple wrong pin, one of the so-called 'soft declines'. It was a funding decline, the last hurdle before a payment was authorised. Restaurant policy dictated that this information wasn't shared. It would be a security risk. Worst still, the card could be stolen. That didn't seem to be the case here, as otherwise it would have been flagged by the system.

The waiter decided to humour Morton, so he cleared then re-entered the transaction. Thirty seconds later the inevitable 'Card Declined' message popped up again.

'Perhaps you have another card you'd care to use, sir?'

'Fine,' Morton dug his MasterCard out of his wallet and virtually threw it at the waiter.

'Card Declined.'

'Again? There's got to be something wrong with your machine, son.'

'It's been working fine all evening, sir.'

'Can we try another machine?'

'We've got a wired PIN machine in the back,' the waiter suggested. Other diners were beginning to turn at the raised voices. The owner would not be pleased if a simple card machine malfunction disturbed the ambiance.

Morton stood, and motioned for the waiter to lead on. The waiter exhaled a sigh of relief at moving the debacle away from the patrons.

Three credit cards later Morton gave up. Sod the card machines. He'd pay in cash, but they damn well wouldn't get a tip. As he counted out the coins, Morton grew progressively angrier. The thought that Sarah would so easily think him a philanderer after three decades together was a grievous affront. He had only strayed once, and that had been over twenty years ago while he was undercover. It had taken her years to forgive that indiscretion, and he had only committed adultery in order to avoid blowing his cover.

'Thank you sir. Have a nice night,' the waiter said.

Chapter 14: 1979

Morton dodged a bullet with this one, Ayala thought with a grimace. In order to store all the paperwork seized at the Keppler Oechslan warehouse, Ayala had commandeered the conference room down the hall from the Incident Room.

In an attempt to impose order on chaos, Ayala had created two piles. The first contained all the documents that were not from 1979. They would be logged and then returned as soon as possible.

The second contained all the purchase records, invoices, tax receipts and warranty registration papers that did have the year 1979 printed on them. Ayala prioritised the work orders for engraving, as many of the watches were sold without personalisation. There was a chance the watch was bought and then engraved elsewhere, but Ayala hoped this would not prove to be the case.

'Boss?' One of the new technicians to join the team, Stuart Purcell, called over from the far end of the room.

Ayala strode over, walking slowly to assert his authority.

'What?'

'I've set up this.' He gestured to a webcam hung above what appeared to be a gutted laser printer.

'What is it?'

'I've stripped down an old laser printer. It's got a lightning-fast roller mechanism and a decent tray-loading system.'

'Get to the point.'

'Fine,' Stuart huffed, more than a little offended the detective had interrupted his stride. 'Paper goes in here.' He pointed to the tray. 'Goes through the roller, gets photographed by the camera, flipped over by the roller, the other side gets photographed, and the paper comes out here.'

'So you can digitise the documents?'

'Yes, but not only that. The camera is connected to some powerful backend servers. An algorithm I wrote then scans the page.'

'What's it looking for?'

'The serial number we found on the watch. Every bit of paper is labelled in the top right with the unique code from the back of the watch.'

'So it'll find our documents for us?'

'Maybe. Some of the records are printed. Some are stamped. Some are handwritten. If the sample is degraded or smudged, it won't find a thing. '

'But it can exclude all the documents we put through it that don't pertain to the case?'

'Yes sir, leaving us with just the documents we do need, and any smudged documents to sort through by hand.'

'Great work. Call me when you've got a name.'

***

'*Available Balance £0.04. Another Service or Return Card?*'

Morton squinted at the ATM. It had to be wrong.

'Sarah!' He called over his wife, 'Please tell me I'm reading this wrong.'

Almost instantly, Sarah's skin paled. The card in the machine was for their main bank account. Only a few days ago, the balance had been over £30,000.

'Don't panic,' David said. 'Let's go inside and check with the bank.'

Thankfully, the ATM was attached to the bank, and they were open over lunch.

They hurried inside to find dozens of customers queued up, waiting to complete their transaction. It was a typical London branch with dozens of self-service machines, but only one cashier working. Bank employees shuffled around the queues, trying to avoid eye contact with the horde of customers.

Morton grabbed the nearest person wearing a bank name badge. 'I need to report a fraud.'

'Bass, t'at ain't my problem. I only do mortgages,' the man replied in an accent that blended East End with Caribbean undertones.

'So who do I need?'

The mortgage broker gestured towards the cashier. 'Just go to the cashier's desk, mon.'

As he walked off, Morton capitulated and joined his wife in the queue.

***

Detective Ayala sat waiting in the Incident Room. He was trying to avoid looking smug, but failing miserably. Over three hundred boxes of paperwork had been catalogued and digitised in less than two days, and he now knew who had bought the Keppler Oechslan watch back in 1979.

Finding that alone was[or 'Merely finding that was'] more than justification for a little bragging, even if the hard work had been mitigated by efficient use of technology, but Ayala had gone much further.

From the name, Ayala had been able to find a death certificate with relative ease. The old man had been gone for a while. A probate search was in the works to find out whom he'd left his estate to, and Ayala was confident that would reveal whom the initials engraved on the back of the watch belonged to. His hope was that someone willing to buy such an expensive watch as a gift would also remember the recipient in their will.

A probate search usually took upwards of four weeks for a civilian, but police requests were prioritised. With his request on the top of the pile, Ayala would have a copy of the Last Will and Testament of Cecil Matthews by close of business.

***

After reaching the front of the cashier's queue, David and Sarah were shown to a pair of thinly cushioned chairs and told that the bank manager would be with them 'in two minutes'. Twenty minutes later, and they were still waiting.

'Look, it's just a mistake, Sarah. I'm not cheating on you. I didn't buy any jewellery,' Morton said for the third time.

'David, let's save it. Until after we've spoken to the manager anyway. Ah, this must be him.' Sarah forced herself to smile as the bank manager came through the open door. He was in his late thirties, with tousled brown hair, and was wearing an elegantly cut suit. At the sight of Sarah, he returned her smile before offering a hand to David.

'Good evening, Mr and Mrs Morton. I'm Lance Peters. I'm sorry to have kept you waiting. I've taken a look at your credit card statement. What I'm going to do is put these charges on hold while we investigate. To do that, I'll need you to sign a declaration that these you are not responsible for these charges.'

'No problem, Mr Peters,' Sarah said.

'As this is a joint account, I'll also need to see both your cards to verify you have retained possession of them.'

Sarah pulled out her purse, and rummaged around until she found a tiny purse.

'Here you are, Mr Peters.' Sarah held out her card.

'Please, call me Lance.' Lance's fingertips brushed Sarah's lightly as he took her card.

Morton threw his onto the desk silently.

'Thank you both. I'll cancel these cards now to prevent any further charges being added.'

'Will we be charged interest on the fraudulent charges, Lance?' Sarah asked.

'No. Of course not. Once we've investigated, we'll either drop the charges if we find them to be fraudulent, or treat the charges as incurring interest from the date of finishing our investigation if they are not fraudulent,' Lance said.

'Of course they're bloody fraudulent,' Morton said.

'Well, then there won't be any problem. We'll call you once we have conducted our investigation. Thank you for coming in, Mr and Mrs Morton.'

David eyed him, tempted to take offense at the summary conclusion of their meeting but Sarah stepped in too quickly. 'Thank you, Lance.'

'No problem, Sarah.'

Chapter 15: Cecil's Legacy

'Thank you for holding. Your call is important to us. You are: first in the queue,' a robotic voice stated flatly at sixty-second intervals in between bouts of classical music. Ayala had been waiting for nearly an hour, and was becoming more irritated every time the automated system spoke, much to the amusement of Detective Vaughn, who took care to hide her smile behind her laptop screen.

The hold music cut out, and Ayala snatched up the conference phone and motioned for silence.

'And? What did you find?' Ayala demanded. He held the phone flat in his palm, with speakerphone mode switched on.

'Sorry sir, there is no will on file for Cecil Matthews,' said the representative from Her Majesty's Probate Office.

'So he didn't leave anything?'

'He could have died intestate.'

'So no will means no records?'

'Have you got a death certificate? If he died recently, his will won't have been through probate yet. If that's the case, we can do a standing search to let you know when his will is probated.'

'Cecil Matthews died at Edinburgh Royal Infirmary on the third of December 1984. I'm pretty sure you'd have got round to it by now.' Sarcasm began to creep into Ayala's voice.

'There's your problem then.'

'Too long ago?'

'No, sir. Wrong country. We only deal with probate records for England and Wales.'

'Damn it!' In his ignorance, Ayala had overlooked that crucial detail, 'So who do I need to talk to?'

'Usually I'd say HM Commissary... but their records don't go back that far. Let me check with my supervisor where records that old go. Mind if I put you on hold again?' He didn't wait for an answer, and Bach blared once more from the conference phone, filling the incident room.

Now that he wasn't concentrating on the conversation, Ayala realised he had created a scene. Instead of working, the junior officers and techs were watching him with amused expressions.

'What are you looking at?' he snarled, and his audience found they had urgent work to attend to.

The music cut out without warning.

'Sir, are you still there?'

Ayala nodded, then realised the other person couldn't see him. He cleared his throat, 'Yes, yes I'm here,' he confirmed.

'It looks like you want the Scottish Records Office in Edinburgh. Want the number?'

'Please.'

Ayala hoped he wouldn't spend another hour listening to tinny hold music. If he was forced to endure that again, then at least one of the techs would feel his ire.

***

'Ah, Mrs Morton, thanks for coming in.' Lance Peters had foregone the suit he had worn the first time Sarah had met him. Instead he was wearing chinos and a v-necked sweater. Spotting Sarah's appraising eye, he explained half apologetically, 'Dress down Friday.'

'It's OK. Your assistant made it sound urgent on the phone.'

'Mrs Morton, my security team have investigated the contested charges. As you may have realised, they were all electronic transactions. My team found that the purchases, all in the name of David Morton, had been done using your husband's e-banking password, the one we issued him so that he could verify his identity online.'

'So you're telling me that David made the purchases?'

'I can't say for sure. Either he made them, or gave out his password, which would constitute authorising the charges. We won't be refunding the charges. I'm sorry.'

'Don't be. It's my husband that will be sorry.'

'Mrs Morton, I'm sorry that you had to find out about your husband like this. If there's anything I can do...' He proffered a business card which had a mobile number scribbled on the back. Sarah took it.

***

David walked into his flat, oblivious to the impending screaming match. As was his custom, he hung his overcoat on a peg beside the door, slipped off his shoes, then made a right turn and headed along the corridor.

By the time he reached the open-plan kitchen and lounge, he knew something was up. There was no tempting waft of dinner coming from the kitchen, and the lights were off.

He entered, flipped on the lights and found his wife sat at their dinner table, a mug in her hand. She looked calm, but David knew this meant she was serious. She was beyond seething.

'Hi,' he said simply.

'Who is she?' Sarah demanded.

'Who is who?'

'Don't give me that. Who's the bimbo you've been screwing around with?'

'Sarah, I'm not cheating on you.' Morton edged towards her, unwilling to move too close. He leant on a chair on the opposite side of the dinner table to Sarah.

'I'm not stupid, David. I spoke to the bank manager today. He knows it was you.'

'How in God's name would he know that?'

'The transactions were yours. You bought jewellery, diamonds in point of fact. Who were they for, David?'

'I told you! I didn't authorise any of those transactions,' Morton protested in vain.

'Then how were the transactions done using your password?'

'I... I don't know. Maybe some sort of technical glitch?'

'It's not a glitch, David. I'll give you one more chance. Who is she?'

'Sarah, I'm not...'

'Liar!' Sarah screamed as she flung the coffee mug at him. It missed by inches, hurtling past him to smash on the wall. Lukewarm coffee exploded from the mug, coating Morton.

'Sarah, I'm telling the truth. You've got to believe me.'

'Once a cheat, always a cheat. Get out.'

'What?'

'You heard me. Get out of my flat.'

'Sarah, it's our flat.'

'No, David, it's my flat. My parents gave us the deposit. I'm going to count to ten. If you're not gone by then, it'll be much more than a mug that'll get broken.'

'But Sarah, I didn't.'

'One...'

David turned, kicked on his shoes, grabbed his coat, and was walking back out the front door by the time she hit ten. When he was gone, she sank to her knees, and began to sob uncontrollably.

***

Ayala perched uncomfortably on the edge of the longest table in the Incident Room. A battered old projector hastily borrowed from the audiovisual forensic team was propped up on an evidence manual. It thrust a fuzzy image onto the wall, and Ayala jabbed his index finger at the projection as he spoke.

'It took me a while, but I got the Will and Testament of Cecil Matthews. The watch he bought was a drop in the ocean for him. He left behind a huge estate.'

'Who were the beneficiaries?' Morton asked.

'His only son got most of it, but the will also provided for a trust fund to pay for his grandson's education.'

'I take it he had no other children?'

'No, not that we know of, sir. Everything went to Mr Eric Matthews and his son, Charles Matthews.'

'Do we have an address for Eric Matthews?'

'No sir. He's dead. I did an Internet search for the name, and a local news article popped up. He died in a car crash a few years back, along with his wife.'

'And Charles?'

'He got taken into hospital, and landed in the foster system. He should currently be with a Mrs Brenda Lattimer in Kennington.'

'Good work. Get all that formally recorded for your report.'

Ayala slumped in defeat as he realised that Morton had no intention of taking him along to visit Mrs Lattimer.

'But boss, why isn't there a missing persons report from the Lattimers? He's been dead for weeks. They must have noticed!'

'That's what I'm going to find out.'

Chapter 16: Cleaver Square

'You want to talk about it?' Tina Vaughn asked as Morton drove.

'Talk about what?' Morton kept his eyes fixed on the road.

'What's eating at you? You've nailed a difficult case; you should be on cloud nine. Instead you're moping.'

'I'm fine,' Morton lied.

'No, you're not.'

Morton sighed, and resigned himself to a long ride to the Lattimer residence. Once Tina zoned in on something, she was like a dog with a bone.

'Sarah and I aren't talking. She's thrown me out.'

Out of the corner of his eye, Morton could see how concerned Tina looked so he continued, 'Don't worry. I'm staying in a Travelodge, the one over by Euston Station.'

'What happened? I always thought you guys were rock solid.' Tina placed a hand on his arm as she spoke, big green eyes fixed on his. Morton shuffled uncomfortably, but he didn't remove her hand.

'Lots of little things. We've been hit by credit card fraudsters; I've been working long hours trying to crack this case. The usual.'

'I know the feeling.' Tina's face was plastered with a wry grin. With two ex-husbands before thirty, she knew better than most the strain being on the job could put on a relationship.

'How about you? How's your life?' Morton desperately tried to change the subject.

'I'm fine. Still single.'

Morton arched a cynical eyebrow, 'How's that happen? Pretty girl like you, thought you'd be fighting them off with a stick.'

'I get attention, just not from the kind of guys I really like.'

'Hold that thought, I think we're here. Is that number 36B?'

Morton pulled his BMW over, and they stepped out into the square. The sun was beginning to set, and a chill was in the air. Morton knew they were only minutes from a major road, but Cleaver Square felt like a world apart from the rest of Kennington. Tall, handsome homes lined both sides of the Square and a green filled with trees shielded each half from the other. A dusting of snow lingered on the trees, coating their bare branches.

He locked the car, and looked around searching for a house number. The nearest homes were marked with names rather than numbers, 'Edwards Cottage' and 'Dappled Townhouse'. Further along, Morton spotted the first house number, 28, and realised that number 36B must be five houses further along.

'This way.'

With Tina in tow, he strode towards the darkened door of number 36B Cleaver Square.

***

Morton walked up to number 36B slowly, careful not to trip on the ice underfoot. He knocked on the door to the last known abode of Charles Matthews.

The woman who answered Morton's knock engulfed the doorframe, obscuring the view into the house. She peered down sternly at the two detectives on her doorstep.

'Mrs Brenda Lattimer?'

'Yes, I'm Brenda Lattimer.'

'My name is Detective Chief Inspector David Morton, and this is my colleague Tina Vaughn. May we come in?'

'It's my Roger, isn't it? What happened to my husband?' Mrs Lattimer's eyes began to water.

Morton felt himself bristle at the speed with which Mrs Lattimer reacted. Crocodile tears? He wondered, 'No, Mrs Lattimer, we're not here about your husband. We're here about Charles.'

Mrs Lattimer still didn't move. 'What's that little twerp done now?'

'It's probably best if we come inside.'

'As you wish.'

They stepped inside but only went as far as the front sitting room. A steaming tea tray sat on a trestle table by the sofa, but their host did not offer them a drink.

'Mrs Lattimer, I'm sorry to inform you that Charles Matthews is dead.'

Morton watched Mrs Lattimer for her reaction, hoping to spot a flash of guilt that would betray her, but his suspicions proved to be off-base. Instead of guilt, grief, surprise or anger, Mrs Lattimer only showed confusion.

'I think you've got the wrong Charlie, officers.' Her voice was firm, unwavering.

Tina took Mrs Lattimer's hand, 'I'm afraid not. We found an item belonging to Charles Matthews on a body in the Marshes. You are the carer for Charles Matthews, twelve years old and the son of Eric and Jacqueline Matthews, aren't you?'

'I am, but let me clear this up for you, officers. Charlie is downstairs playing with my son right now. Would you like to come and see?'

Morton's muscles tensed as he and Tina followed Brenda Lattimer, half-expecting her to attack them or run: the denial could simply be a ploy to distract them. Instead, Mrs Lattimer led them to a stairwell. The stairs creaked heavily under her weight as she descended.

Morton and Tina followed slowly, forced to go single file by the treacherously narrow steps. At the bottom of the stairs, they reached an open-plan room. Sure enough, as Mrs Lattimer had so vehemently declared, two boys were splayed out on beanbags, lazily mashing buttons on their video-game controllers. The larger boy was the spitting image of his mother, the Lattimer genes evident in his ruddy complexion. The other boy was so slim that he appeared diminished in comparison to James Lattimer's ample bulk.

The boys continued to play their game, ignoring the shadows cast by the three adult intruders.

'Charlie, pause that, will you... son?' Mrs Lattimer demanded, stepping in front of the screen. She hesitated slightly as she added son, almost as if she had added a term of endearment for the officers' benefit.

Morton's eyes darted to Tina's face. She looked as confused as he felt. All the evidence pointed to Charles Matthews being on a slab in the morgue. If Joe Bloggs wasn't Charlie then who was he?

Charlie looked up, and then hit the pause button on his remote. He was emaciated, sullen and not at all pleased to have his game interrupted, but he was definitely alive.

'These nice officers are here to see you,' said Mrs Lattimer.

Morton turned to Vaughn. This was completely unexpected. For the first time in his career, he was speechless.

Sensing Morton's hesitation, Tina stepped in, 'Hello, Charlie, we're here to check on you. Is everything OK?'

Tina's training in dealing with child witnesses paid off; improvisation worked, and Charlie nodded meekly, blissfully unaware of the real reason for the presence of two police officers.

An awkward silence filled the room as the detectives pondered their next move.

Finally, Tina said: 'Mrs Lattimer, could we have a word upstairs again?'

Mrs Lattimer shrugged in an accommodating manner and the trio ascended the rickety stairs to the ground floor hallway. Away from Charlie, Morton began to zero in on the details.

'Mrs Lattimer, how long has Charlie been with you?'

'Oh, I'd say six weeks now.'

'And before that?'

Brenda looked around warily, wondering if it was a trick question. 'With another foster family. Charlie lost his parents a while back, so he spent some time with short-term foster carers. I'm not trained to deal with trauma cases. I'd much rather have a nice, quiet, long-term thing.'

Morton chewed a nail thoughtfully, his brows furrowed. Then he asked, 'Has Charlie ever worn a gold watch?'

Mrs Lattimer shook her head. 'Not that I've seen. He only had two bags on 'im when he got here, and they only had clothes in, and a ratty old teddy bear.'

'Mrs Lattimer, would you consent to us interviewing Charlie to confirm that?'

'Like I said, he ain't got a watch. But yeah, no skin off my nose.'

'We'll have to arrange for a social worker to attend. My colleague here, Miss Vaughn, will conduct the interview. Are you available to come to the station tomorrow?'

'Not 'til after three. I can bring him down after school? Children's Services will have my guts for garters if I pull 'im out of school.'

'Why would they have a problem with that?'

'He's already behind, isn't he? Probably down to being bounced around a bit, and what with what happened.'

'What happened?'

'One of his previous foster families, they died in a house fire.'

Morton nodded. He'd read the report on the Dalkeith Grove fire in which Mr and Mrs Grant had perished.

'We'll see you and Charlie at the station tomorrow at half past three.' Morton handed her a business card. 'Call me if you need to change the appointment, or need us to arrange transport.'

'I've got a car, thank you very much!' Mrs Lattimer protested indignantly.

'Yeah, and going by the size of your stomach you drive everywhere,' Tina jibed under her breath, too quietly for Mrs Lattimer to hear.

***

'Well, that was unexpected. If our Joe Bloggs Junior isn't Charlie Matthews, then who is he and why the hell does he have Charlie's watch?' Morton said as he and Tina returned to the car.

'Could we have made a mistake with the watch?' Tina asked.

'Maybe, but it appears to be a one-off, totally unique. Let's try and track down when and where that watch changed hands.' Morton unlocked the saloon with a beep then climbed into the driver's seat.

'Won't the kid be able to tell us himself in tomorrow's interview?'

'Sure. But before the interview, I need you to go over Ayala's paperwork and make sure we've not made any silly mistakes. I don't want the interview to be a complete blunder like today.' Morton's voice trailed off as he wondered if Charlie might be fond of playing with matches.

'Isn't it odd that the both his real parents and his foster parents die in tragic circumstances, and then he appears to be murdered. What are the odds of that?'

'It is peculiar, but murder always is. I'll be in late tomorrow, so get started without me. I need to go see my bank manager.'

'Leave it to me.' Tina patted Morton's knee reassuringly.

Chapter 17: Homogenised Milk

Shortly before nine o'clock, Morton stood outside the Westminster branch of his bank and waited for it to open. At the moment Big Ben began to ring out on the hour, the doors opened and Morton strode in, and made a beeline for the corridor leading to Lance Peters' office. He made it past the row of cubicles housing mortgage advisors without issue, but mere steps from the manager's office a giant of a man appeared from a side door.

'That's off limits, that is,' he declared, physically interposing himself between Morton and the manager's office.

'I'm here to see Lance Peters,' Morton bluffed, as if he had an appointment. The security guard leant to the right so that he could see through the glass door into the manager's office. Lance Peters was deep in conversation with two businessmen. He was pacing back and forth, gesticulating wildly.

'Mr Peters is busy. Talk to his secretary.' The guard gestured towards a cubicle near the mortgage brokers.

Morton sighed, pulled out his police badge and said, 'I'm going nowhere. Get Mr Peters for me, please.'

'Got a warrant?'

'No, but...'

'Then talk to his secretary.'

Morton flushed red. 'This is important. Get Mr Peters. Now.'

'Calm down.'

'Calm down? I am calm.'

'Sir, don't take that tone with me.'

'Take what tone?' Morton said, a little louder than he had intended. The occupants of the cubicles rose to see what all the fuss was about, a sea of faces suddenly watching Morton.

'I'm not going to ask you again. Calm down or I'll have to escort you off the premises.' The security guard reached out to grab Morton's arm, intending to steer him towards the exit.

Morton batted his hand away and shouted, 'Lay a hand on me, and I will arrest you.'

At that moment, the businessmen exited Lance Peters' office, followed by the man himself.

'Is there a problem?' he asked mildly.

'No sir, just escorting this gentleman off the premises,' the guard replied.

'No, you're bloody not. Mr Peters, do you have a moment?'

Lance glanced at his watch, then nodded briskly, 'Very well.' He beckoned with his index finger for Morton to follow him, then disappeared back into his office. Morton followed, then closed the door behind him with an audible click.

'So what do you want?'

'I need you to tell my wife I didn't cheat. I didn't use my password. Those aren't my transactions,' Morton said bluntly, without any preamble.

'Mr Morton. Let's walk through this logically. Have you given your password to anyone else?'

'No.'

'Ever write it down?'

Morton remembered the copy he kept in the safe for Sarah. 'No,' he lied.

'I know from your account details that you're an online banking customer. Do you keep your computer clean? I don't mean dusted,' Lance laughed at his own joke, 'I mean do you run security scans, anti-virus software and the like?'

'Yes, of course.'

'Do you download using peer-to-peer systems?'

'No.'

'Do you, ahem, use adult entertainment sites?'

'No,' Morton said, more vehemently this time.

'Then do you use any other computers?'

'No, I don't. Where are you bloody going with this? I didn't authorise these transactions.'

'Mr Morton, I'm simply trying to establish how this has happened; if you didn't authorise these charges someone else had to have done so.' Lance Peters sounded sceptical.

'I didn't,' Morton said through gritted teeth.

'OK. Do you stream live sports events on your laptop?' Peters asked with the air of a man taking a stab in the dark.

'Yeah,' Morton shrugged.

'Legally?'

Morton remained silent for a moment. Come to think of it, the cost for watching those games was a bit on the cheap side... way less than a Sky Sports subscription. Morton hastily retreated back onto safer grounds: 'Look, I didn't authorise those transactions. I've got my card still. I know my rights. You're liable.'

'Not if you didn't act reasonably we're not. I think you've taken up enough of my time. I'm not going to waive these charges.'

'That's fraud!'

'I suggest you take that up with the police.' Lance smirked.

***

'Date of birth?' The police clerk's voice was monotone, never wavering out of a low octave.

'October 14th, 1961.'

'Driver's licence?'

'Here,' Morton slid a scan over, notarised as a true copy at the desk in the Fraud Squad's foyer. Since this was a branch of the City of London Police, Morton didn't expect to receive the deferential respect he enjoyed at the Met.

'National Insurance number?'

'LN 29 AB 6D 0.' Morton passed a second scan across.

'Telephone numbers please – work, home and mobile.'

Without comment, another piece of paper went across the desk.

'Bank account details – name, numbers, any customer service and investigators' names from the banks. We'll also need copies of any communication, notes of any conversation including the times of said conversations, and a chronology of the frauds.'

Morton repeated the clerk's request in his head, trying to discern if he had all the papers he had been asked for. 'N, N, CS, C, NC inc T + C,' Morton mumbled, using an archaic police memory trick to recite the request.

He flicked through his folder, taking out a copy of all the requested documents. Finally satisfied he had everything, he handed them all over. His gut churned with the realisation he had just handed over everything a criminal would need to rob and defraud him to a mere police clerk. Morton often chastised those who were too free with their personal data, but it appeared he had just joined their number.

***

'Homogenised Partially Skimmed Sterilised Milk,' Morton read aloud to the empty room; 'delicious.'

Like almost every other budget hotel Morton had stayed in, the walls were beige. Even the bed linen matched the walls. Only the blue hues of a plastic chair and desk broke up the monotony.

The room had no minibar, but Morton had stopped off at a convenience store on the way back for a bottle of Laphroaig. A generous portion sat in front of him in one of the hotel's coffee mugs. In one quick motion, he tossed back the amber liquid. A smoky fire engulfed his mouth and slowly travelled down his throat with a satisfying warmth.

Morton grabbed a pen, and held his hand over a blank page. If he couldn't take Sarah away for a second honeymoon then he'd go back even further. He had barely finished his police training when their paths first crossed. He'd written the attractive way-out-of-his-league Sarah a poem, and agonised for days about sending it to her. His poetry had first won her heart over thirty years ago. His hand hovered over the paper, then began to briskly dance across the page recording the words that could   never   be   spoken.

Chapter 18: Question Time

The half past three appointment quickly became four o'clock as Morton struggled to assemble the right people for Charles 'Charlie' Matthew's interview. He would take an observer role in the interview, as dealing with child witnesses required specialist training. Morton, along with Detective Ayala and Dr Jenkins, would observe from the Incident Room. One of the investigation boards had been turned around to reveal a matte white surface. Ayala's borrowed projector lay on one of the benches painting a low-resolution picture from a nearby laptop. There were no speakers free, so the team was relying on the laptop's tinny built-in speakers.

'Shh. I think we're finally on,' Morton addressed the Incident Room in a hushed tone.

On the video, Morton could see three chairs set up in a rough triangle with an ankle-height table between them. The room was only one floor up, but could have been virtually anywhere thanks to the video link. A similar set-up could be found in a guest waiting room which had been made available to Mrs Lattimer. She had declined to watch, however, opting to take the opportunity to chain-smoke outside the building.

'Hi, Charlie. I'm Tina.' Tina Vaughn spoke softly, forcing the detectives to lean towards the tinny laptop speakers.

'Hi.'

'And you already know Hank, don't you, Charlie?' Tina indicated the social worker who would play a passive role in the interrogation, speaking up only if he felt Charlie needed him. Charlie's eyes flickered over the social worker, and then stopped as if transfixed by a spot behind him.

'That's a nice shirt. Do you support Arsenal, Charlie?'

Silence met Tina's attempt to build rapport. Charlie continued to stare off to one side. Tina twisted to see where he was looking, but there was nothing there.

'Do you know why you're here, Charlie?'

Charlie bit his lip nervously, and then shook his head.

'Charlie, I'd like to ask you about watches. Do you have a watch?' Tina lifted up her arm to indicate hers. Almost immediately, Charlie mimicked her, showing off a plastic Casio watch.

'Is that yours, Charlie?'

Charlie nodded, a slight smile indicating he was starting to relax.

'Have you ever had another watch, Charlie?'

Charlie pursed his lips as if he wanted to speak, and then shrugged.

Tina hesitated. Child witnesses were prone to being led, and she was keen to keep asking open questions to prevent any issues with defence counsel at a later date. At some point, she'd have to show him the Keppler Oechslan watch. That could wait.

'Where do you live, Charlie?'

'Number 36B, Cleaver Square,' he replied slowly, as if struggling to pronounce each syllable.

'Who do you live with, Charlie?'

'James. And Mrs Lattimer.'

Almost as soon as Charlie had finished speaking, Morton's voice buzzed over the radio reminding Tina that he lived with Mr Lattimer too. She ignored his advice, and pressed on towards the detail she really wanted.

'How long have you been there?'

'A little while.'

'Did you move before or after Christmas?'

'Before.'

'Do you like it there?'

Another shrug, 'I guess.'

'Charlie,' Tina paused for a moment to double-check the printout of Charlie's care history that Ayala had cajoled from the local authority, 'where were you before that?'

'Another house.' Charlie shifted in his chair, sitting on his hands to stop them fidgeting.

'Who were you staying with?'

'Lots of people.'

'But who was looking after you?'

'Adrian and Pru.'

Tina nodded. Adrian and Prudence Lovejoy were Charlie's short-term foster carers after the fire at the Grant residence. The next few questions could be delicate. Tina glanced at Hank Williams, who nodded almost imperceptibly.

'Charlie, tell me about the fire.'

Charlie frowned, his forehead scrunching up as he did so.

'What happened, Charlie?'

'The house burnt,' Charlie said. His expression was vacant, as if recalling something that had happened to someone else.

'Where were you, Charlie?'

'Downstairs. I felt sleepy.'

'Then what happened?'

'Firemen came and squirted water all over the house.'

'And then?'

'Then I got taken away, to hospital,' Charlie said matter-of-factly.

Morton hit mute on the video.

'Did anyone else have a chill run down their spine?' Morton asked those in the Incident Room.

'It was weird, boss, almost cold — detached even,' Ayala replied.

'That was my take it on it. He was totally dispassionate. What do you think, Jenkins?'

The psychologist was deep in thought, 'Huh? Oh. Right. He could be in shock. Trauma like that can easily cause post-traumatic stress. He appears to be in a dissociative state. He's not properly feeling the trauma of seeing his foster family burn. I'd like to get him in for a session.'

'It's not going to happen, Doc. Not without parental consent.' Morton flicked the volume back up as Tina took the watch out from her bag. All eyes turned back to the big screen.

'Charlie,' Tina held up the Keppler Oechslan watch, 'do you know what this is?'

She watched his eyes for a glint of recognition.

'A watch?' he offered tentatively, as if afraid he was being tricked.

'Who owns the watch, Charlie?'

'The police.'

'Why do you say that?'

'It says so on the bag.'

Tina glanced at the evidence bag; 'Police' was indeed printed across the bag.

'So it isn't yours then, Charlie?'

'No.'

'OK, Charlie, that's everything then. Thank you for coming in today.'

Hank led Charlie from the frame, and Morton killed the projector.

'What do we make of that then, lads?'

'Could be he's forgotten the watch. God knows when he was separated from it. He's only twelve, and he's been in the system for most of that time. Stolen, sold, or lost. Take your pick,' Ayala offered.

'Maybe. But it's not an easy watch to pass on. Very distinctive,' Morton said slowly. 'It's also a big jump going from lost or stolen to ending up on another dead child. It's not exactly likely that a second kid found or bought it, then decided to wear it, and then got murdered. That stretches plausibility.'

'Where do we go from here?' Ayala said. 'We've got an unknown dead kid, with a watch which we know was bought by a gentleman, since deceased. The heir apparent to the watch doesn't recognise it, so it has to have been moved on while he was pretty young.'

'He doesn't appear to recognise it,' Jenkins interrupted. 'Memory is fallible, and he's been through a great deal of stress. He could be suppressing memory of the watch.'

'Even so. How did our watch get from the kid to the dead body? Whether Charlie remembers it or not, he should have it. It was his granddad's gift to his father, and it went with Charlie as far as the Grant residence. They were paying to insure it when they died last year. It didn't have long to go AWOL,' Morton thought aloud.

'Could the dead kid be related to the Grants?' said Ayala, his voice wavering between octaves.

'Doubtful. Probate records show they left everything to Charlie. He was with them seven years, and they have no other family,' Morton said, his lips pursed. He had to be careful not to phrase his rebuttal too strongly. Ayala had been responsible for the grunt work that led them to the dead end in Cleaver Square, and he'd take any implied insult personally.

'Our research hasn't turned anything up. Charlie doesn't look anything like the facial reconstruction we've been handing out. If we could get a sample of Charlie's DNA, it would make this so much easier. It might be Charlie has a twin brother,' Ayala said.

'That seems unlikely, Bertram. We'd have seen some sort of documentation,' Jenkins quipped wryly. Morton silenced him with a glare. The group sat awkwardly in silence for a moment, none willing to volunteer an idea lest it be shot down in flames.

It was down to Morton, ever the conciliator, to break the silence: 'We'd need permission from the guardian for DNA anyway, and that Mrs Lattimer didn't strike me as the co-operative sort.'

'We could at least ask,' Ayala said.

'True enough, Ayala. No harm asking.'

***

'Absolutely not,' Brenda Lattimer's reply gave no room for doubt. It was clear she wouldn't budge. Smoke emanated from Mrs Lattimer's cigarette, her third since arriving at the station.

'Mrs Lattimer, it isn't going to hurt Charlie in any way. All we need is a cheek swab. Or a comb he uses. Or his toothbrush.

'I said no. Charlie's one of my charges, ain't he? I can't be giving away his DNA. You want it, get a court order.' Mrs Lattimer walked off, leaving Morton standing outside New Scotland Yard with Tina Vaughn.

'Any bright ideas?' Morton asked, not expecting a response.

'Actually,' Tina replied, 'I do. The kid had a can of coke during our interview. It's probably still in the bin. If we're quick, and a bit lucky, then we'll have our DNA sample. It's a bit clichéd but who's to argue if it works?'

'Tina, I could kiss you!'

Chapter 19: Running in Circles

Before the team assembled for the morning briefing, Morton and Tina met in his office. Every few moments, Morton checked his email again. There was still no word from DNA. A long-since-cold bagel lay next to Morton's laptop.

'David. You know if the Travelodge gets too much, there's always room at mine,' Tina said.

Morton barely heard her; he was too busy concentrating on the New Message notification that had popped up on his screen. He snatched at his mouse, and then clicked to open the email.

'Damn!'

'No match?'

'No match, zero alleles in common. Well, there goes the sibling theory. Joe Bloggs and Charlie Matthews are not blood relations,' Morton said.

'Give yourself a break, David, we'll get there.' Tina laid a hand on her boss's knee.

Morton glanced down, mentally deciding whether or not to remove her hand. In the time it took him to decide, Tina noticed his apprehension and withdrew her hand.

'Who the hell is this kid? We've run down all the leads, and there's absolutely nothing tying him to a missing child. How does a child disappear and not one person bother to try and find him? Not a teacher, a social worker, a parent or even a friend.'

'I don't know. The kid could have never been in the system. You know, a Fritzl-style case. The kid gets born at home, never registered with the authorities. Then killed by the parent and dumped.' Tina referred to an infamous Austrian case in which a woman had been held captive by her father for twenty-four years, giving birth to seven children in a dark basement.

'Maybe, but there's no sign of abuse or malnutrition. We don't even know how he died; no bone breaks, no evidence of foul play in the toxicology report.'

'That doesn't mean much. You could stab someone without hitting a bone if you were lucky. He could have bled out. He could have frozen to death. He could have been smothered. We only had limited tissue samples to work with.'

'All valid points, but that still leaves us with an unknown victim, an unknown assailant and no obvious leads.'

'We'll get there. You haven't let us down yet, Chief.'

***

Ayala tried not to stare when his boss walked into the meeting. Morton looked terrible. His eyes were bloodshot with deep bags hanging underneath them, and those shoes with that suit... what was the boss thinking?

'We're back to square one, people,' Morton began the morning briefing. 'We've got ourselves a dead kid in the park with a watch. We traced the watch through to the purchaser to the recipient of the watch, and from there to his heir: Charles 'Charlie' Matthews. The child who inherited the watch has no knowledge of it. Simply put, we've run down all the major leads. If our Joe Bloggs Junior isn't Charles Matthews, then who the hell is he?'

Silence ensued, every member of his team avoiding eye contact.

'I can't prove it, but there's something just plain off here. How did the watch leave Charles Matthews' possession? There are no indications it was sold, and no crime reports. If someone had stolen a watch worth over fifty grand from me, I'd be damn sure to report it.'

'But Chief, if he was young when the parents died it could have gone AWOL while he was in the system and too young to remember it. Just because the Grants had it insured doesn't mean they physically retained possession of it. Even at black market prices, it would have made a few bob.'

'Good thinking, Ayala. But that still doesn't explain how it ended up on a dead pre-teen in Hackney Marshes. If you steal or buy something that fancy, and it is obviously expensive, then you don't give it to a kid. Even at scrap prices, that watch is valuable.'

'What if our Joe Bloggs Junior is a pickpocket?' Ayala tried again.

'So you're thinking it was stolen twice? I'm not buying it. I can't prove otherwise, but there's something odd going on here. Ayala, I want you running down anything the social worker knows about Master Matthews. Something about that kid doesn't sit right with me. Vaughn, look into this house fire. Find out what happened and see if it explains the kid's reticence. All clear? Good. Get to it.'

***

The office space Hank Williams occupied courtesy of Children's Services was part of a hot desk system that had been introduced to help curtail the running costs of the services' administration. Rather than allocate every social worker a small cubbyhole-style office, someone in the ivory tower had decided that a pooled space, shared between all local authorities, was the most efficient way to do things. The move had been rather successful; with so many staff out on site visits to their charges, the hot desk system introduced had freed up space for a new computer system to be installed on-site.

'Can I ask an idiotic question?' Ayala led with his favourite interview tactic. Rather than jump in and ask what he wanted to know, he made the interviewee feel secure by implying his own ignorance. Criminals could be arrogant, and arrogance breeds carelessness.

'Sure, if you don't mind an idiotic answer.'

Ayala chuckled appreciatively. 'What does your job involve? I know the basics, but how does the set-up work?'

'It's pretty simple – I'm ultimately responsible for the welfare of the children in my care. I look after around twenty kids at a time. I place them with foster carers, seek adoption where appropriate and follow up on any feedback from schools, foster carers and from your own colleagues. I make sure they're reasonably happy, healthy and get any help they might need, or I try to anyway,' Hank Williams replied.

'And you cover the whole of London?'

'Yep. Pretty much everything central anyway. If it's within an hour on the tube from Marble Arch, I could get assigned it. I work part-time for multiple Local Authorities, so I get to travel quite a bit.'

'Right. So Charles Matthews is one of your twenty?'

'Yep. I took him on a few months ago.'

'How's that been?'

'About average. The kid is a bit quiet. I drove him to the Lattimers from the Lovejoys. The Lovejoys never take them for long. They just provide a safe haven after a trauma. I know Charlie is having a bit of trouble at school. They think he might score highly on the autistic spectrum, or possibly suffer from dyslexia. He's doing brilliantly in maths, but everything involving language skills has him stumped. We're waiting on an educational psychologist to see him, but the waiting times can be a bit insane in the months preceding the exam season.'

'At least he's too young to be doing exams this year,' Ayala smiled, trying to look as sympathetic as possible.

'That is one saving grace. If I'd lost my parents, then my foster parents, I'm sure I'd be struggling too.'

'How'd his biological parents die?'

'Car accident, I think. It's in his file. I can check if you like.'

'Thanks. What would be really handy would be getting a copy of that file,' Ayala said.

'No can do. You want that, you've got to talk to Children's Services Head Office, and they never give out our files unless lawyers get involved.'

'I guessed as much.' Ayala paused to find a business card. 'Thanks for your time, Hank. If you think of anything else then let me know.'

As he turned to walk away, Ayala shrugged. Nothing unexpected, although he had hoped to get a copy of Charlie's complete file.

Chapter 20: Dalkeith Grove

'This was the point of origin,' Lucien Darville, Fire Investigator, indicated a particularly charred spot of flooring in the corner. Ash covered the scene. Metal and burnt wood were strewn all over the house. Where once a Victorian terraced house stood, Dalkeith Grove now had a gaping hole with only the structural husk left. Smoke had licked the adjoining homes, leaving dark stains on walls that were never intended to be exposed to the elements. Plastic coverings and metal pins had been put in place to prevent any structural issues, but gave an impression of post-Blitz London.

'What started the fire?' Tina inquired. She glanced down at the Dictaphone in her hand to make sure a red light was lit to indicate that it was recording.

'We found the carcass of a fan heater. The cheap kind you get in catalogues.'

'I know the type; my Mum has one and has it on constantly. It costs a fortune to run.'

'Ha-ha, you should buy her a jumper. See if she gets the hint. Or show her a picture of this place. That ought to scare her enough to unplug it.'

Tina took Darville's advice, and snapped a picture on her phone. It would double up for the investigation file anyway.

'Did the heater malfunction?'

'I don't think so. We had it inspected, and our expert could discern no fault. More likely it was too close to something flammable. Newspapers, magazines or the like.'

'That simple?'

'Yep. Simple but deadly. The house is timber-frame construction. When carbon-heavy material burns, you get carbon monoxide gas. It's lighter than air, so it rises. We found Mrs Grant upstairs in the master bedroom, and Mr Grant in the upstairs office. They would have passed out before they knew what happened, never to awake. Cause of death was obvious before the coroner pronounced; a pink corpse is a sure sign of carbon monoxide poisoning.'

'Where was the kid?'

'Playing in the garage, which probably saved him. There was an internal door to the house, but it was shut. He got taken to the hospital for a once-over that afternoon as I recall, but he wouldn't have suffered any permanent physical damage from the fire. His mental state, on the other hand, could easily have suffered.'

'Why didn't the fire alarm go off? Don't tell me they didn't have one.'

'They had one, but the batteries were dead.'

'Christ, I'd better check mine,' Tina said as images of a lobster-pink family shuffled through her mind; to think that a simple battery failure could kill two people, and irrevocably change the course of a third life.

'You do that. Anything else you need to see here?'

'Nope. Just to make sure, you think this is an accident, right? That's how it's listed on the report.' Tina tapped her vintage shoulder bag, which had a printed copy sticking out of the outside pocket.

'That's my report. Of course I think it was an accident. No sign of foul play here. We looked for it, but most arson involves some sort of accelerant and there was no evidence of that here. Besides, neither of the victims had any known motive to set a fire. The place isn't insured for anything beyond replacement and rebuild costs, and they didn't have any financial difficulties. I'd say there's a 95 per cent chance this was just plain old bad luck. I see at least two or three of these fires every week.'

'Thanks, Lucien,' Tina stared up doe-eyed at the wreckage of the Grant family home, trying to comprehend how two or three families could suffer such a terrible fate week in, week out. It was almost worse than investigating a murder. At least with a murder, there was always someone to take the blame. It was just a matter of catching them.

***

James and Charlie were enjoying a brief respite from the presence of Brenda and Roger Lattimer. It had become an increasingly common occurrence. The downside was the extensive list of chores they'd been left to complete. To get the house clean would take all evening if they didn't speed up, and neither boy wanted to risk the inevitable punishment should they fail to live up to the exacting standards expected of them.

'Pull your socks up, Charlie!' James Lattimer urged Charlie on as they polished the woodwork in the kitchen.

Charlie bent forward, rolled up his trousers and tugged his socks higher up his legs. James burst out laughing as Charlie stretched the socks further towards his knees.

'Not literally, you moron.'

'You moron,' Charlie parroted, copying James' mocking tone.

'How you doing anyway? Tired yet?'

'Fine thanks, mate,' Charlie replied.

James frowned. Charlie always seemed to say exactly the same thing. Always.

'Charlie, are you doing banana gorilla OK?' James fought to keep a straight face as he tested his theory.

'Fine thanks, mate.'

'Do you want to throw my PlayStation out the window while doing the Macarena?'

Recognition flickered in Charlie's eyes at the mention of the games console. 'Sure.'

James grinned. He was right.

Chapter 21: Keep Digging

'Kiaran, I know this is unorthodox but we're hitting dead end after dead end. Joe Bloggs Junior is not a match for Charles Matthews. I need to know how Charles' watch came to be on our corpse. What are the odds of exhuming the parents of Charles Matthews to confirm his identity? There's something off about that kid.' Morton paced up and down in his office, using his BlackBerry's hands-free kit to talk.

'You've got to be joking, David,' Kiaran replied. The line crackled as he replied. He too was using a hands-free kit, but rather than pacing he was clicking hastily through a legal precedent database looking for a reference for an unrelated case's skeleton argument.

'Deadly serious. I've got a dead kid, and absolutely no idea who he is. There's a connection there with the Matthews family, but I'm not sure what it is. The watch was last in the possession of Mr Eric Matthews, deceased. His son doesn't recognise the watch. So how did it end up with our Joe Bloggs?'

'Chief, you're fixating way too much on this watch. What if it was just coincidence? It could have gone missing anytime in the decade between the death of Eric Matthews and Joe Bloggs Junior's being found. We only have Robert Lyons' word that the watch was on the body rather than near it.'

'Where else can I look? We're running out of evidence. The public appeal has gone nowhere. Besides, if he'd been buried only near the watch then Lyons would have been able to keep the watch as a lawful find rather than evidence. He had no reason to lie,' Morton said. The line went quiet, and for a moment Morton thought he had lost Kiaran. In the background, he could faintly hear the prosecutor clicking furiously. 'Kiaran?'

'You're the cop, David. I'll make an application to the Ministry of Justice, but I really don't think they'll let us disturb the dead on a hunch. Find me something solid, and I'll make it work. Until then, what else have you got?'

'Bugger all. My gut says that the watch is the key to cracking this case wide open.'

'You said that about the search warrant,' Kiaran jibed.

'Same strand of the investigation. As a toddler, Charles Matthews lost his parents in a car crash, then his foster parents died in a house fire last year. Aren't you the least bit curious?' Morton cajoled.

'I'll take a look at the coroner's report,' Kiaran replied dubiously, 'But these are cold leads, David. You'd better be right if we're going to start digging.'

***

Charlie waited nervously, fidgeting in his seat. The waiting room was a colourful affair, with toys and a television. He knew he wasn't there to play; Mrs Lattimer had intimated as much. The other kids in the waiting room were sitting with parents and teachers, but Mrs Lattimer had dropped Charlie off and gone. Charlie hoped she would come back to take him home, otherwise it would be a long walk.

The door to the psychologist's office opened a smidgeon, and a pretty brunette leaned through the gap. 'Charles Matthews?'

Charlie stood, leaving his school bag in the waiting room under the chair. All he needed was a pencil.

Once he was inside, he took the seat nearest the door. There was a school-style table between him and Doctor Wagner.

'Hi, Charlie, we're going to do a few exercises today.'

Charlie glanced at the document on the table labelled 'Wide Ranging Assessment Test 4', and wondered what the afternoon had in store for him.

'The first thing I'd like you to do is read out this card for me. There's no rush, so take your time.'

'The dog ran over the road to the house,' Charlie began. Each word was pronounced slowly, as if he had to mull over how to pronounce it properly.

After a few paragraphs, the doctor had assessed Charlie's reading age as being well below average. In the writing test, in which he copied out the same words, he was quicker. Charlie's biggest difficulty was the spoken word. Doctor Wagner watched him carefully as he worked, noting the neat cursive in which he wrote. Few boys had such pretty handwriting.

'That's great, Charlie, thank you. We're going to do something a bit different now.' The doctor placed flash cards depicting shapes on the table. 'These cards show a shape made up of cubes. I'm going to give you a card with one shape on it, and a set of cubes that make up that shape. I want you to assemble the cubes to make the same shape as on the card. Do you understand?'

Charlie nodded, already turning a piece of the plastic puzzle over in his hands.

'Now, the first one is just a practice so I know you know how to do it. After the first one, I'll time how long you take. You'll be given sixty seconds per puzzle, and we'll see how many you get through. You ready? Go.'

Charlie picked up one part of the puzzle, an L shape with three cubes on the longer side and two at one end. He looked at the other parts, and tried to visualise how they would fit together to make the cube depicted in the drawing. Then, without hesitating, he twisted the pieces together to form a perfect cube and set the completed puzzle upon the desk.

Charlie proceeded to complete every puzzle given to him. His spatial awareness was exemplary.

He was a very unusual child indeed.

Chapter 22: Insurance

A rich aroma filled the incident room as Colombian coffee percolated through the coffee machine and dripped softly in the pot below.

Morton found himself poring over paperwork once more. This time, it was the Grants' insurance documentation. Morton ran a finger down a page entitled 'Inventory List' which was sandwiched between several other appendices to the Fire Investigation Report written by Lucien Darville. The more Morton reread Lucien's words, the more convinced he was that the fire had been an accident.

The insurance looked pretty standard at first. The 'building' element covered only the estimated rebuild costs, and the estimates were modest. It was the contents that had drawn Morton's attention.

Inventory List: Disclosed high value objects (Replacement value only)

- *1 x Dell XPS 8190 Laptop (£2000)*
- *1 x Panasonic DPT59X:LN Plasma Television (£1450)*
- *1 x Diamond engagement ring, 1.04 CT VVSI (£4750)*
- *36 x Cases, Vintage Wine Collection (£13,000)*

'Well, that explains how the fire spread so quickly.' Morton flipped back to the incident summary which read 'The property included an extensive cellar which was used to store vintage wines and spirits which acted as accelerants.'

Morton sighed inwardly at the pretension. When would people learn to buy wine then drink it rather than letting it sit getting dusty for a decade or two. Morton turned his attention back to the Inventory List.

- *1 x Art Collection (Full inventory located at addendum F) (£19,000)*
- *Audiovisual equipment (£800)*
- *Sports Equipment (£450)*
- *Watch collection (Full inventory located at addendum G) (£72,000)*

'Seventy-two thousand?' Flipping pages, Morton quickly uncovered addendum G.

'Watch collection comprises four watches (as photographed) including Citizen Eco-Drive (Men's) (£900), Citizen Eco-Drive (Women's) (£1100), Rolex Abyss (£12,000), and Keppler Oechslan (£58,000).'

Morton punched the air. 'I knew that bloody watch was important!'

He grabbed his phone, hit the number nineteen speed dial for Kiaran O'Connor and waited impatiently.

'Kiaran, I've got the evidence to prove Charlie inherited the watch. He had it when he was with the Grant family, whom he left last year. He should have known about it. We need to exhume Mrs Matthews. Get down to the incident room. Now.' Morton hung up without waiting for a reply. He knew he couldn't give orders to the CPS lawyer, but he also knew that curiosity would get the better of Kiaran. The CPS prosecutor had an office in a nearby building, less than fifteen minutes' walk away.

***

'Charlie exhibits some of the core indicators for dyslexia. He has difficulty with reading and spelling. This difficulty is particularly pronounced when he attempt to utilise multisyllabic words. He further shows difficulty processing instructions without supplementary aids. His reading is inaccurate, and his completion speed for language comprehension exercises falls well below the normal range.

'Despite this, Charlie shows an astonishing aptitude for mathematics. This segment of the test alone indicates an extremely high IQ. Charlie completed spatial awareness tasks quickly and easily, suggesting strong problem-solving skills, and above-average manual dexterity. His handwriting further demonstrates this. Although he writes slowly, and has great difficulty spelling, his writing is exceptionally neat.

'During the two-hour assessment, Charlie rarely smiled and seemed reluctant to make eye contact. His speech patterns were slow, and he paused often. His syntax was punctuated with 'umms', which could indicate that Charlie is high on the autistic spectrum, though such analysis falls outside the immediate concerns of the Wide Range Assessment Test.

'In conclusion, I recommend Charlie is given Special Educational Needs status, and accorded help in exam situations, as well as weekly support classes to help him with his schoolwork.'

Doctor Wagner finished typing, slender fingers pulling away from the keyboard. Something about Charlie bothered her, but she couldn't put her finger on what exactly. She hit print, readied her pen to sign, and then waited for the printer to churn out her report. It was a flat-fee gig, and every extra minute she spent thinking about work was a minute she wasn't getting paid.

***

Kiaran entered the conference room to find David Morton practically bouncing around. As soon as he saw Kiaran, he skipped over, the balls of his feet barely connecting with the floor.

'Afternoon!'

'Hi, David. You rang?' said Kiaran.

'I've got a break. That watch...'

'Not the damn watch again?' Kiaran interrupted.

'Yes, the damn watch. The damn watch the kid didn't remember. It was insured at the Grant residence.'

'The home he was in for several years? Remind me again what the chronology is.'

'After Charlie's parents died ten years ago, he spent three weeks with a temporary family. The usual trauma support placement. Then on to the Grants, where he spent several years. Then the Lovejoys for a short stint after the fire, and now he's with the Lattimers.'

'They really do bounce around the system,' Kiaran observed wryly.

'Yep, but you only insure a watch if you know it exists. So why didn't Charlie recognise the watch? I've played the interview video back over and over. His eyes don't even flicker when Vaughn takes the evidence bag out. If I'd lost my parents, I'm sure I'd remember the only heirloom.'

'I suppose so. So how did the watch get from Charlie to Joe Bloggs Junior, and why didn't Charlie recognise the watch?'

'Could the Grants have kept it safe for him?' Morton thought aloud.

'Or from him,' the lawyer remarked dryly. 'If they did, they didn't do a great job. It ended up buried in the Marshes, after all.'

'There was no safe at the Grant residence, not according to the fire investigation report. So the watch must have been worn.'

'Mr Grant might have worn it. Could have been stolen.'

'But then you'd claim on the insurance.'

'Unless it wasn't long before he died.'

'I'm not buying it. A guy gets robbed, and then he gets burned to death. Then the thief either dies, or sells it to a kid who dies? Doesn't make sense, you wouldn't fence a watch worth over fifty-thousand pounds to a kid.'

'So what do you want me to do with this?' Kiaran asked.

'Get Mr Matthews exhumed.'

'Why not Mrs Mathews?'

'Ayala did some digging; she's been cremated. We'll have to use DNA to confirm there's no familial link between the Matthews and our Joe Bloggs Junior. An heirloom like that would naturally end up with a relative.'

'I'll give it a try. The Ministry of Justice might be swayed. We don't need a criminal standard of proof, but even a bureaucrat will need some convincing to let us dig up a body.'

'Keep me posted, Kiaran,' Morton said as the lawyer departed. Morton sat down, suddenly deflated once more. When will this case break?

Chapter 23: Second Time Lucky

Kiaran crossed his fingers, and hit the send button, causing his application to whizz through the ether to the Ministry of Justice.

'S25 Burial Act 1857 Application to Exhume

'For the urgent attention of Her Majesty's Principal Secretary of State for Justice.

'An application is made herein for a licence to disinter the body of Eric Matthews for the purpose of a DNA test to confirm his relationship to a deceased child found buried in Hackney Marshes. Mr Matthews is the only possible relative that could be disinterred for this comparison as the child's mother, Jacqueline Matthews, was cremated and as such her DNA is unavailable.

'The child was buried with a watch that belonged to Eric Matthews and was known to be in the possession of Eric's son in November of last year. This has been confirmed by insurance documentation.

'In this active investigation, the DNA link is the cornerstone in identifying a murder victim. It has not been possible to contact Eric Matthews' next of kin, as the decedent left behind no relatives...'

The application was not the most elegant ever made by Kiaran O'Connor, but he rarely had cause to exhume a body. From his previous experience dealing with extra-judicial applications, and civil servants in general, Kiaran thought it might take days, if not weeks, to get a reply. Even then, it would take a day or two to organise the exhumation.

***

The laptop screen cast a pale blue glow on David Morton's face as he sat in the dark. David was still at the Travelodge, where he hid under the covers in room 212 as he perused his credit file. Where a nice round 900 had previously been, his score now read 36B7. Even recent bankrupts can manage better than that, he mused.

'Victim of Impersonation – CIFAS' stood out in bold typeface at the top of the screen, just under his full name, David Gareth Morton. From a brief text message exchange, he knew Sarah's record was similarly inscribed. She still wasn't talking to him, despite a bunch of flowers sent to her office using a credit card he'd pilfered from expenses.

For a mere twenty pounds a year, CIFAS put David on their Protective Registration service. Now, all credit applications would require an extra step to verify it was really him. David thought it was closing the stable door after the horse had bolted, and the cost was simply rubbing salt in the wound. He and Sarah had argued about that too. Everything was an argument lately.

***

Eric Matthews was buried in non-consecrated grounds, which made the job of Henry Larkin much easier. As an employee of the Ministry of Justice, Henry spent his whole life dealing with the politics of the Anglican Diocese. If a body was buried in consecrated grounds, then Henry could not simply grant a licence as the diocese had to agree to any exhumation on church grounds. The process for getting their permission made the Ministry of Justice's process look like the Gatwick Express. Electronic applications for licences gave way to local ministrations holding ecclesiastical meetings to determine the right way to decide. Certain older priests were known to pray on a decision for days or weeks at a time.

Despite being a bureaucrat, Henry was different. He'd received an application from Kiaran O'Connor at the Crown Prosecution Service at half past four. By quarter to five he'd made his decision. There would be no fallout from the church, and there were no relatives to complain or apply for a judicial review. Henry didn't care about the rights of the dead, but he did care about his own career, and having an ambitious young prosecutor on his side couldn't hurt.

Henry signed the licence, and dropped it in his out tray. A secretary would fax a copy back to the CPS first thing in the morning. Until then, Henry was a free man. God bless the civil service nine-to-five. He grabbed his umbrella from the rack by the door and headed home.

***

They arrived on the dot of 8:08 a.m., the break of dawn. Frost danced across the grassy knolls, bathed in the orange glow of the sun.

'Get that marquee up,' Morton barked as the pole framework of the structure was dumped unceremoniously from the back of a police van. The cemetery was not due to open until nine o'clock but they were taking no chances. If the media realised they were digging up a body then they'd want to know why. Any story could tip off the killer that they were onto him.

Once the marquee was in place, they began to dig. The topsoil came off quickly as a mechanical digger did most of the work. Once they approached the six-feet depth at which the coffin was buried, they switched to manual excavation to avoid damaging Mr Matthews' remains.

It was unlikely that any soft tissue would remain after the better part of a decade, so getting a DNA sample would probably mean removing one or more of the teeth. DNA could survive for a long time inside a tooth, protected by the walls of calcium. If they could get a match between Mr Eric Matthews and Joe Bloggs Junior then that would explain how he came to possess Eric's treasured watch, as well as giving them a lead on who Joe Bloggs Junior might be. It would also confirm if Eric was in any way related to the child living in Cleaver Square.

Morton preferred to think of the investigation in old-school terms. Who, what, why and when? So far, he had very little. He didn't know who had been killed, who the killer was, how the victim died or why he was murdered. All he had to go on was a loose timeline. The watch would be the key to cracking open the who, he just knew it. Morton leant back in his pop-up chair, letting the younger detectives do the digging. He'd crack this case wide open soon enough.

Chapter 24: Follow the Money

With his aversion to lawyers, Morton could rarely be found in a solicitor's office. Yet, thanks to his wife's insistence, he had called in on Mr Theodore J Edmonds. He had known Teddy in another life, when they'd stolen cigarettes and downed cider in the woods with the local girls. The man sitting opposite him couldn't be further from the boy he had once known. Teddy sat in an executive office chair; his stark grey suit pinstriped with silver exuded an air of success and confidence.

The image was deliberate: in Teddy's mind, it was what everyone looked for when they consulted a lawyer. Sarah had c   hosen   to   sit equidistant between her husband and Teddy. She had not yet forgiven Morton.

'Well David, it looks like we've got quite a big mess to unwind here. Do you want me to start with the good news or the bad news?'

'Bad,' Morton replied as his wife simultaneously asked for the good news. Morton jerked his head towards Sarah, indicating deference to her choice.

'Okay. Essentially we can split up the identity thefts into two groups. Group number one is where your own money was taken. That's all the unauthorised charges against your debit cards, bank account transfer, and the sale of your stock portfolio. Group number two is where someone else's money was stolen via the victim's credit. That's anything that was taken using credit in your name, so: credit cards, loan applications, that sort of thing. The latter we can sort easily. The relevant law, which is called the Consumer Credit Act, says you're only liable for the first fifty pounds of an unauthorised transaction. There are twelve transactions here, so your liability is capped at six hundred pounds. We'll send out a letter asking the issuing bank to waive the charges entirely. If they refuse, I'd recommend you pay the statutory fee. It will be cheaper than challenging it in court.'

'That's the good news?' Sarah asked incredulously.

'I'm afraid so, Mrs Morton.' Teddy turned towards David. 'Do you know how common identity theft is from your work with the Met?'

'One victim per hundred people?' David guessed. Financial crimes were not his forte.

'One in four. Quite often it's fairly inconsequential, something like a rogue charge on a credit card, or a flipped electricity supplier. Most credit card providers simply reverse the charge if they are notified promptly. The problems occur when the victim doesn't notice. Looking at your statement, we can see there was a negligible charge of ninety-six pence to PayPal. This is common in identity theft as the thieves check to see if a card is active.'

'But how did they get all the details they needed to use the card? Didn't his PIN protect him?'

'You never need a PIN online. There are different kinds of credit card charge. First, we have the basic charge in person. That uses a PIN to verify the card owner's identity. Though I'm sure you guys remember signing your own name!'

The Mortons nodded. Signing had been much easier than remembering dozens of four-digit combinations for different cards. At the thought of PIN combinations, it was Sarah's turn to blush a fierce shade of red.

'Sarah, got something you want to share?' her husband teased.

'I changed all my PINs to the same code,' she whispered conspiratorially.

'You silly mare!' Morton's anger surfaced swiftly.

The lawyer raised a hand to regain control. 'The PIN doesn't matter. These weren't PIN transactions. For those they'd need to either steal your card, or clone it. That isn't what happened here. You've still got your cards, so you wouldn't be liable for a PIN transaction.'

'See. Not my fault, David. You are such a drama queen.'

'Sorry,' David mumbled inaudibly.

'Come again, I didn't quite catch that,' Sarah goaded.

Morton ignored his wife, and tried to steer the conversation back on track. They were paying by the hour, after all. 'So what happened?'

'The thieves used 'customer not present' transactions.'

Morton must have looked confused because Teddy went on to clarify, 'Like when you buy things online. So if you order from Amazon, that's a customer not present transaction as you aren't physically there to type in your PIN.'

'So anyone with the card number can order stuff using my card?' Morton's mouth hung open in surprise.

'Not quite. If the billing address and the delivery address are different, that's a flag. If the name isn't identical, that's a flag. If the landline number is registered elsewhere, that's a flag. Now, flags don't immediately stop transactions. Retailers set their risk level according to their needs. Gift transactions, mistyped names, use of short names or omission of initials. All of those can be perfectly legitimate but still raise a flag.'

'I'm not sure I understand. What is a flag?'

'It's like a warning. Each is weighted so some are more important than others. Too many warnings, or a critical warning, and the transaction isn't processed.'

'So they just posted themselves gifts?'

'Again, it's not that simple. They could have – that's up to the police to investigate. They could have drop-shipped, i.e. bought something for someone else and shipped straight there. Or they could be funnelling money through payment processors. None of your charges seem to be retailers, just payment gateways. No way to tell where the money actually wound up. Western Union is almost entirely untraceable. A fake identity card, or a lax member of staff, and the thieves can pick up the money at any Western Union affiliate worldwide.'

'So, can we reverse it with the bank?'

'I spoke to the banks directly after you called me last week. They're saying it's your fault. The banking code says that you're only liable if you have treated your details 'without reasonable care'. The problem is that it's a woolly phrase, totally ambiguous.'

'So they're arguing it's my fault because I streamed a Chelsea game or two?'

'That's the tall and short of it.' The lawyer avoided eye contact.

'Oh, come on. I wasn't stealing. The site asked for my details, I handed them over. We're not even sure that the streaming site is how they got my details anyway. This is pure speculation.' Morton shuffled in his seat.

'David, as your friend I have to warn you. If you argue this in court, you'll have to declare to the world that you used an illicit streaming service. Whether you meant to do anything wrong or not, you know the newspapers will have a field day with it. They'll run a headline like "Famous cop cops free football". They're banking, excuse the pun, on you just keeping schtum. You might have a reasonable legal case, but this isn't a purely legal decision. You are a high-profile policeman. If you generate negative publicity towards the Met, then you might come under pressure from above to go quietly into the night.'

'Can we trace where the money went? Surely the bank would know that,' Morton said.

'They would. I'll send them a request, but chances are the money has been forwarded on several times by now, possibly even through other victims' accounts. We may never know where it ended up.'

'Then let's fight the bank.'

Sarah said nothing. If Morton had paid more attention to his wife's expression, he'd have realised that she valued her reputation much more than mere money. She didn't like the sound of losing her savings, but she knew her family would bail her out if she needed them to. It wasn't worth having her name dragged through the mud.

Chapter 25: Smile

Dirk Raoult's polite smile deteriorated into a scowl once the constable delivering an evidence bag left his lab. In his opinion, the lab did all the hard work just so that the detectives could swan in and take all the credit. The real work was done under strict conditions that let the evidence do the talking. Supposition might have a place out in the world of policing, but in Dirk's domain the forensics were key.

Dirk set the evidence bag on the table, used tweezers to remove the tooth, then surveyed it at 10x magnification. He scribbled on an A4 pad as he observed the tooth, 'Adult molar. Significant wear. Evidence label declares that it belongs to Eric Matthews (deceased).'

So this was why Dirk had been asked to stay late. As the only dental forensic specialist in-house at Scotland Yard, Dirk saw more displaced teeth than anyone else he knew. A lesser specialist might have been tempted to crush the entire tooth. It was a functional method, but far from elegant, and it would have destroyed the whole sample.

Instead, Dirk opted to take a horizontal section at the cervical root of the tooth. By taking only a small slice, he negated the need to fill in all the paperwork necessary to document methodology when destroying the whole sample. If a defence lawyer wanted to challenge his work, they could redo the examination using their own expert.

'Upper First Left Molar, 136B0mg. No visual indication of fillings or caries.' Dirk alternated between examination and documentation. Just because the methodology wouldn't be going to court didn't mean that he could be sloppy.

The tooth was treated with 10 per cent natrium-chloride. Dirk then cut the tooth precisely along the enamel dentine joint using a motorised diamond plate. He drained the pulp, setting it aside in the regulation Eppendorf tube. Dirk powdered the roots, and mixed the result with sterile water using a centrifuge.

Satisfied his work was done according to procedure, Dirk added an extraction buffer. The sample would need to rest at precisely the right temperature before the final step. Once the incubator was set at 56°C, Dirk placed the sample inside. In precisely eighteen hours, he would add proteinase, spin it all again, then dry the sample out. Then, and only then, could he test the DNA.

It was boring, but it was specific, scientific and reliable. Just like Dirk.

***

'Ladies and gents, good morning. I have progress for you today. Forensics were able to pull DNA from Mr Matthews' tooth. No match for his purported son, Charles Matthews of Cleaver Square.'

The room collectively groaned, confusion spreading through the ranks.

'Was he adopted, sir?' Ayala asked.

'Or did Mrs Matthew get around a bit?' Tina said.

Morton shrugged. With Mrs Matthews having been cremated, they've never be able to answer Tina's question definitively.

'But curiously enough, it was a match for Joe Bloggs Junior. Joe is Eric Matthews' son. My impostor theory is looking more and more plausible.'

'You're saying Joe Bloggs is Eric's son, and therefore he must really be Charlie Matthews. If the kid we met in Cleaver Square isn't related then he can't be Charlie. Are you sure the samples didn't get mixed up, boss?' Ayala asked incredulously.

'Absolutely. The samples were digitised days apart. The Charles Matthews we met is not a relation to Eric Matthews. The dead body is, which explains why he had his father's Keppler Oechslan watch. What it doesn't explain is who the hell the Charles Matthews we met is.'

'Switch-up at the hospital? Two kids called Charles Matthews, that could easily confuse a maternity nurse on a double shift, couldn't it?' Ayala tried for a third time.

'That's not possible. The boys don't share mitochondrial DNA. They have different mothers. We know Joe is Eric Matthews' son, and he has Eric's watch. Eric died when Charlie was a toddler, so he can't have passed his watch to the wrong boy three years before then.'

'Ah,' Ayala replied.

Morton continued: 'I'll admit that we can't disprove Tina's 'the mother cheated' theory. It doesn't seem likely though. The only scenario that works is if Jacqueline cheated on Eric when she became pregnant with Charlie, and Eric had Joe with another woman.'

'Then, with all due respect, sir, what's your theory?'

Morton's eyes steeled at the obvious challenge to his authority, then slackened as he realised the team still didn't know much. It wasn't truly insubordination, but a genuine question.

Tina spoke up, 'I'm still a little confused here. Am I right in saying that we know Joe Bloggs is related to Eric Matthews, and Charlie isn't related to either? We don't know which boy, if any, Jacqueline is related to as we don't have her DNA. She can't be related to both, as the boys don't share their mitochondrial DNA. I'm starting to like your impostor theory. But if Charlie isn't Charlie, who is he?'

'I don't know. The only reason to take someone's identity is to hide your own, or profit from the victim's identity. We know that the real Charlie, whoever he may be, is in line to inherit a substantial sum. That could be a motive,' Morton said.

'There has to be a record of the second child's birth somewhere. He's about twelve. You can't just hide a kid for that long. A neighbour would have noticed,' Ayala said.

Morton paused. The kid's English was awful. What if he isn't from around here?

'Right you are. Go and see the Grants' neighbours. See if they recognise our facial reconstruction photo. Tina, you're with me. If Charlie is an impostor, we need to find out who he is.'

As Morton barked fresh orders, he could feel the energy in the room rising. It was the buzz of closing in on a difficult case. They were finally getting somewhere.

Chapter 26: Stakeout

Morton was watching a reality television program and contentedly taking sips from a bottle of beer when Tina flicked the television set off without warning.

'Hey! I was watching that.'

'My flat, my rules, big boy,' Tina smiled.

'After I cooked you dinner. Again. That's just mean.' Morton pulled a face, sticking his tongue out like a child.

'Ha-ha. I'd rather talk, and you're the only one here to talk to.'

'That I am.'

'So, what do you really think?' Tina Vaughn pouted, crimson-stained lips elongating the 'o'.

'About what?'

'Who is Charlie Matthews, and how do he, Eric Matthews and our Joe Bloggs Junior all fit together?'

'I think it's too early to be sure; we know Charlie isn't a blood relation, but the other two are. Father and son. If Charlie is not related to the couple we thought were his biological parents, then maybe he has contact with his real family. We need to watch out for any phone calls he makes, any text messages or emails, and see if he has access to a bank account. If he's an impostor, he must have something tying him to his real identity.'

'Or someone. This sort of identity theft would require real planning. How was the victim identified? When did they get switched?'

'Our victim, if he is the real Charlie, was in the system. No one was looking out for him. We already know he's changed foster families multiple times. He would have been pretty vulnerable. I've ordered Ayala to talk to Charlie's former neighbours which should tell us when. I'm more worried about who our faux-Charlie could be. He's too young to have a record.'

'But not too young to break the law. One of the kids I nicked last month for possession lived with his sister, his mum, his grandmother and his great-grandmother. All of them were smoking weed when I walked in. Oh, and his sister, all of sweet sixteen, was with child.'

Morton met her gaze. 'And London has the highest crime rate in the country. Is it any wonder? I wouldn't have been responsible enough to look after a child properly when I was sixteen.'

'You had your first at twenty-five didn't you?'

'Yes. In wedlock. Stephen first, and Nick two years later.'

'How are they doing? I haven't seen them since your barbecue last summer. You still haven't given me the recipe for those ribs...' Tina leant in as she spoke, closing the distance between her and David.

'Err, thanks, I guess. That recipe is a family secret.' Morton blushed in surprise at the belated compliment, then his expression darkened. 'I haven't seen Stephen since then either.'

'Why's that?' Tina asked.

'I don't want to talk about it,' said Morton.

'Fine. Just making conversation.' Tina folded her arms across her chest, leaning away as she did so.

'Sorry, it's just a sore subject.' Morton swigged the rest of his bottle then set the empty down on the table with a thud.

'OK, we'll talk about something else then,' she paused, her mind unable to conjure a good topic of conversation. Eventually, she reverted to the old stand-by, work. 'What's the plan on the Joe Bloggs Junior investigation?'

'Tomorrow, we'll follow Charlie. If he isn't the real deal, hopefully we'll be able to spot that. We can't talk to him without a parent or guardian present, but there's no harm just watching.'

'What's he going to do, walk home from school wearing a sign that says 'I'm an impostor'?'

'Very droll. We've got no other leads. There's no harm sitting on him for an afternoon.'

'No harm, but also no point.' Tina sounded sceptical.

'Last time I checked, I was in charge. So it's happening.'

'I do love it when a man in uniform gives me orders,' Tina drawled.

Morton rolled his eyes. As if he hadn't heard that line before. 'Right, I'm going back to my hotel. Thanks again for inviting me over for dinner, even if I did have to cook it.'

'Stay.'

'I can't,' he held up his hand, his wedding band catching the light, 'besides, I've already paid. See you tomorrow afternoon for the stakeout. If you're at a loose end in the morning, start looking online for anything connected to Charlie. If he's like my kids, he'll be on every social media site known to man.'

Morton moved to grab his coat from the back of the kitchen chair, acutely aware of Tina's eyes following him as he made good his escape.

'David?' Tina said breathlessly.

'Yes?' He turned back towards her.

She stepped forwards, so close that he could feel her breath on his cheek, 'Night.'

'Goodnight, Detective Vaughn.'

***

The clock ticked towards lunchtime as Ayala sat engrossed in his iPad. Screen after screen of scanned birth certificates flew by as Ayala flicked the screen to move between records. Finding Charles Matthews' birth certificate had been easy enough. With the advent of digital records, it had taken a simple search for *'Charles Matthews'* + *'DATERANGE: 1997-2013'*. But that birth certificate had been disproved by DNA already. Charles Matthews of Cleaver Square was not the son of Eric Matthews no matter what the official records said.

'How's it going, handsome?' a Welsh voice called out.

Ayala peered over his iPad to see Tina Vaughn take an opposing seat at the conference table. A bundle of documents landed on the table with a thud as she sat down. School records, social media printouts. Everything she could get without having to resort to a search warrant.

'Slow. I can't find a second son, or other male relative.'

'Well, he's probably not Jacqueline's son,' Tina replied simply.

'So who is Charlie?'

'Start looking for other kids in the system of the same age. The impostor had to come from somewhere.'

'I can't find anything to suggest that. No adoption records. Not even a birth certificate yet.'

'I haven't found anything either.'

'Nothing at all? What kind of kid doesn't have Facebook?'

'Exactly. This just keeps getting stranger and stranger. Who is Charlie Matthews?'

***

'David, what the hell are we doing here?' Tina Vaughn leant towards the middle of the car, reaching for the drinks holder.

'Watching. Charlie ought to be home soon, and I want to see if he walks home alone; if he comes back out, and where he goes if he does.'

'Right... But why? We know he isn't related to Eric Matthews but you can't seriously be thinking he's involved in the murder of our Joe Bloggs Junior?'

'I'm not suggesting the kid is a murderer. But if he's an impostor, he's got to have had help. That help is probably responsible for Joe's death.'

'Hey, I'm getting paid either way.' Tina reclined her seat then kicked back and closed her eyes.

After an eternity of silence, Morton roused Tina from her nap, 'It's 4:15 p.m., and he's just walking down the south side of the square towards number 36B.'

Tina sat up. 'Not alone. Is that the Lattimer kid?'

'Looks like it.'

'Damn. I doubt Mrs Lattimer would be any happier us talking to him than Charlie.'

Morton shrugged. All they could do was wait until Charlie next emerged from the Lattimer residence.

Chapter 27: Waiting Game

'He's not coming out. Let's go,' Tina pleaded.

'We're not leaving after three hours,' Morton said flatly.

'But I need to pee!' she protested for the third time that afternoon.

Morton tossed a bottle and a funnel in her direction. 'Women.'

Tina caught the bottle one-handed. 'You've got to be kidding me?'

'Yeah, I am. There are a few bars on the Kennington Road. Go to one of those.'

'But there's a pub right there.' Tina pointed towards the corner of the square.

'Yes. Right past number 36B. If you walk the other way, you won't be seen.'

'David, you're taking this far too seriously. It's just a kid. He's hardly going to have any counter-surveillance training.' Tina smirked. 'What are we even watching for?'

'I'll know it when I see it.'

Tina twirled her curly brown hair around her index finger. 'Is this just a ploy to spend time with me?'

Morton glared, not dignifying her with a response.

'It is, isn't it?'

Morton continued to stare at the Lattimers' front door, acutely aware of the heat between them. Tina leant in, notes of sweet vanilla perfume wafting towards him. Almost without conscious thought Morton turned his head, meeting her gaze. Ivy eyes drew him in, their pupils widening visibly as the distance between them closed to mere centimetres. At the last moment, Morton turned his face away.

'I can't.' He glanced guiltily at his wedding band.

'You can't fight how you feel forever, David.' Tina reached for the door handle, then stepped out of the car. Once she was outside, her posture sagged, and she took short quick strides into the darkness, obviously keen to put distance between them.

Chapter 28: Rock Bottom

The orange light of dawn illuminated the copper coinage that had tumbled onto the bed. The pile included only a smattering of gold and silver coins. It was like being a kid smashing open his piggy bank all over again. Morton pushed his reading glasses up on his nose and surveyed the amassed shrapnel. To his eye, it looked like less than twenty pounds. He had half a tank of petrol, and the room was prepaid for another night. Once the bank confirmed the credit card charges were waived, he'd at least have some credit. But he'd had nothing back from either the bank or the fraud squad about his own money, and his lawyer, Teddy, had not been optimistic about a speedy resolution.

Morton picked up his mobile and dialled, tapping his foot impatiently as he waited for the phone to ring at the other end.

'Nick? It's Dad. Can I borrow your sofa?'

***

Amelia Laker rearranged the conference table, shifting around the laptop and paperwork. It was totally unnecessary, but it was a nervous habit and Amelia was exceptionally nervous.

It had started out like any other day, with the usual assortment of arrogant motorists making her bicycle journey into work as hellish as ever. But the fun of London travel had paled when she arrived for work.

Instead of 'Investigation', 'Trend Analysis' and 'Reach Projections', her Outlook Calendar had been cleared to make way for an appointment labelled 'DCI David Morton'. It was a perplexing appointment. What would a Detective Chief Inspector want with a mere fraud investigator? Not just any DCI either, but the legendary David Morton.

Amelia double-checked the conference room. Laptop, check. Wi-Fi signal, check. Projector and VGA cable, check. Comfortable chairs, check. She had liberated those from one of the other offices in place of the usual furniture.

A window opened out onto the street below, pedestrians scuttling along like ants. Being on the thirteenth floor came with a real feeling of power. Three sharp knocks roused Amelia from her thoughts.

'Mrs Laker?' A deep voice emanated from the doorway.

Amelia turned to see a less-than-immaculately presented detective. 'It's Miss Laker, but please call me Amelia.'

'Thank you.' The detective took a seat without waiting for an invitation, opting for the chair nearest the door.

'Coffee?'

'Please.'

For a moment, neither spoke as the clang of spoon on china filled the room.

'You're probably wondering why I'm here,' Morton said.

'Yes sir. It's not every day my diary gets cleared for a last-minute meeting.'

'This is actually a personal matter. I'm not here in a professional capacity.'

'Then, with all due respect, why are you here? And why was my diary cleared without consulting me?' Amelia's nostrils flared as her hope of career advancement dissipated.

'I was the victim of identity fraud. In the last two weeks every bank account I own was systematically emptied. Every credit card maxed out. Loans were applied for in my name. Even my shares and pension funds were cashed in.' Morton could have been reading out a restaurant menu. It was dispassionate, factual. Amelia had seen emotional burn-out a few times before, and the man sat opposite her was showing all the signs. Her anger vanished as she imagined the hell he would be going through; it was strange to put a face to the victim in her line of work.

'OK,' Amelia flipped up her laptop, and began typing. The projector on the ceiling buzzed as it whirred to life and threw a replica of Amelia's screen onto the whitewashed wall at the north end of the conference room.

'Are these details correct?'

Morton nodded. A scanned copy of the report he had filed stood larger than life on the wall.

'OK. I see you've been issued with a crime reference number. I assume the banks have agreed to cancel the credit charges?'

'I'm expecting confirmation of that any day now.'

'And you've got CIFAS protection?'

'Yep.'

'Then, what do you want to get from this meeting?'

'I want to know what you're doing to catch the criminals that did this.' Morton spoke slowly, as if explaining to a child. Surely it was obvious?

'Mr Morton, if I may be frank with you... We don't generally do much beyond this point. Let me explain what my role is. I am a data analyst. I look at all the information we gather, like your report, but from hundreds of victims. I look for trends – which banks are being hit, any commonality between victims such as visits to the same shops or use of the same cash machines. Their purchase histories get compared with tens of thousands of other purchase histories. We ask why these people have been subject to fraud. Generally, we trace things like duplicated cards easily. If all our victims ate at one restaurant, then it's easy to identify the location the crime was committed. If they all belong to the same gym, likewise.'

'So, does the crime I suffered match any other profiles?'

'Not exactly. Your losses aren't localised, nor are they consistent with suspected local criminals. Initial investigations would suggest your details were stolen online. The Internet is a big place, Mr Morton. We know you probably weren't one victim in a group as no one else has come forward with the same problems. You could have been specifically targeted.'

'So you've done basically nothing?'

Amelia looked like she'd been slapped, but recovered quickly. 'I'm sorry you feel that way. I'm only one person, and there's only so much time in the day.'

'Yeah? Well, thanks for sparing a whole five minutes of it.' Bile rose to Morton's lips, his ire at the injustice bubbling just beneath the surface of his usually cool demeanour.

Chapter 29: Prying Eyes

Dark skies gathered long before Ayala surfaced from Kennington tube station. It was a short hop on the northern line from Ayala's apartment near the Barbican, and had seemed easier than trying to park. The sight of the clouds gave Ayala pause; at least a car would have kept him dry.

Less than two minutes away from the station, Ayala almost missed the turn-off for Cleaver Square tucked alongside the local art college. Some Internet research had told Ayala that the neighbours were likely to be affluent and middle class. With properties costing well over a million pounds, the square was the preserve of the rich despite being a simple terrace design that dated back to 1789.

Unlike most London roads, the square was set out sequentially, with house numbers 36A and 37 adjoining the Lattimer residence. The floor had been set a little higher at number 37 compared to the others, an outlier among an otherwise neat row of arched doorways. Ivy ran around the lintels.

Ayala hoped the neighbours would be a useful source of information. Terraced homes were notorious for thin adjoining walls, and noise would carry easily. Ayala knocked smartly on number 36A, the home of a local politician according to Ayala's research. A 'Vote Conservative' plaque could be seen in the kitchen window. There was no answer. Ayala knocked again, rain starting to fall as he waited. Beads of water began to form where they lay on his overcoat. If he didn't get inside soon, he would be soaked. There was no light visible through the half moon of glass above the doorway.

Number 37 yielded more luck, an elderly lady answering the door an eternity after Ayala heard 'Just a second!' called out from the back of the property.

'Hello?' With greying hair tied neatly in a bun, the homeowner appeared to be in her late sixties. Yellow gardening gloves covered her hands, with her wrinkled skin visible between the end of the gloves and the start of her sleeves.

'Good afternoon, ma'am. I'm Detective Ayala with the Metropolitan Police. May I come in?'

'Has something happened?' Rheumy eyes widened in anticipation of bad news.

'No ma'am, just a few questions I'm hoping you can help me with.'

The woman's relief was palpable. 'Please officer, do come in.'

The sitting room looked as if it had been lifted from the fifties. A collection of tea cosies studded the shelves, with no television or laptop in sight.

'Would you care for a cup of tea? Oh dear, where are my manners. I'm Ethel Hawkins.' Now that she knew Ayala's presence was benign, Ethel looked positively delighted at the prospect of company.

'Yes please, Mrs Hawkins.'

'English breakfast or Earl Grey?'

'Earl Grey, please, Mrs Hawkins.'

'You'll be taking that with lemon then.' It wasn't a question.

'I suppose I will. Could I have two sugars with that, please?'

Once his thirst was quenched, Ayala settled back in an armchair. 'I'm here about the boy next door.'

'James? He's a lovely kid, fetches my paper for me every evening.'

'No ma'am, I'm here about Charlie Matthews, the Lattimer's foster child. Do you know him?'

'I didn't know his surname, but I've met him.'

'How would you characterise him?'

'Lonely. He sometimes follows James around like a puppy. Never says anything. I've seen him sat out in the square, lost in his own little world.'

'Where in the square?'

'On one of the benches. Usually the one on the opposite side of the square, right in the middle.'

'Is this him?' Ayala showed her the facial reconstruction of Joe Bloggs Junior.

'Oh no. That's not the boy I know.' Mrs Hawkins' voice wobbled as she tried to work out whether she was mistaken.

'How about this picture?' Ayala showed her a copy of Charlie Matthews' photo from his Children's Services file.

'Oh yes, that's him!'

'Have you ever seen him wearing a gold watch?'

'No, never.' Mrs Hawkins hesitated, as if unsure whether to add something more.

'Is there something else?'

'He talks to himself. It's not even a conversation. I walked past him, and he was just saying 'Fine, thank you' over and over again.'

'Hmm, that's very interesting. I'm not sure if it's germane but we'll look into it. Thank you very much for your time, Mrs Hawkins.'

'You're welcome, dear. Feel free to stop by anytime for a cup of tea.'

***

Morton slept fitfully. His mind ran in circles trying to work out what he was missing in the Joe Bloggs Junior case. Ayala's visit to Cleaver Square confirmed that the impostor had been in place for as long as Charlie had been living with the Lattimers, which was no surprise. The body had been in the ground longer than that.

He eventually dropped off a couple of hours after midnight, only to be awoken by his son drunkenly coming through the front door not much later. A shadow accompanied him, indicating Nick was not alone.

By the time Morton's half-past-six alarm went off, serious bags had formed under his eyes. He stretched as he woke, trying to work the knot out of his lower back. A five-foot sofa and a six-foot man meant a foetal sleeping position that was not conducive to a healthy back.

The kitchen was at the rear of the property, just off the living room. It was cramped, but Morton easily found eggs, bacon and a frying pan.

'God, that smells good.' A female voice flitted through from the lounge. Turning towards the sound's source, Morton saw a nubile blonde towelling off her hair, nothing covering her modesty.

Seeing David, she screamed.

'Nick! There's a fat old man in the kitchen!' She ran from the room, hands trying to cover her modesty. Her towel remained wrapped around her hair like a turban.

Morton would have found the scene highly amusing, if he had not just been called fat. He ran his fingers over his stomach. Perhaps he could stand to lose a few pounds.

Nick came running down the stairs, tennis racket in hand.

'Crap. I'd forgotten you were coming over.' He turned towards the stairs, 'Mia! It's OK. It's just my dad.'

'Humph!'

'So, Dad. You staying long? I can see this getting a bit awkward.'

Morton eyed up his still-drunk progeny. 'No son, I'll find somewhere else to doss.'

Chapter 30: Time to Talk

'What we need are Charlie's fingerprints or at least one more interview now that we have questions to ask him,' Morton said.

Coffee cups littered the conference table. The entire Murder Investigation Team had been assembled to discuss how to move forward, but most of the room were avoiding DCI Morton's gaze.

'David, how are we going to get Mrs Lattimer to agree to that? She's already brought him in once. And what exactly are we going to be asking him this time that we couldn't have asked last time?' Tina bit her lip, expecting swift reprisal but Morton merely smirked.

'Last time, we didn't know he wasn't related to Eric Matthews, his supposed father. We had no idea he might be an impostor. We didn't even question him on his poor English. There has to be some sort of hole in his story. I think if we keep him talking long enough, he'll give us something inconsistent that we can pursue.'

'That's not going to be easy. Don't forget we're limited by the ABE guidelines. He's not an adult so we can't deliberately railroad him, nor is he guilty of any crime. It just doesn't seem fair.

'You think it's unfair? We've got a dead child without a name. That child deserves dignity in death, even if he didn't have it while he was alive. As to staying within the rules, I have every confidence in your ability to coax it out of him. We'll have his guardian and his social worker on hand to keep things above board. If we overstep, I'm sure they'll object on Charlie's behalf.' Morton glanced around the room at his team, looking for any further objections. 'You guys satisfied?'

'Yes, but how do we get Mrs Lattimer to agree?' Tina asked.

'We don't. Ayala does. We know how much he loves befriending middle-aged women, don't we?' Morton winked at his junior officer, careful not to directly reference the Christmas office party.

'Fine. I'll do what I can.' Ayala glared.

Morton grinned. If looks could kill.

***

Ayala licked the back of his hand, and then sniffed. Reassured that the breath mint had worked its magic, Ayala pressed the button for floor 14. He took a moment to straighten his tie as the lift silently ascended towards the office of Ogden & Thwaite, Chartered Accountants.

The double doors slid open, revealing a large hallway divided by floor-to-ceiling glass which separated the various offices sharing the fourteenth floor of the Canada Water skyscraper. At the end of the corridor, the space opened onto a viewing deck with panoramic views over Canary Wharf.

Ayala approached a rounded visitor's desk set between the offices. 'I'm here to see Mrs Brenda Lattimer of Ogden & Thwaite.'

A svelte redhead looked up from her magazine, then drawled: 'Do you have an appointment?'

'No, but...'

'Then you'll have to make one,' the redhead interrupted Ayala before he could explain his presence.

'Miss, I'm a plain clothes detective,' Ayala thrust his ID at her, 'and I need to talk to Mrs Lattimer as soon as possible.'

The redhead flicked her hair. 'Wait here.'

She disappeared into the door behind the desk, reappeared momentarily behind the glass wall to Ayala's left, then vanished completely through another door.

Once she was out of sight, Ayala leant over the desk and tugged out a thick red diary marked 'Appointments'. It was in chronological order, and the current day was marked by a gold ribbon. It fell open to the right page, and Ayala scanned through Brenda Lattimer's schedule. She had an appointment booked at midday for one hour, but the next hour was clear on the diary. Ayala checked his watch; it was quarter to one. He wouldn't have to wait long.

Out of the corner of his eye, Ayala saw the redhead reappear on the other side of the glass, coming back towards the desk. Ayala hastily stuffed the appointments book back onto the desk, careful to close it as he did so.

The secretary reappeared. 'I'm afraid Mrs Lattimer is unavailable, and won't be able to see you.'

'Is there a time that would be more convenient for me to come back?' Ayala said.

Without even checking the appointments book the redhead replied firmly, 'Mrs Lattimer is fully booked for the rest of the week.'

'Right. Thanks anyway.' Ayala walked away. If that was how Mrs Lattimer wanted to play it...

Outside Canada Water, the tube station beckoned to Ayala. Under the Canary Wharf shopping centre, the lunchtime foot traffic was coming and going from the small eateries and coffee shops. More office workers were loitering outside smoking.

Smoking! Ayala was struck by inspiration as he watched the group puff away. Mrs Lattimer was a known smoker. She had got through at least three cigarettes in the half hour Charlie was at the police station last time. With the law prohibiting smoking inside public buildings, she'd need to leave the comfort of the fourteenth floor in order to get her fix. It was odds-on she'd come down in the one to two o'clock break in her calendar for a nicotine fix. All Ayala had to do was wait.

***

It didn't take long for Ayala's hunch to pay off. The burly frame of Mrs Lattimer trundled out of Canada Water at precisely five past one, and immediately produced a pack of slim cigarettes from the depths of her enormous purple handbag.

She seemed unaware of the 'No Smoking Within 5 Metres of This Building' sign she had chosen to park herself near, and it wasn't long before dirty grey smoke began to emanate from her lips.

'Mrs Lattimer?'

Mrs Lattimer turned around, searching out the person calling her name.

'You. What do you want now?'

'I'd like to talk to you, if I may, Miss Lattimer.' Ayala deliberately adjusted his salutation in an attempt at flattery. It didn't work.

'You know I'm Mrs Lattimer. And I don't have anythin' to say to you.' She turned to go, and Ayala was forced to bluff.

'Before you go, could you read the big sign to your right for me?' Ayala pointed.

'No Smoking.'

'That's right; I do believe that's a sixty-quid on-the-spot penalty fine.'

'This is harassment, this is.'

'I might be minded to forget I saw you smoking if...'

'If what, officer?' said Mrs Lattimer.

'If you agree to let us speak to Charlie again.' Ayala flashed what he hoped was a winning smile.

'What do you want with tha' little twerp now?'

'Just to talk. We think he can help us clear up some inconsistencies.'

'But 'e ain't in trouble?' Mrs Lattimer was obviously mindful of her annual foster parent performance review, which Ayala had discovered was due shortly.

'No, it's just a chat,' Ayala lied.

'And you'll forget the ciggies?'

'Absolutely.'

'Go on then.'

Ayala smiled, content at having scored a minor victory over the manipulative witch. Upstairs she should have just agreed to see him.

***

This time around, Morton was alone in the Incident Room while Tina conducted Charlie's interview. He was using the same video-link technology, but a simple radio was on hand so that he could prompt Tina if needed.

Charlie sat straight-backed at the low table set out for the interview. He was still wearing his school uniform despite the five o'clock start time. Hank stood to Charlie's left with his hand resting reassuringly on Charlie's shoulder.

Mrs Lattimer had been cajoled into sitting in, but had insisted on having "her ciggie" before they started. When she deigned to waltz in five minutes after the scheduled start, the pungency of nicotine wafted in after her like a cloud, though she seemed oblivious to the smell, as did Hank.

Tina's sniffed, but she remained silent. This was to be a voluntary interview, and any perceived insult could see it terminated prematurely.

'Hi, Charlie.'

'Hello.'

'Do you remember me? I'm Detective Vaughn.'

Charlie glanced at his social worker, who nodded encouragingly, before replying, 'Yes.'

'How was school?' Tina needed to build on the rapport she had established in the last interview if she had any chance of getting Charlie to open up.

He shrugged. 'Fine.'

'What lessons did you have today?'

'Maths.'

'Just the one class today?' said Tina.

He shrugged again. Clearly, rapport was hard to come by in Charlie-ville.

'Charlie, what's your favourite subject at school?'

When Charlie didn't reply, Mrs Lattimer interjected, 'He's been doing very well in art.'

Tina silenced her with a glare. 'So you like drawing then, Charlie?'

'Yes.'

Morton's voice crackled in Tina's ear, 'Like dragging blood out of a stone, eh?'

'Tell me what you like to draw.'

'People.'

'Who do you draw?'

'My friends.'

'Tell me about your friends.'

'There's James.'

'Ohh...'

'And Marcus.'

'I'm really interested. I'd like to hear more.'

'And Mr Neil. He's always nice to me.'

'That's good. Charlie, I'm going to ask you a few questions today, just like last time. If you don't know the answer to a question, it's OK to say 'I don't know'.'

'OK.'

'Let's just practice that. What's my dog's name?'

'I don't know.'

'Good. And if you don't understand a question, what would you say?'

'I don't understand.'

Tina smiled, glad that Charlie was getting to grips with the ground rules. A few more, and she'd be able to get onto the meat of the interview, but it was key not to rush.

'And if I get something wrong, you'd correct me, wouldn't you, Marcus?'

'My name's Charlie!'

'Perfect. Now, just to confirm. You do know the difference between truth and lies, don't you?'

Charlie nodded; he'd answered the exact same questions the first time around. But Tina needed to get it on tape.

'Let's take an example. If I say, 'I am a man,' is that the truth or a lie?'

'Lie.'

'If I say, 'I am a woman,' is that the truth or a lie?'

'Truth.'

'Perfect. I see you understand the truth. While we're talking today, I need you to tell me the truth, and only the truth. Will you do that, Charlie?'

'Yes.'

'Tell me about where you live.'

'Number 36B Cleaver Square, Kennington.'

Tina's brow furrowed as Charlie spoke. The way he spoke was slow, laboured, almost to the point of being rote.

'What's Kennington like?'

Charlie shrugged, 'Fine thanks, mate.'

Unconvinced that Charlie was really responding to her questions, Tina decided to test him, 'Charlie, isn't Kennington the home of the new zoo?'

Morton's laughter boomed in her earpiece, and Tina had to bite her lip to avoid joining in.

'Yes,' said Charlie.

'Are you sure?'

Charlie nodded, though he looked suddenly uncertain, as if thrown out of his depth. He looked over at his social worker searchingly.

'Perhaps you could ask a more pertinent question, Miss Vaughn?' Hank spoke for the first time, his hand still lingering on Charlie's shoulder.

'OK, Charlie. Tell me about the people you've lived with before Mrs Lattimer.'

Charlie glanced up at his social worker, looking for reassurance, 'I was with the Lovejoys. They had a big house, lots of kids coming and going. No one stayed long.'

'How long were you there, Charlie?'

'About a month.'

'And before you were there, where were you?'

'I will be...' Charlie glanced again at his social worker, who nodded almost imperceptibly, 'with Mr and Mrs Grant.'

Morton's voice flashed in Tina's ear, 'A decade living with them, and he still refers to them as Mr and Mrs Grant, not Mum and Dad? And what's with the tense change?'

'Charlie, what was it like there?'

'Happy.'

'Tell me about Mr and Mrs Grant.'

'They were nice. Very nice.'

'So, what did you like to do together?' Tina tried to dig deeper.

'Movies. Football.'

'Where did you play football, Charlie?'

'Garden.'

Morton's voice buzzed in Tina's ear yet again, 'The Grants had a tiny plot. No way was he playing football in that measly garden.'

'Where was this garden, Charlie?

'Outside.'

'Where, though?'

'I told you. Outside,' Charlie said.

'Miss Vaughn, perhaps Charlie meant 'at the park'?' Hank volunteered.

'Mr Williams, if you can't remain silent and observe properly I will have to ask you to leave. Do I make myself clear?' Tina leant forward and spoke quietly towards Mr Williams, her voice pitched an octave higher despite her attempts to restrain her annoyance.

'Miss Vaughn, if you ask me to leave, I will terminate this interview.'

'We'll discuss this outside – if you interrupt again, I will arrest you for perverting the course of justice.' Tina turned back to Charlie. 'Did you mean 'at the park', Charlie?'

'Yes.'

'Which park did you go to, Charlie?'

'The one near our home.'

'Did that park have a name?' Tina shifted tack, unable to advance the interview any further through free narrative.

'I don't know, miss.'

'Did you go there often?'

'Sometimes.'

'What was it near?'

'Some shops.'

'Do you remember the name of any of those shops?'

'No.'

'OK, Charlie. Tell me about your parents. Do you remember them at all?'

'Miss Vaughn, he would have been a toddler. Far too young to remember,' Hank interrupted yet again.

'Perhaps, but if Charlie could answer me that would be great.' Tina smiled politely.

'Don't remember,' Charlie parroted Hank's response.

'You don't seem to remember very much, Charlie. I understand you were young when your parents were around, but don't you remember anything about this park? Was it near a tube station?'

'I don't know!' Charlie began to cry.

'You're not really Charlie, are you?' Tina said over Charlie's sobs.

'Miss Vaughn, I'm terminating this interview in the best interests of the child. We won't be talking to you again.' Hank rose, tugging Charlie to his feet like a rag doll. The pair headed for the door, with Mrs Lattimer following blindly behind with her ear glued to her mobile.

Tina hit the 'press to talk' button on her police radio. 'David, what did you make of that?'

'Bloody strange, wasn't it? He didn't remember anything about the first twelve years of his life. Not even his favourite park. That bloody social worker didn't help either – the kid parroted his responses. That wouldn't hold up well under cross-examination. We're still no wiser as to who he really is. It's almost like he's a blank slate that appeared out of thin air.'

'It's so frustrating. He's clearly not the real Charlie. Where do we go from here?'

'Let's run down his family history. See if we can corroborate when and where the lives of Charlie and Joe Bloggs Junior intersected.'

Alone in the incident room, Morton placed his head in his hands in despair. Who was the child pretending to be Charlie Matthews?

Chapter 31: Nightcap

'Thanks Tina, I really appreciate this.' Morton accepted a glass half filled with ice, and a drizzle of single malt. He took a swig, sighed contently and leant back in the recliner.

'No problem. Dinner should be here any minute. I'm not much of a cook, but O Sole Mio does the best pizzas. Romana thin, free salad and a generous portion of truffle pasta on the side.' Tina set her own glass down beside Morton's, and curled up on the sofa opposite him, clutching a throw pillow.

'Sounds delicious. I should get thrown out by the wife more often.' Morton grinned lopsidedly, the whisky starting to mellow him out.

'You really should. She's totally out of order throwing you out. It's not like the identity theft is your fault.'

'Try telling that to the bank.'

'If we started holding all victims of fraud to account just because they'd downloaded copyrighted material without paying, we'd never get a fraud prosecution ever again,' Tina observed dryly.

'I suppose pirate football is pirate football, whether the site is English or Greek. I didn't know it wasn't legit. What am I going to do? She clearly thinks I'm going to apologise and take responsibility for it all, but our relationship has been rocky for ages.' Morton drained his whisky glass.

'The 'You should retire while you still have life and limb' thing again?'

'Yep, that old chestnut. She knew when we met I was a copper, and I've been in the police ever since. We've had the argument dozens of times. She keeps trying to set me up with a job at her old man's firm.'

'You, become a lawyer? You'd have to be insane. You'd have shopped half your colleagues by the end of your first week.'

'It'd make an interesting change from giving evidence, that's for sure. But if I'd wanted that, I'd have taken their offer three decades ago. I'm not going to change now, and she's not being realistic if she thinks I am.'

'So, tell her that.'

'I've tried. She thinks I should just take the early pension, and then sit around at home.'

'You'd be bored out of your mind.'

'You know me too well.'

'Well, that's what happens when you spend fifty hours a week on the job together. Besides, going after murderers is one of those situations where you can't help but become familiar with your colleagues. I know you and Ayala better than my own family.'

Morton nodded. 'We're the same. Though that's not saying much. Nick's off doing his own thing. I see him every now and again, usually when he's short on the rent.'

'You were on his sofa last night.'

'You've got me there. Thanks again for putting me up, by the way. I might have to dangle my feet over the end of your sofa, but it beats waking up on Nick's sofa with a naked woman in the kitchen.'

'No way! That really happened?'

'Yeah. She wanders in, thinking I'm Nick. Guess he forgot to tell her that he had a house guest.'

Tina's face creased up with laughter as she pictured the scene.

'That is hilarious. What's up with you and Stephen?'

'I'm not sure. He just doesn't talk to me. No calls, no texts. Doesn't answer the door if I go over there. When I emailed him and Nick asking for help when our accounts were frozen, he wired me a hundred albeit with the note 'Pay me back ASAP'.'

'But no reply to the email itself?'

'None, not a 'Sorry', not a 'Hope it gets sorted'. Just 'pay me back'.'

'He could have ignored you,' said Tina.

'True. I suppose it shows he still cares... Or he doesn't want to be disinherited,' Morton chuckled. 'Anyway, enough about me. How are you?'

'Like I said the other day, still single.'

'No suitors on the horizon?'

'Ha-ha, who says suitors? David, you're a relic.'

'Now who's evading the question?'

'There is one guy...'

'Aha! Who is he then?'

'I'm not saying. He's married to his job, and pretty much emotionally unavailable.'

'You sure can pick 'em.'

Tina threw the cushion at him. 'Men!'

Chapter 32: Camden Market

Tina rose early on Saturday morning. She dressed quietly, preferring to sacrifice fashion on the altar of practicality by opting for a woollen jumper. It was January after all. She tiptoed towards the door, being careful not to disturb her guest. She'd left a note, and her spare keys, on the table next to him.

Her getaway would have been unimpeded if it were not for Morton's tendency to sleep light. One half-open eye watched Tina as she crept towards the doorway and begun unbolting the front door.

'Going somewhere?' Morton stretched languorously as he spoke, a yawn following his greeting.

'I'm going to run down this ID fraud. If the City of London Police won't do anything for you, then I will.'

'Tina, that's really kind, but it's the weekend. For once our off days line up with the Monday to Friday crowd. You should make use of that.'

'So should you.'

'I intend to. I'm going to go and try and make up with my wife.'

'David, that's great. OK, the weekend it is. But you need to get on top of this fraud stuff. You'll do that, won't you?' Tina fluttered her eyelashes in a mock-persuasive manner.

'Yes. First thing on Monday, I'll chase my lawyer for a progress update. I promise.'

'Right. I'll see you later then – spare keys are on the table.'

'OK, thanks.'

Tina left the flat and jogged down the stairs and out towards Oval.

'Lawyers. Sod that,' Tina muttered as she headed for the tube.

***

Tina Vaughn took a right immediately after she emerged from Camden Town, glad to be free of the sweat and claustrophobia of the northern line. A misty morning greeted her, the hustle and bustle of Camden Market buzzing through the fog. As usual, student types had congregated to buy knock-off jewellery, cheap electronics and clothing no real adult would be seen dead in. Merchants called out, hawking whatever tat they had to sell.

'Oi, love. Pretty necklace for a pretty neck?' One balding vendor called out, holding gold-plated jewellery out for Tina to see.

'No, but if you ever speak to me like that again then I'll snap your neck. Got it?'

'All right, love, no need to PMS.'

Tina flashed her badge, and the skinhead disappeared back to his market stall as quickly as he had emerged.

DiamondJewlz was listed as being on Camden High Street, not far from the Regent's Canal. When Tina finally arrived at the address, she found it no more than a door to a second-floor flat. Tina gingerly pressed the grimy off-white security buzzer to the right of the door, and waited for a response.

'Hello?' A female voice answered over a crackly intercom.

'Hi, I'm looking for,' Tina glanced down at the information sheet she had printed from DiamondJewlz' website, 'Mr Craig Linden, the manager of DiamondJewlz.'

'Well, he ain't here.'

'Do you know where he is?'

'Do I look like a map?'

'That retort would work better if I could see you.'

'Err, yeah. I guess it would. He's just over the road – the big jewellery stall next to Voluptuous Vintage Fashion.'

'Thanks.' Tina twisted one hundred and eighty degrees and marched towards the morass of stalls. The smells of a dozen varieties of street food wafted through the air as she closed in on the northern end of Camden Market. There was no map of stalls around; the stall-holders changed far too frequently for one to be practical, but many of the more established stalls had unfurled PVC banners to advertise. The purple and gold banner of independent fashionistas, Voluptuous Vintage, hung high enough to be seen above the parapet.

Tina made a beeline for the banner, and then glanced around searching for her destination. A black lace corset on display at Voluptuous Vintage caught her eye. Tina could just imagine the reactions in the squad room if they knew she were[since she isn't actually wearing it now] wearing that underneath her uniform.

DiamondJewlz finally came into sight with the churn of the crowds moving on. The calibre of jewellery on display did not live up to the company's moniker. Nearly everything in sight was simple fashion jewellery, and would not command the £1922.44 price tag that had been charged to David and Sarah Morton's MasterCard.

Tina sauntered over, and pretended to admire the goods on display.

'These aren't real, are they?' Tina asked of the stallholder.

'For £14.99? Definitely not.'

'Do you have any real diamonds?'

'You got money?' Linden asked in a hushed tone.

'Of course. I'm looking for something a bit special.'

'What sort of price range?'

'About two grand,' Tina invented.

'You're in the wrong place. Does it look like we sell high-end gems?' He chuckled.

'So you can't do me a special order?' Tina said.

'Did someone send you?'

'David Morton,' Tina ventured, hoping the seller wasn't in on the fraud.

'Ah, him. Yeah, we can talk. Want to come up to the flat? I don't keep anything good out here.'

'Lead on.'

'Great. I'm Craig, by the way but you probably already knew that. One second.' Craig turned to an adjacent stall. 'Yo, Barry. Watch the stall for me?'

'Sure thing, boss.'

The duo weaved through Camden Market in silence, the din of early morning shoppers rendering it impossible to have a private conversation. Eventually, the pair were back at the flat on Camden High Street. Craig fished inside his jacket for a short bronze key, and led Tina up the stairs to the flat.

'Mind the banister. It's a bit loose,' Craig said as they ascended.

He was breathing heavily by the time they reached the second floor, leaning heavily on peeling wallpaper as he unlocked the inside door. An open door to Tina's left revealed a broom-cupboard-sized bedroom.

Without that tiny box room, the flat would have been a bedsit. Tina could only imagine it had been marketed by the estate agent as a cosy apartment.

Opposite the entranceway, Tina could see a kitchenette which combined a small refrigerator, stove top and a sink into one unit. A sofa and chest of drawers rounded out the furnishings. There was no sign of the woman whom Tina had spoken to less than half an hour previously, and the place looked barely lived-in. No clothes were strewn about despite the lack of space.

Craig began rifling through the chest of drawers. 'You looking for anything in particular? Something big enough to cut or you want something to flip?'

'What've you got? I need to move about two grand without anyone noticing.'

'Got these, but they're two-and-a-half grand each.' Craig held out a solitaire.

'Got certificates?'

'No. It's a VSI diamond, but it's been cut down to shave the laser engraving. You'll be entirely untraceable with one of these. You want to sell them as certificated, you'll need to get them reappraised, but that won't cost much.'

'Are they conflict diamonds?' Tina asked, mindful of the Kimberley process.

'Nah, nothing like that.'

'What about the rest of the details?'

'Brilliant cut, white colour, a little over a carat.'

'Why so cheap?'

'Why do you think? You don't cut a gem down for no good reason.'

'Are they from that big warehouse bust in Antwerp a few weeks back? I hear they're going for half value. Not easy to trade 'em.' Tina had seen the Interpol bulletin about a robbery, but had no idea what the street value on them would be.

'Half? What you been smoking? Yeah, they're lifted. I'll do you one for two thousand if it's cash, today. That work for you?'

'Yes, it does. Craig Linden, you're under arrest for the possession of stolen goods. You have the right to remain silent; anything you do say can and will be used against you in a court of law.'

'Shit. Morton was an informant?'

'I'll be asking the questions – down at the station.'

***

'What the hell did you think you were doing?' Kiaran jabbed at Tina, his eyes furrowed into slits.

'I arrested a criminal after he admitted possession of stolen goods.'

'And what, pray tell, were you doing at said criminal's apartment, on your day off? On my day off.' Kiaran jabbed a finger at Tina.

'Following a lead.'

'On what case?'

'An identity theft...'

'Oh, so that's what you were up to, chasing down your precious chief's errant credit card charges? Did you bother to check in? No. You didn't. The folks in Organised Crime have been sitting on this guy for weeks, and you've spooked the entire chain. Now Mr Linden is in custody, and we've got no chance of getting his suppliers without cutting him a deal.'

Tina stared at her shoes, unable or unwilling to look the prosecutor in the eye, 'Sorry, Kiaran.'

The lawyer huffed, suddenly deflated. He wasn't done yelling, but little would be gained from berating Detective Vaughn further.

'Right. Well, get in there and get what you can out of him. He's lawyered up, so I'll have to cut some sort of a deal but let's put out feelers first, see what he's after. And see if you can get info on this identity theft into the bargain.'

Craig Linden was leant over the desk, his head twisted towards his lawyer. The moment Tina opened the door, the hushed whispers ceased.

She glanced at her watch: 1:58 p.m. 'Good afternoon. Detective Tina Vaughn.' She extended her hand to the lawyer, pointedly ignoring the suspect.

'Elliot Morgan-Bryant, Cutler & Kass.'

'How'd he afford your fees?' Cutler & Kass were famed for their exorbitant fees. A simple possession charge didn't warrant spending six hundred pounds an hour on such esteemed council, and Morgan-Bryant didn't seem the type to volunteer to work weekends for a pro bono client.

'That's between me and my client. What's on the table here, officer?'

'That depends on what information Mr Linden has for us.'

'Is immunity on the table?'

'That's down to our prosecutor. You give me something to take to him, and I'll see what he's willing to give up.'

'As a goodwill gesture, we'll give you a taste. The diamonds are from Antwerp, my client has already indicated as much. If he gives you the names of those involved, will that buy his freedom?'

'We'll need more than that.'

'I'm not advocating Mr Linden accepts any deal that is contingent on you getting a conviction, if that's what you are suggesting.'

'No. I need details on his buyers as well as his suppliers.'

'That we can do, right, Craig?' said Morgan-Bryant. His client nodded immediately, not realising how unhappy his paymasters would be.

'Give me a moment. I'll run this by the prosecutor.'

***

'Provided that what you've got is good, I'm prepared to offer s71 immunity from prosecution for the possession of stolen goods charge. If your client is about to admit a part in the robbery, then we can talk about a suspended sentence recommendation. So, cards on the table time, Elliot.' Kiaran O'Connor had taken a seat next to Tina in the custody suite, and immediately begun to take control of the interview.

'My client wasn't involved in the original theft, but was merely one of the fences contracted to cut and move the goods. He can give you the names of his suppliers, the times and dates of handovers, and he'll surrender all remaining evidence. In return, he wants complete immunity and you don't seek to recover any illicit profits he may have made so far. Is that acceptable?'

Kiaran nodded, then slid a document across the table. 'This is an Immunity Notice. You comply with the conditions outlined in it, which broadly reflect what you've just said, and we will drop all the charges.'

Elliot Morgan-Bryant pushed his reading glasses up on his bulbous nose as he skimmed the document. 'Everything appears to be in order.' He nodded. 'Craig, time to start talking.'

'I got the gems from the Bakowski brothers. One of their lot did the hit, I don't know who exactly. They laid low for a while, shipped me the gems a couple of months after the heist.'

'How'd they ship the diamonds?'

'In tennis balls. They bundled a few gems inside each ball, plus some lightweight padding. I imported a whole pallet of sports goods including a crate of tennis balls. I had to spend a whole weekend cutting the lot up to find my shipment. They weren't marked, for obvious reasons, see.'

'How much did you import?'

'Seven or eight hundred carats. Mostly larger pieces. Had to shave 'em to take off the laser identifiers so I got them well below market rate.'

'How much?'

'Two hundred grand for the lot.'

Kiaran whistled, 'That's a nice profit. Easily worth half a million on the open market if they're all like the gems Detective Vaughn seized.'

'Yeah, they were.'

'Were? You expect me to believe you offloaded the lot?'

'I'm at the end of my stash. Got a few more in my safe. I'm sure you've found that already, though.'

'The one under the carpet?' Kiaran asked shrewdly. A search team had been dispatched the second Tina called in her arrest.

'That's it.'

'And who did you sell the rest of them to?'

'Loads of people. All word of mouth, mind you. Not wise to tout stolen gems with coppers looking for 'em.'

'Where's the money you made now?'

'Used it. Had to pay off my creditors.'

Kiaran looked sceptical, 'I need the names of all your buyers.' He tapped the immunity notice requiring disclosure as he spoke.

'Got a list. Most of 'em were under the table, but some were via our website.'

'How'd the website customers pay?'

'PayPal invoice. They contacted us, we sourced what they wanted and invoiced 'em. Then they picked up from the flat, or we posted them depending on what the customer wanted.'

'Did many pick up?'

'Nah. Most wanted the gear posted out of the country. Good luck tracking them down. Only one guy picked up in person this month. That was your snitch, Morton.'

'He wasn't one of ours. What did Morton look like?' Kiaran said.

'Damned if I know. Shelley was there when he picked up. She has no idea my stuff is stolen, just thought he was a customer.'

'Who's Shelley?'

'My wife. She's often in the flat when I'm not. She's used to customers coming to pick up parcels.'

'We'll need to talk to her.'

'Fine with me. Am I free to go?'

'For now. I'd better not hear you've been selling stolen goods again.'

'You won't.'

Linden and his lawyer left, leaving Kiaran alone with Tina.

'There's no way he's got rid of half a million in diamonds, then squandered the cash,' Tina said.

'I agree. As this is your mess, you're going to clean it up. Find me those gems so I can bust him, immunity notice or no immunity notice.'

Tina smiled, 'Consider it done.'

Chapter 33: Trail

The evening of Craig Linden's arrest, his wife ignored Tina ringing the doorbell over the intercom, and Tina resorted to buzzing a neighbour in the downstairs flat. She identified herself as a police officer, and was let into the building. She strode up the stairs to the Linden flat once again, purposefully avoiding reliance on the wobbly banister.

'Shelly Linden! It's the police. Open up.'

'I'm coming, I'm coming. Don't break the bloody door down.' It was the same voice Tina had spoken to when she first set out for DiamondJewlz.

The rattle of a chain followed, along with the shunt of three security bolts being undone. The door finally swung open to reveal a young woman. She had platinum blonde hair, but the brown roots gave away her natural colour. Carefully tweezed eyebrows contrasted with an un-ironed camisole and fluffy slippers. Despite it's being a Saturday night, Shelley Linden had not planned on going out or receiving visitors.

'Shelley Linden? My name is Tina Vaughn. I'm with the Metropolitan Police, and I'm here to talk to you about a man who picked up a package from you.'

'My husband did text as much. Daft twat, letting a copper into his flat.'

'Quite.' Tina couldn't help but like the woman.

'You'd better sit down.'

Tina took a seat. 'I'm looking to identify a man you would have known as David Morton.'

'Doesn't ring a bell. What was he collecting?'

'It would have been a small package. Sometime on or around the sixth of January.'

'Last Saturday? Didn't have any packages then.'

'What about shortly after?'

'There was one bloke on Sunday. Internet order, as always. It's much easier to post the stuff.'

'What'd he look like?'

'White feller. About six feet tall. Not fat.'

Great, Tina thought. That only fits a million Londoners.

'Would you work with a sketch artist?'

'What's in it for me?'

'Us not busting your husband for possession?'

'Nice try. He's immune. If you can't do better than that, I'll have to ask you to leave.'

'Look, I can't force you to help. But if you ever need a favour, a legal one, I'd be in your debt.'

'I don't need anything from you. I don't do anything illegal.'

'But your husband does.'

'Then ask him for a favour. Not me. You want to talk to him, come back tomorrow. He has a lunch break about midday most Sundays. Otherwise, get out.'

Tina stood, and held out a business card to Shelley Linden. When she didn't take it, Tina threw the card onto the coffee table. 'Call me, if you change your mind.'

***

Craig Linden ambled through Liverpool Street station, appearing to admire the row of shops above the main concourse. As he drew nearer to the fast food joint at the rear entrance, he turned and walked towards the counter. A quick glance in the polished glass lining the storefront assured him there was no one following him. His reflection was suitably nondescript: jeans, trainers and a plain t-shirt. A white cap rounded out his attire.

He ordered, and then took his meal to a table in the corner where he began to dissect the burger, tossing aside the pickle and tomato. He took a bite, and then looked around surreptitiously to make sure he was alone. It would be just like the police to let him leave, then follow him. But there were no signs they'd been that crafty. Perhaps it was simply Saturday staffing.

With his burger, which was now oozing ketchup, held aloft in one hand, Craig delved into his jacket pocket with his other hand. He pulled out a mobile phone which was remarkable only for its plainness. This was no Smartphone. It could text, and make calls, but had none of the technology that could betray its user later in life.

Craig manually entered the number with his free hand, and then began to punch in his text message old-school style. Multiple number presses yielded one upper-case letter at a time, until he had managed to peck out his warning:

'THE POLICE ARE ONTO YOU. GET RID OF THE DIAMONDS.'

For the life of him, Craig could not find the caps button. Not that it mattered. The client had paid extra for a warning if the police ever came calling, and the customer was always right.

Craig hit send, and then returned his attention to his beef burger.

Chapter 34: Panic

'You look like crap.' Tina tossed her coat onto the rack by the door, and muttered a curse as the coat missed the bronze hook and fell to the floor in a crumpled heap.

'Uh, thanks. Kick a guy when he's down, why not?' Morton said as Tina scooped up her coat, and hung it neatly.

'Hey, it's Saturday evening and you're lazing around in a t-shirt watching reruns.'

'I like reruns.' David clutched protectively at the eighties box set beside him. Sometimes, the oldies were the best.

'But you already know how they'll end! Where's the fun in that?'

'Tina, it's about the journey, not the destination. You ever go to the cinema just to watch the closing credits? Thought not.'

Tina's mouth gaped open, and she tried to think of a retort.

'Besides, what else am I going to do with no cash?'

'I can think of a few things.' Tina winked.

'Tina, I'm a married... Ah, you meant Monopoly.' Morton blushed as he spotted her grabbing the board game from the top of the bookshelf behind her.

'No, I meant Vodkopoly.'

'Come again?'

'Every time you pass Go, you do a shot.'

'You cannot be serious.'

'Deadly. If you're still melancholy by the end of the game, I'll shoot you myself.'

'All right. But no cheating or I'll fire you on Monday.'

***

In any normal setting, Dimitri Bakowski would have been considered a giant. At over six foot, and tipping the scales at nigh on twenty stone, he was a hefty man. His idea of a run was barely ambling, but his right hook meant sprinting was never on the cards.

However, he was the runt of the Bakowski litter. His elder brothers, Nicodemus and Pavel, both topped six foot six and had mockingly christened him 'Tiny'.

The only thing that was little about Tiny were his eyes, which were small, black and beady like a raven's. They perused the warning the brothers had just received from their London contact, and the vein on Tiny's neck began to throb a dangerous purple.

The diamonds wouldn't give them away, but that Linden scum just might. He had never been their first choice of fence. He wasn't part of the family, and that meant no warnings and no second chances.

Tiny tapped out a reply, pudgy fingers clicking against keys, 'Take care of it.'

***

With a whoosh, flames burst into life atop the gas cooker, and the frying pan began to sizzle with melting butter as Morton sleepily depleted Tina's store of bacon and eggs. Saturday night Vodkopoly had resulted in the inside of Morton's head pounding like a rock concert. Even the sound of the egg cracking into the pan seemed to shoot through his very soul.

He grimaced. Being old sucked. Back in his twenties, he never had a hangover. By thirty, he needed a paracetamol in the morning after a night out. At forty, the mornings disappeared in a haze of pain. Now, in his fifties, the light seemed to sear his retina with the brightness of a supernova, and Tina's footsteps coming from the bedroom were the drumbeat of war.

'Mm. Smells good.' Tina looked aggravatingly upbeat; her brunette locks were tousled above her head in a neatly tied towel.

'Ugh,' Morton said, unable to form a complete sentence.

'Have a shower; it'll do you the world of good.'

'You're too cheerful in the mornings. You want fried bread?'

'Eww. No way. I've worked very hard on this,' Tina engulfed her wasp-like waist with two dainty hands, 'to ruin it over some grease. Just the bacon for me please, and do be a darling and cut off the fat, won't you?'

Morton bit his tongue. He wanted to argue, but he was her guest, and he was eating her food.

'Fine. You doing much today? I'm not fit for anything more than sofa duty.'

'Again? That sofa will have an imprint of your bottom on it soon.'

Morton glared, and then turned back to the cupboard that he had been searching.

Tina continued, 'Anyway, I'm going back to chase down some loose ends for Kiaran. I know what you're going to say. 'It's the weekend, I'm off duty blah blah blah.' I can't do this on the clock, so it's now or never. And you're in no fit state to do anything for yourself.'

'No arguments there,' Morton replied on autopilot, barely listening to Tina, and continued to pull things out of a cupboard at random. He pumped his fist in the air as he found what he was looking for. 'Aha! Ibuprofen!'

'That won't do much for a hangover, it's an anti-inflammatory.'

'Don't care. Need something.'

'Fine. I'll be back for dinner. You mind cooking? I might be back quite late.'

'Yeah, no problem.'

Morton flipped the bacon twice, inspecting both sides for crispiness. 'Hungry?'

***

Church bells rang out from St Mary's Church at the top of the hill as Hank left his flat. Hank chastised himself for his non-attendance at morning Mass. He would have to make it to the evening communion instead. It had taken him considerable effort to force himself out of bed.

Eliminating Craig Linden had never been in the plan, but what Tiny wanted, Tiny got. He cursed his bad luck that his sister had married into 'The Family', as Tiny called it. Tiny ran The Family with an iron fist: it was blood in, blood out.

Hank checked his watch: eleven o'clock. So much for Sunday being a day of rest.

Hank wasn't carrying a weapon, but he didn't need one. His gloves, which were conveniently normal in January, would be ample to strangle the life out of Craig Linden.

Hank bowed his head, drew his forefinger across his chest to make the sign of the Cross and muttered to himself, 'God forgive me.'

***

Thoughts the task ahead occupied Hank on his tube journey. He knew Craig would be on his stall from ten until twelve, and then break for lunch, as always. Hank aimed to arrive at the flat well before midday, in order to dispose of Shelley Linden. She would otherwise raise the alarm too soon, and the window of opportunity to dispose of Craig would be too narrow. Craig's wife would be an unfortunate, but necessary, by-product of his death.

Hank deliberately travelled one stop too far on the tube, opting to disembark at Mornington Crescent. The police would be sure to check the Camden Town station footage first, and this might buy him extra time. From the station, he walked south to Crowndale Road, then doubled back north via Bayham Street. He kept his head bowed as if struggling against the wind, and made his way to the Linden apartment.

Gaining entry to the flat proved remarkably straightforward. Hank simply rang the bell, and announced he had a parcel for Craig. Shelley's buzzed him in straight away.

Adrenaline pumped through Hank as he raced up the stairs three steps at a time.

As he made it to the landing, Hank could hear the click of locks being undone, then the door swung open to reveal Shelley Linden wearing only a woollen dressing gown. She was barefoot, and beckoned him in immediately. As soon as Hank was inside, Shelley pushed the door shut and the locks clicked back into place automatically.

Inside the flat, steam rising from a mug of tea on the counter caught Hank's eye.

Shelley saw him looking. 'You want a cuppa?'

Hank smiled, 'Sure.' Anything that would distract her would make it quick and easy.

'All right. Give me a mo, love.'

Shelley walked into the kitchenette, flicked a switch then rummaged in the small cupboard above the kettle. It was now or never. Hank slipped off his bulky overcoat, tiptoed up behind her and raised his arms.

Just as she turned to put milk in the mug, Hank struck.

In one fluid motion, he placed one hand either side of the small woman's head, then twisted sharply. She was dead before she hit the floor. No screams, no mess.

Hank tossed her limp body over his shoulder, walked into the solitary bedroom, then threw her on the floor on the other side of the bed from the door, out of sight. Now all he had to do was wait for Craig Linden.

***

Craig Linden's arrival was like clockwork. He had left his stall at exactly twelve, turning it over to a part-timer he hired to cover his lunch. At five past the hour, his key rattled in the door to his flat. The bottom lock clicked first, and then the top.

At the sound of the first lock being undone, Hank positioned himself to the left of the doorway, almost at right angles, the toes of his right foot resting on the rubber doorstop embedded into the floor. He held his breath, keeping deadly still to avoid detection.

Craig pushed the door, swinging it inwards towards Hank.

'Shelley?' Craig called out for his wife, stepping forwards into the living room. He seemed totally oblivious to the man waiting for him. Hank stepped up behind Craig, and reached for his neck. His hands were poised as they were with Shelley Linden, ready to execute Craig in one smooth twist.

The opportunity to strike loomed, then vanished as Craig sensed that something was wrong. Craig spun, acting out of instinct. He clawed at Hank, aiming for his eyes. Hank turned his head, leaving Craig's fingernails free to claw Hank's right cheek.

Hank suppressed the urge to roar in pain, instead swinging a pendulum-like hand towards Craig, catching the side of his head and sending him tumbling to the floor.

Hank leapt after him, using his immense weight to pin him to the floor, then used his right arm to crush Craig's windpipe. Craig struggled in vain against the larger man, then began to convulse as his oxygen supply was cut off. Eventually, Craig went limp and life deserted his body. Hank collapsed on top of the body, exhausted from the struggle.

***

'It's done.'

Tiny grinned at the text message from Hank Williams, displaying a mixture of crowns and decaying teeth. He was glad Hank had learned to obey his order. He would be handsomely rewarded for services rendered, once he had disposed of the bodies.

Tiny's flabby fingers pecked out a reply, 'Cut and chicken wire.' One simple text, sent from one disposable pay-as-you-go phone to another, condemned the remains of Craig and Shelley Linden to be treated like garbage. The cut and chicken wire technique was simple. The bodies would be dismembered, each piece wrapped in chicken wire and then dumped in the nearest body of water to rot, out of sight.

***

A generously proportioned meat cleaver from Shelley Linden's kitchenette and a full-size bathtub made Hank's job easier than he'd expected. There weren't many one-bedroom flats with a proper bath in central London. He'd have to go out and buy chicken wire, but as long as he was careful coming and going that wouldn't increase the odds of being associated with the crime too much.

As he was cutting up Craig Linden's corpse, the buzzer rang. Someone was outside the flat. Hank ran into the living room, cleaver still in hand, and stared at the door. His perception drifted to the entry phone buzzing to the left, an arrogant red LED flashing rapidly. He eyed the 'Do not disturb' function, and puffed a silent sigh of frustration, wishing that he'd had the foresight to turn it on before beginning his grizzly task.

Hank's mind raced as he ran through his options. Then the buzzing stopped. The visitor had given up. Hank allowed his body to sag with relief, and then tensed again when he heard the front door swing open. Someone else had let the visitor in.

Hank tiptoed to the flat's front door, and then pressed one bulbous eye to the peephole, getting a fisheye view of the stairwell.

He began to sweat as his body went into fight or flight mode. He knew the woman climbing the stairs: it was Detective Tina Vaughn. She was in plain clothes and hopefully unarmed. Hank had to act quickly lest she break down the door and find him. He looked down; his clothes were covered in blood. If she saw him, it was over.

Hank heard a knock at the door. 'Craig Linden. This is Detective Tina Vaughn. Open up.'

Hank shook his head with regret. The panic began to subside as he realised what he had to do. He had no desire to be a cop killer, but it looked like he would have to deal with Tina Vaughn.

He snatched up a frying pan from the kitchen, took up his position behind the door, then opened it inwards, crouching slightly so that his hairline was not visible above the door. As Tina stepped through, he swung the pan, hard. It connected with the front of her skull with a dull thud, and she dropped to the floor.

Hank dragged her inside, and then slammed the door before anyone could see her. He leant down and felt for a pulse. She was still breathing, but she was out cold. He could get away long before she regained consciousness. He grabbed his phone. Tiny would be sure to know what to do.

Chapter 35: History

Pitch black greeted Tina as she regained consciousness. Pain flickered through her body as she squinted into the darkness, trying to make out where she was. Then, slowly and stiffly, she flexed her muscles in a vain attempt to move. She was bound tightly, with cotton wool stuffed inside her mouth to stifle her screams. Harsh cold metal pressed against her from her left, with little room to move. There was something plastic squished against her right side, but Tina had no idea what it was.

She felt vibrations underneath her, the soft rumblings of an engine. Despite the darkness and her disorientation, it dawned on Tina that she was in the boot of a car. She strained to recall where she had been before waking up. She remembered the trip to Camden High Street, even as far as ringing Craig Linden's doorbell. So how did she end up in the boot of a car? Did it belong to Craig? None of that mattered right now. She had to escape, and fast.

Taking a deep breath, she focussed on her situation. Her mind flashed back to her police training. Morton's instructions echoed in her mind: Kick out the car's rear lights, then try and signal for help. It was easier said than done; her feet were bound tighter than a nun's vagina.

Tina wriggled, worm-like, and tried to angle her feet towards the corner she hoped contained the car's rear lights. She rocked back and forth, constrained by the rope. Little by little, she gained momentum until she was ready. As she rolled towards the corner, she kicked out as hard as she could. A muffled yelp escaped her as her toes collided with solid metal, and her eyes watered.

She changed tack, trying instead to feel for the right direction. Her fingertips met the soft, lukewarm object wrapped in plastic that she had noticed earlier. With a shudder, she realised that she was not alone in the boot. She was on top of a corpse.

***

Morton sat at a small fold-out dinner table, a relic with three legs that would have wobbled uncontrollably if not for the phone book used to steady the shortest leg. He rested his elbows on the table, and stared at the empty plate before him. He'd have to dish up soon, before dinner burnt.

She should have been back by now, he thought as his hairs stood on end. In his heart, he knew something was wrong but it was too soon to raise the alarm. She was only a couple of hours later than she had said she'd be. It wouldn't hurt to check in with a few of her friends to see if they'd heard from her, would it?

Morton plucked his mobile from his jacket pocket, and dialled the one man who was always attached to his phone. Ayala answered after just two rings.

'Ayala, it's David. Have you heard from Tina? She was supposed to be back a few hours ago, and it isn't like her to be late.'

'Back? What are you doing at her place, boss? Something you want to tell me?' Ayala's voiced was muffled, with a nasal quality.

'Never mind that. Have you heard from her?' Morton rose from the table, and began to pace with his mobile held at arm's length on speakerphone.

'No. I've been in bed all day, not spoken to a soul.' Ayala let silence hang in the air then felt compelled to break it: 'Bit of flu; awful weather; isn't it?'

'Yeah. OK. Well, if you speak to her, tell her to call me.'

Morton hung up, neglecting the niceties of saying goodbye. Where was she? He allowed himself to mull over several scenarios. It was cold out; she might have stopped for a hot toddy. Or worse, slipped on the ice. That could be it. He'd give it a few hours, and then try the hospitals. There was no sense getting worked up over nothing.

He resolved to follow the logic his mind dictated, but his gut still squirmed as he returned to the dinner table alone.

***

Tina leant heavily against a wall with her legs tucked underneath her as if she was praying. She was in a room barely larger than the car boot. It was lined with fluffy carpet, and more strips of carpet hung from the ceiling like stalactites.

Her journey from the car had been uneventful. While she was still bound, she had been yanked roughly from the boot, and a bag had been placed over her head then tied around her neck.

She had time to glimpse the inside of a double garage with shelving running along the wall, and an old boiler in the corner. Her captor was tall, but the bag stopped her from seeing any more than that. She'd been dragged over his shoulder and lugged down steps into a basement before being thrown into the room she now occupied. A trapdoor had slammed shut above her the moment she landed on the floor.

While she had not yet freed herself of all her bonds, she had managed to wiggle the gag free and spit out the cotton swabs. It didn't do her any good. Her makeshift cell's carpet lining muffled the sound too well, not that it stopped her from yelling herself hoarse.

There appeared to be no exit, but a gentle breeze flowed through an open grate somewhere above, tickling Tina's nape. The silence was the worst part. It isolated her from the outside world, and made it hard to tell how long she had been alone. Hunger pangs lanced through her, and thoughts of Morton's cooking pervaded her imagination. Would he be missing her?

She strained again, trying to think of the last thing she knew for sure had happened before she found herself in the boot, but her mind resolutely refused to serve up those memories.

***

In the Incident Room, Morton watched the hands of the clock tick by. He had a ten o'clock meeting with the Superintendent to justify keeping the Joe Bloggs Junior investigation live, but it was barely five past nine, and his wits had already deserted him.

He listlessly stirred sweetener into his coffee, desperately willing Tina to walk through the double doors unharmed. He'd tried the hospitals. She hadn't been admitted to any of the major London Accident and Emergency departments. He'd checked the drunk tank too, just in case. It was virtually empty, as was usual on a Sunday. He'd even tried to phone her next of kin, but her sister Catrin hadn't answered.

Soon, twenty-four hours would be up, and he'd be able to formally have her listed as missing. Until then, he just had to get through the day.

***

The Superintendent was running late for Morton's ten o'clock meeting. Morton could see him through the window in the office door, yapping into his phone and jabbing his index finger at thin air and otherwise doing his best to look busy. In reality, Morton suspected he was simply talking to his mistress.

Despite his misgivings, Morton waited patiently in the corridor outside the Superintendent's office. It was an odd antechamber in the eaves of New Scotland Yard where few other offices were to be found. The Crown Prosecution Service nominally reserved one area, and a media suite took up half the floor. The remaining two rooms were split between a conference room and the Superintendent's private office. Naturally, the Superintendent occupied the largest room.

Each room was lined with solid oak walls. Decorative motifs wended their way around the cornices, and police chiefs of yesteryear adorned the walls in oil portraits. Pure decadence, Morton scoffed. Such extravagance, when he was there to justify the continued investigation of a child's death.

At twenty past the hour, the Superintendent waltzed out of his office, garbed in a daring silk waistcoat that did nothing to conceal his pot belly, 'Ah, David. I hope you haven't been waiting long.'

'No sir,' Morton lied through gritted teeth.

The Superintendent spotted Morton looking at the waistcoat, and mistook his revulsion for interest. 'Lovely, isn't it? My wife had it made for me by a friend of hers. He's got a shop down on Jermyn Street. Wouldn't normally shop there, oh no,' the Superintendent shook his head as if London's second most exclusive street of tailors was beneath him, 'Saville Row all the way normally, but Marcus is a dear friend to my Becca. Shall we?' He gestured for Morton to open the door, and then followed him through.

'Now then,' he continued once he was settled, 'this case, Joe Bloggs Junior. What's it all about? You've had staff running left, right and centre but from what I've been told you're getting nowhere.'

'I'm not sure who told you that, sir,' but Morton knew. It had to be the newcomer, Detective Inspector Mayberry. The rest of his team had been with him on and off for eons, and knew better than to rat him out to the bureaucracy.

'Never you mind that, my boy,' the Superintendent replied.

Morton's teeth gnashed together at my boy; He was a grown man in his fifties, thank you very much.

'But I need to know there's a reasonable prospect of a conviction in the pipeline here. We're throwing dozens of men behind it full-time, and you don't appear to be getting anywhere. Even the CPS has logged well over a hundred man-hours on this.'

Morton bit his tongue, paused, then responded diplomatically, 'Well sir, it's an unusual case. The body was dumped in the Marshes towards the back end of last year. No name, nothing to identify him forensically. We thought we'd found his identity when we linked his watch to a Charlie Matthews, but apparently Charlie is alive and well. He's currently living with a foster family in south London. '

'So how did Joe come to possess Charlie's watch?'

'That's where this case takes another interesting turn. The watch originally belonged to Eric Matthews.' Morton paused to collect his thoughts while his boss looked deep in thought.

'Eric is legally Charlie's father, but their DNA has no alleles in common. On the other hand, DNA confirms that Joe is Eric's son, so it makes sense that he was wearing his father's watch. The last record we can find of the watch was with Charlie's long-term foster family, the Grants. It's perplexing in all honesty, sir. We've got one dead boy whom we have no record of but is definitely related to Eric Matthews, and then we have Charlie, the legal son of Mr and Mrs Matthews, who is not biologically related to his father.'

'Sounds like they've been switched somewhere,' said the Superintendent

'That's a possibility but how it all fits, we don't know. What I do think is that if we can run down how these boys' lives are intermingled then we'll be able to give Joe back his identity at the very least. It might even lead us to Charlie's real identity. This could be much bigger than a simple murder case.'

'Very well. How do you propose doing that?'

'I'm going to run down Charlie's past, and see who he really is.'

'But if the investigation into Master Matthews yields another dead end, the trail ends?'

'Potentially, sir, yes.'

'Then you've got until you exhaust that lead to find something that justifies our continued allocation of resources to this case. This isn't the only investigation we have open. Find something and quickly or this goes to the cold case team, and you know what kind of backlog they've got.'

'Very well, sir. I'll update you when I know more.' Morton turned to leave. He'd invent something to appease the Superintendent if he had to. He wasn't going to leave the dead boy without a name, and he certainly wouldn't let a child's identity be usurped.

'And Morton?'

'Yes sir?'

'Do go check out Marcus' Tailors. You look awfully scruffy, old chap.'

Chapter 36: Little Hatters Wood

The Lovejoy household was a middle-class suburban affair. The Lovejoys took in so-called trauma cases, those children who had lost their parents or guardians to accident, injury or homicide. The Lovejoys never kept children for long. They were specially trained counsellors, and in so much demand that their charges typically only spent around a month in the Romford suburb.

La Casa Lovejoy, as Adrian Lovejoy affectionately called it, had started out as a simple four-bed semi-detached home. It was seconds from the local bus links in Whitchurch Road, and, being in the middle of an oval block, enjoyed an enormous garden.

Demand for the Lovejoys' expertise exceeded the space they had available to care for their charges. The Local Authority had stepped in to help the Lovejoys, allowing Adrian to obtain a mortgage for the house next door. The combined houses formed a home big enough for the extended family.

Adrian spent his days clearing up after the children, while his long-suffering wife Pru tried to keep the house in order amidst a constant whirlwind of activity.

Despite the biting winds, Adrian was outside when the police arrived. He was lovingly he rims of his people carrier's tyres, oblivious to the visitors standing above him.

'Mr Adrian Lovejoy?' Morton's voice oscillated as his teeth chattered in the cold, having had to suffer Ayala's unfathomable preference for keeping the heating off on their drive from New Scotland Yard in order to 'improve fuel economy'. Ayala was studying his manicured fingernails, sheepishly avoiding eye contact with his partially frozen superior.

'Good morning!' Adrian beamed, enthusiastic for the chance to have an adult conversation. The smile, combined with rosy red cheeks, gave Adrian the appearance that Santa Claus would have sported had he gone on a serious diet, and burned several thousand calories a day chasing small children around.

'Hello, sir, we're here to talk to you about a former charge of yours, one Charlie Matthews. Might we step inside?'

'Yes, yes, of course. Do forgive my manners. My office, I think. Anywhere else is likely to be bedlam. Do you know we've got eight children with us, right now? What are they thinking? It's just Pru and I. We can only chase after so many charges at one time! Three under-fives, for God's sake! One minute we're running a nursery, the next we're trying to stop the older ones from sneaking out and smoking. Utter lunacy,' his words came out in a rush, a verbal machine gun of conversation.

'Quite. We're a little stretched ourselves, sir,' Morton observed dryly.

'Ah yes, I saw the newspaper. Didn't get a chance to read the whole article. One of the little ones upchucked all over it at breakfast. Fussy little eater, that one. Didn't it say something about the Met being short of funds, cutting basic pay and all that? Bonkers if you ask me. If your bobbies are broke, they're much more likely to be on the take.' Adrian continued to aim a barrage of questions and comments at them as he led the way to his study.

Ayala looked like he wanted to agree, and Morton was forced to silence him with a glare.

'I can't say I agree with that, sir, but the logic is faultless,' Morton said tactfully.

'Here we are.' Adrian ushered them into his office, clicking the door shut behind them.

'Mr Lovejoy,' Morton began after they had sat down.

'Please, call me Adrian.'

'OK. Adrian, do you remember Charlie Matthews?'

'Oh yes. We had him here for about a month. Only left a few weeks ago. Lovely lad, a bit quiet. He ate his own weight in chocolate given half an opportunity. Is he in trouble?'

'No sir, we're just following up some routine enquiries. Nothing to be concerned about.'

'Thank goodness. I was quite fond of the little tyke. He was a whizz at fixing electronics. See that computer over there?' He pointed at an old machine tucked away in the corner,.'Helped me put that back together. Took to it like other kids play with Lego.'

'Is this Charlie?' Morton produced the picture of Charlie Matthews supplied by Children's Services.

'That's him,' Adrian confirmed.

Morton unrolled a copy of the facial construction. 'What about this boy? Do you know him?'

'No,' he replied almost too quickly, and then continued hesitantly, 'Should I?'

'We believe he may be a relative of Charlie's. Did he ever mention a sibling?'

'Not once. But he barely said anything.'

'In that case, I think that's everything. Thank you for your time, Mr Lovejoy.' Morton rose, proffering a handshake.

'You're going so soon? But I haven't even had time to offer a coffee. One for the road?'

'No, thank you. We'd best be getting back. Thanks again.'

Back outside, they climbed into Ayala's aging Mercedes.

'Well, that was a waste of time,' Ayala volunteered.

'Maybe, maybe not. They only had Charlie for a month.'

'Shame the Grants are dead.'

'They are, but their neighbours aren't. Charlie was there for almost a decade. Let's see if they remember anything.'

'Right you are, boss.' Ayala turned the ignition, blasting frigid air around the car.

'Bloody hell, that's cold.'

'Bet you wish you'd said yes to that coffee now, eh boss?'

***

'You have reached your destination,' a robotic voice emanated from the satellite navigation system, prompting Ayala to pull over and kill the engine.

'This road looks like an old Roman road, don't you think?' said Morton. Dalkeith Grove was as straight as an arrow.

'No idea. Looks like modern suburbia to me, not much different to the place we just came from.'

'You know, for a detective, you've got no sense of subtlety.'

'So, how's this any different?' Ayala demanded.

'Well, for a start it's more affluent. Every house is detached. Some are mock-Tudor in style; you don't find that on a council estate. Most of the driveways are full, many with two or three cars.'

'Looks just as icy to me.'

'Just shut up, and get out of the car. That's an order.' Morton swung his door open, and placed his right foot gingerly on the ice, causing it to crackle underfoot.

No repairs had been carried out at the Grant residence. At first glance, it didn't seem too damaged. The walls were still in place, barely stained with a lick of smoke. Closer inspection revealed melted uPVC lintels, and warped glass. The only obvious damage was that the roof had collapsed inwards, but even that would not be discerned by a casual passerby, thanks to the angle from the street.

The neighbouring homes had minor smoke stains, but had been saved by the actions of the Fire Brigade. Morton veered towards the house to the left of the Grant residence. A trampoline in the garden, the kind designed for one, suggested they had a child, and might therefore be more apt to remember the boy next door.

They rang the neighbour's doorbell, and heard a chime reverberate throughout the house. A 'No solicitation' sign was prominently displayed in the front bay window.

A woman answered the door, a sleeping baby cradled in her arms.

'Hello, I'm Detective Chief Inspector David Morton, and this is Detective Ayala. Do you know a Charlie Matthews?'

'I knew a Charlie, but I don't think his surname was Matthews. He lived next door,' she shifted the baby up and down as she spoke, willing it to stay asleep.

'Perhaps you knew him as Charlie Grant?' Morton wondered if the Grant's had imposed their surname on their adoptive son.

'Yep, I knew the Grants. Mrs Grant and I used to go to spinning classes together. Sad what happened to them.'

Morton pulled out a picture of Charlie. 'Is this him?'

'Sorry, that's not him. That's not the boy who lived next door.'

Morton switched the photo for the facial reconstruction of Joe Bloggs Junior. Recognition dawned on her face immediately. 'That's him! The hair's a bit different, but that's unmistakeably the boy from next door.'

'Are you sure?'

'Yeah, I'm sure I am. Hang on; I might have some photographs from the Diamond Jubilee Street Party we threw last summer. Shall I go look?'

Half an hour later, the detectives were headed back to New Scotland Yard. The photographs were definitive: Joe Bloggs Junior was Charles Anthony Matthews, son of Eric and Jacqueline Matthews, and grandson to one Cecil Matthews.

'If our dead kid is the real Charlie Matthews, who the hell is the impostor?' Ayala's question hung in the air of the saloon. Morton had no answer.

Chapter 37: Gone

Twenty-four hours after Tina had been expected to return home, Morton formally registered her as missing. Morton had hoped that the twenty-four hour deadline elapsing would galvanise Missing Persons into action, but that assumption was to prove overly optimistic.

'Sir, we have two hundred thousand missing persons every year. We can't simply send half the department on a wild goose chase across London. We've got all the pertinent details. I suggest you continue to make your own enquiries.'

All Morton had to go on was a slightly nasal telephone voice, but in Morton's mind the clerk he was talking to was a snotty-nosed, zit-faced jobsworth. He was clearly irked at having to go off-script and actually deal with the complainant.

'This isn't a mid-life crisis case. She hasn't upped and left without a word to her friends or family. Tina Vaughn is one of our own.'

'I appreciate that, sir,' the clerk said.

'Do you? What you're telling me is that your department is going to do next to nothing. Get me the Initial Investigating Officer. Better yet, send him up to my office. I'll be here until ten tonight.' Morton hung up the phone, knowing he'd made a ridiculous demand.

Morton tried to think what more he could do to find Tina beyond wandering the streets aimlessly. She'd been expected back at dinner time Sunday, and it was fast closing on 8 p.m. Monday. She wasn't the kind to disappear without notice.

He dug into his drawer and pulled out a yellow legal pad then laid it in front of him on his desk and began to jot down his thoughts in an attempt to organise them.

Missing Person: Tina Vaughn

Relatives: One sister, Catrin Vaughn (Next of Kin)

Friends: All in the force (?)

Relationship status: Single

Medical conditions: None

Financials: Cards untouched; Alerts placed on all accounts

Photographs: On file

DNA: On file

What was she doing when she went missing? Unknown.

Morton underlined the last point. It was the million-dollar question. Morton thought he'd heard her say she was running errands for Kiaran, but the prosecutor denied he had assigned her any such task.

He racked his brains for their last conversation, but the only other detail he could recall was that she'd promised to be back for dinner. She hadn't gone into work; her security card was last logged as entering Scotland Yard on Saturday. Her phone was not connected to the network, but that could be simple battery failure. A request had been sent to Tina's network provider to see if they could find her last known location. It wouldn't take them long to respond given the simple geometry involved. All they needed to do was use signal strength to guesstimate how far she was from the three nearest masts, then triangulate her location.

It wouldn't be much help if she was last seen at a tube station, but it would be a starting point. The only problem was the wait. Morton snorted into his coffee. The chance of getting a response that night was about as good as the Initial Investigating Officer traipsing up to his office.

Knowing that he could do little for Tina until the morning, Morton decided to take one more look at the Incident Room data wall before calling it a night.

The door to the incident room was ajar when Morton arrived, light spilling out into the hallway.

'Ayala. What are you doing still here?' The junior detective had been off the clock for over three hours now.

'Evening. I knew I wouldn't sleep, so thought I may as well spend the time trying to be productive.' Ayala's eyes were bloodshot, with dark bags hanging underneath them.

'Worried about Tina?'

'Yeah, and this case. Who the hell is our impostor?'

'No idea. Who would want to impersonate a child?'

'I'm sure I heard of a case where a thirty-year-old woman pretended to be a child. Could we have another one of those on our hands?' Ayala said.

'I doubt it. The kid has barely hit puberty. You can't fake not having hit adolescence.'

'So, what's your theory?'

'I think there's money involved. Someone helped our impostor become Charles Matthews. What if they saw the watch, and realised just how much our orphan was due to inherit?'

'But where did the kid come from?'

'I don't know. No one is missing a child, and our faux-Charlie seems to have a poor command of the English language. He could be from anywhere.'

'Then we talk to Children's Services,' Ayala suggested.

'Eventually we'll have to, but I'd like some idea of how they got switched first. We also need to work out if this is a one-off, or if it could be more systematic than that. The switch has to have happened after the fire at the Grant residence, as the neighbours knew Joe rather than the child with the Lattimers. I can't rule out the Grants being involved, but they're dead. Sometime between Dalkeith Grove and the end of Charlie's stay at the Lovejoys the boys were switched.'

'You think the Lovejoys are in on it, boss?'

'Maybe,' Morton replied cautiously. 'We're going to have to tread carefully here. It could be a simple mix-up. If our fake Charlie has a criminal record, then he might have seen such a switch as an opportunity. If he noticed the real Charlie disappear, he could have assumed his identity to get away from another foster parent or something,' Morton postulated dubiously.

'That doesn't ring true. He's barely above the age of criminal responsibility. Besides, wouldn't his prints be in the system?'

'He'd have been tried in the Youth Court, everything sealed.'

'But that negates any need to impersonate someone else.' Ayala stifled a yawn.

Morton shrugged. 'I'm pretty much spit-balling here. I've never heard of a case where one child has impersonated another. I doubt any child would know how records work in Youth Court anyway. We can't assume a twelve-year-old would act logically.'

'So, why are we assuming it wasn't the Lattimers?'

'I can't see how they'd have had the opportunity to substitute in a fake Charlie. They haven't had him long, and surely their son, what's-his-name?'

'James,' Ayala supplied.

'James would have noticed. As would social services, and the school,' Morton concluded.

'Then the switch has to be before then. Are we concentrating on the Lovejoys?'

'I guess so. We'll start our investigation bright and early tomorrow morning. For now, out of my Incident Room. You need to be rested up for tomorrow.'

Ayala nodded curtly at his dismissal, and then left Morton in silence. Alone with his thoughts, Morton pondered where to spend the rest of the night. He didn't relish the thought of spending the night alone at Tina's, but there was always the slim chance she might come back. Stranger things had happened. Morton rose, flicked off the strip lighting and plunged the incident room into darkness. He should heed his own advice, and be fit for the coming investigation.

***

Pangs of hunger lanced through Tina's stomach. She had been left alone since being knocked out except for one brief visit by her captors. The sound of something heavy had preceded the opening of a trapdoor overhead. For one glorious moment, Tina thought she was free. Something was thrown in, landing on Tina's chest with a painful thud. Then the trapdoor slammed shut, and the darkness conquered her prison once more.

Tina twisted, trying to manoeuvre the object towards her hands. It was a plastic bottle of water. Good. That meant they weren't intending to kill her. At least, not immediately. An overhead screech reverberated as whatever was being used to weigh down the trapdoor was dragged back into place.

Her sense of time had been warped by the darkness. Only Tina's hunger gave her any indication how long she might have been kept in the dark.

'Aha! Got you.' Tina grappled the bottle between her fingertips, constrained by the ropes around her wrists. Somehow, she had to get the bottle back up to her lips in order to drink.

The bottle was half empty by the time she had contorted herself to bring it to her lips. She held the bottle between her teeth, then chugged back a swing. It wasn't much, but she had to make it last. She settled the bottle down next to her, propped up against the carpet hanging from the ceiling of her cell. Surely someone would come for her.

Chapter 38: A Room With a View

It was Hank Williams' first-ever visit to the London residence of Dmitri 'Tiny' Bakowski. Hank had expected something oppressive, broody and vaguely imperial. Instead, the duplex was clean, minimalist and even empty. Over two thousand square feet of open-plan space, but barely any of it in use.

Hank sat on the edge of a curvy leather sofa, one of a pair positioned right in the middle of the room. The furniture was clearly designer. Other than a television, which hung on a floating wall in front of him, there was no other clutter in sight.

'Like it?' Tiny's voice startled Hank.

Tiny appeared from the kitchen wearing shorts and an open-cuff shirt. Tiny's casual attire sharply contrasted with Hank's own, which included a thick cashmere overcoat that was much more practical for someone living in London in the depths of midwinter.

'It's gorgeous,' Hank gushed, 'but did you just move in?'

'No. It's meant to be like this. Minimal. Some like to display their wealth.'

'And you don't?'

'I do, but I'm doing it by the absence of stuff.'

'Eh?'

'This is Hyde Park One, the most expensive building on the planet. Being able to have this much space, and not use any of it, makes me stand out.' Tiny spoke slowly, as if talking to a child.

'Ah. Right.' Hank's expression betrayed his confusion.

'So, what do you want? A bonus?' Tiny reached into his pocket to pull out his wallet. He had no qualms about rewarding family loyalty.

'Umm. I need your help.'

Tiny's eyes narrowed with suspicion. 'What with?'

'The Linden job wasn't, um,' Hank watched Tiny's face for any sign of impending violence, wary of his cold stare. 'Well, it wasn't as clean as it could have been.'

'You whitewashed the scene?'

'Yes.'

'You ditched the bodies as directed?'

'I ditched the bodies downstream, near Tilbury. Thanks for sending a car, by the way.'

'Outside the Met's jurisdiction? I like it.' Tiny's yellowed teeth, long since stained by cigarettes and poor personal hygiene, protruded from his lips in a victory snarl.

'Yeah. The Lindens' deaths won't trace back to you, don't worry.'

'Then what's the problem?'

'When I was cutting up the bodies, someone else entered the flat.' Hank's words came out in a rush, only just decipherable.

'And? You had to ditch one more body. No big deal.'

'I didn't kill them.'

'Why the hell not? What did you do, convince them with your silver tongue: "Oh hello, I was just cutting up these bodies... for the local medical school. Would you mind giving me a hand?" You stupid bastard.'

'I knocked her out.'

'Her? Pretty, was she?'

'No. She was a bloody cop!'

'What the hell have you done with her?'

'She's in the basement of our place in Crystal Palace,' said Hank.

'You've kidnapped a cop, and shut her up in my basement? Has she seen your face?'

'No.'

'A minor miracle. You've got two options. One, kill her and dump the body with the others. Two, drug her and dump her somewhere to be found. Number two only works if you're certain she can't identify you or my place or otherwise link back to us.'

'She was blindfolded the whole time. On the way back from the Linden flat, I stopped off for a while. Bitch did a bit of damage to my boot.'

Tiny cackled. 'Thought she was going to escape, did she? Nice try. Kill her, she's too much trouble to let live.'

Hank hesitated. It was one thing to off the competition, but killing a cop would paint a bright red cross on his back for life. Hank's reluctance must have shown in his expression, as Tiny frowned and asked: 'You need a hand?'

'N-n-no, boss. I'll take care of it.'

'Good. Now get out. Crystal is waiting for me.' Tiny gestured towards the kitchen.

Hank looked over to see one of Tiny's floozies loitering in the doorway, her ample chest barely concealed under the fabric of her top.

'Right. Thanks, Tiny.'

***

It took almost a whole day for Tina's mobile phone network to respond to Morton's request. The last time her phone had been connected to the network, it had bounced a signal off several towers from the Barbican up to Essex Road and east to Shoreditch High Street. Studying the report, Morton realised that the epicentre of the signal activity was Old Street Station. Morton cursed. It looked like Tina had lost signal when going underground on the tube, and had either never resurfaced or lost battery power while in transit.

Morton traced the laptop screen with his finger. Old Street was on the Northern Line, two changes away from virtually any station on the underground. The signal had gone dead at 12:32 p.m., which was presumably when she descended the escalator to the platform buried deep underneath the silicone roundabout.

Morton had been to Old Street Station every day since he'd begun occupying Tina's sofa in Hoxton Square. He'd always taken the north-east entrance to the station, and then gone through the ticket barrier towards the tube. Each morning he saw a morass of commuters, dressed for the January weather, congregate like sardines in small carriages. The shorter travellers suffered. They had the misfortune to stand underneath the sweaty armpits of taller commuters holding onto the ceiling-mounted rails.

Sunday probably wouldn't have been quite so busy. Morton logged onto the Transport for London database. As he waited for his session to load, Morton cracked his knuckles impatiently. It was even slower than the Met's system. Morton stood, and then paced the Incident Room, traversing the small space repeatedly as he waited for the screen to refresh.

Eventually, he was in. It wasn't as simple as typing in 'Tina Vaughn' and bringing up her travel history. Not that Morton didn't try that. He entered her name, crossing his fingers that she had taken the time to register her Oyster Card. No such luck. Like everyone else Morton knew, she'd just paid the five pounds deposit for a pay-as-you-go card, and gone on her merry way.

Morton clicked back to the menu screen, wondering if he'd be able to find her Oyster Card from her credit card details. Surely she had topped up with her card at some point.

'Damn!' Morton swore. Payment data wasn't available on the system he had access to. He'd have to call someone.

'You losing at solitaire again, boss?' Ayala hung in the doorway, propped up against the frame and lazily watched his superior officer's growing frustration.

'Very funny,' said Morton. Ayala had taken Morton for almost a hundred pounds at a poker game he'd organised. Morton still swore Ayala could count cards. 'I'm trying to find out where Tina went. Her mobile signal died at Old Street Station at lunchtime on Sunday.'

'Checked her Oyster travel history?

'Can't. It's pay-as-you-go.'

'Her bank must have payment details for top-ups?' Ayala suggested, following the same logic Morton had.

'Got to subpoena those sorts of records.'

'OK. Let's try again. What time did you say she lost signal?'

'12:32 p.m., why?'

'It takes what, roughly a minute to go from the ticket barrier to the platform? How many cards went through the gates in the period 12:30 to 12:32?'

'I like your thinking.' Morton ran the query, which flashed up results almost instantly. Maybe the TFL system was better than the Met's after all.

'Eighteen,' Morton read from the results screen.

'And how many of those are registered?'

'Seven.'

'If we exclude those seven, we've got eleven candidate numbers. Close, but no cigar,' Ayala said.

'How's the CCTV coverage around there?'

'Awful; I can see Tina going into the tube station but I lose her once she's inside.'

'Right. I'll bring up the eleven cards that could be her. Between them we've got one departing at Angel, two at Waterloo, one at Piccadilly, one at Regents Park, one at Camden Town and even one way out in West Finchley. The last four got off the tube at Oxford Street.'

'Sounds like those four were a group. How closely grouped were their times near the barrier?'

Morton checked the screen, 'Seconds apart.'

'Right. So let's park those four for a minute. The other seven: all of them will be on CCTV exiting those stations. They're all pretty thoroughly covered, except maybe West Finchley. I've never been up that way.'

'I have. Bunch of champagne bloody socialists.' Morton spread his fingers wide, hands held aloft, in a 'What can you do?' gesture.

'Let me guess. The in-laws live there?'

'Used to. They've got a place on the riverfront in Hammersmith these days.'

'Nice.' Ayala didn't envy Morton for being married. He'd sooner be dead.

'Aha!' Morton cried, 'I've got her. She left Camden Town at just after 12:43.' Morton checked the Oyster database again to get her Oyster Card number: 056056259473. 'No activity on her Oyster Card since.'

'Then it's time we paid Camden Borough Council a visit and see if we can track her down on their CCTV. Which way did she leave the tube?'

'She came out on the west side of the station; looks like she was heading north,' Morton said.

'Towards Camden Market then. Sunday afternoon shopping perhaps?'

'Let's find out.'

***

Tina kept slipping in and out of consciousness. When she came to, her head pounded as if she was suffering from the worst hangover of her life. It was pitch black, but her eyes still saw an inky black haze shimmering around her.

The only upside was that the thirst was gone. That wasn't because she had water. The bottle thrown in with her was long gone. She was simply too far gone to feel it. Her tongue felt swollen and dry, as if a sandpaper balloon had been inflated in its place.

The pain wasn't too bad either. The bindings had slackened a little, not enough for her to effect an escape but enough to afford a modicum of comfort. Tina's limbs simply tingled. It was like the pins and needles she'd been fascinated by as a child, and had sometimes deliberately leant on one arm to achieve; but now the sensation seemed to have taken up permanent residence.

A sound came from above. It was the same scraping noise she had heard before. As the trapdoor swung open, light rushed into the tiny cell. For a brief moment, she thought she had been saved. A shadow reached down and picked her up, drawing her into the light. Her eyes burned as the sudden light seared them. She instinctively tried to kick out against her captor, but she was too weak to have any effect.

Her eyes slowly came into focus as she was carried up and out of the basement. Back in the garage, she had one last glimpse of freedom before she was thrown back into the boot. As the boot closed, Tina's world went black.

Hank chugged along the A2199, with his hands firmly planted at ten and two on the steering wheel. He was not normally such a cautious driver, but he was anxious not to get pulled over while he had a woman in the boot. He checked the speedometer, and gently lifted his foot just enough to bring him back within the speed limit. The roads were empty. He had to dump her somewhere unconnected to the Bakowski family. New dump sites were hard to find, but sometimes hiding in plain sight was enough.

He indicated left, a gloved hand briefly activating the turning lights. Hank always wore gloves in winter, but instead of owning one pair he kept sets of three. He had to use an un-gloved hand to put on the first glove, which meant it could end with fingerprints on the first glove worn. He kept a third so that he could put on the pair he really wanted with his contaminated first glove. It was convoluted, but it helped Hank sleep more soundly.

The girl had to go. He should have just killed her in the Linden flat. The blessings of hindsight.

Still, a little voice in his head kept on arguing, she hasn't seen you. She didn't even see the Linden corpses. Why not just let her go? Why risk a murder rap when you could just dump her? Even Hank's more ruthless side was calculating enough to see the benefits of letting her live.

Hank pulled over onto Brockwell Park Gardens, pulled up on the curb and killed the engine. There was no one around. He'd expected as much. It was four a.m. If he'd been any earlier, there might have been drunk students stumbling home. Much later, and the fitness nuts would be out in force.

Hank chewed his lip. He didn't want to kill. That had never been the plan. All he ever wanted was a better life for the kids than he'd had.

Hank pulled his scarf tight above him, obscuring his face. Then he rose from the driver's seat, still unsure of his final decision. He opened the boot slowly to keep the noise down.

She was pitiful. Bedraggled, covered in her own sweat, urine and faeces. She was bound tightly, gagged and unconscious. She was no threat. Screw Tiny. He didn't need to snap her neck.

Hank pulled out a pocketknife, and slit her bonds. They fell back into the boot. The gag was likewise removed, revealing puffy purple lips. Hank lifted Tina, a little more gently this time.

Tiny would punish him, if he ever found out. He carried Tina towards the south-west fence of Brockwell Park Gardens, lifted her easily over the knee-high fence, and then propped her up against the fence. He crouched next to her. Both the road and the jogger's path on the other side of the tree line were visible. Confident that she'd be found shortly, Hank scurried back to his car.

***

Ayala nodded, 'I think we've got it from here. Thanks.' He nodded at the CCTV tech who loitered awkwardly until he realised his presence was no longer required.

'Well, call the front desk if you need anything, Just dial one on the intercom,' the tech said as he walked out, leaving Morton and Ayala alone with the bank of screens. There were thirty-two smaller screens displaying the insides of various council buildings, plus a larger screen in the middle which had been left for their use.

'How do you work the facial tracking on this thing?' Morton said.

'Been watching crime dramas again? These cameras were put in back in the early nineties. The resolution is awful. I've seen higher-quality video taken using mobiles,' Ayala replied.

'The old-fashioned method it is, then. Where are all these cameras?'

Ayala pointed at a map of the area on the wall behind them. 'Each of those pins is a council-owned camera. The yellow triangle on the top shows which way the cameras are facing.'

'Are they all the same model?'

'Nope. So we've got different fields of view covered. Some of them are narrow-lens cameras. I think they're mostly pointing at doorways in and out of public buildings. What we want is a camera on Camden High Street, as that was where Tina was headed.'

'What about that one covering Inverness Street Market?'

Ayala pulled up the feed on the largest monitor, and then found the footage from 12:43 p.m. Sunday.

'There she is, right at the back of the image. On the opposite side of the road, next to the 'One Way' sign.'

'Looks like she's headed towards Camden Market.'

Morton glanced up at the map of camera locations. 'We've got two cameras on the market. Get those up.'

A processor whirred as it fetched video archives from the computer's memory banks. The file began to buffer, and an image of Camden Market sprang to life.

'Wide-angle lens. Looks like we've got the whole of the frontage covered,' Morton said.

'Yep, and there she is!' Ayala grabbed Morton's arm and pointed. Tina could be seen disappearing between the shoe store on the corner and the clothes stall next to it.

'And after that, nothing. Too many stalls in the way.' Morton checked the map to see if there were any other cameras covering the inside of Camden Market, but there were none to be found.

'Right. So, the question is: did she leave Camden Market under her own volition? There's no sign of foul play so far, which suggests anything that has happened would have been after that.'

'Fast forward a bit, and we'll see if she comes back out.'

The pair sat in silence as the feed flashed by at quadruple speed.

'There! Rewind a sec. I think I spotted her.' Morton pointed at the left-hand half of the screen, showing the northern half of the market's front elevation.

'Good spot, Chief; so she carried on north. Where's the next camera?'

'There are traffic cameras at the intersection of Camden High Street, Hawley Crescent and Jamestown Road. Get those up.'

Ayala tapped away at the keyboard once more and the intersection camera feeds sprang to life. The detectives watched the feed for an hour, still playing the recording at quadruple speed.

'No sign of Tina,' Morton summarised after watching.

'Perhaps she went into one of the pubs or eateries along that strip of shops. Almost one o'clock sounds like lunchtime to me,' Ayala said, realising how hungry he was.

'Maybe. You keep looking through the feed, I'm going to get down there and talk to the shop owners. Someone might remember her.'

'OK, boss.'

'And Ayala? Thanks for all this help. I know it's off the clock.'

'She'd do the same for us.'

***

It was a bitterly cold night, but Tina's shivering had stopped. She had been dumped at four in the morning, but in the depths of January the sun didn't rise until a little after eight. In a brief moment of lucidity, she had curled up into a foetal position to conserve the modicum of warmth she had left.

Eventually, she became aware of people nearby. First were the joggers, music blaring from their earphones, totally oblivious to Tina's plight. Then came the dog walkers, striding briskly along the path nearby. None stopped to help her.

Tina's skin was pale, and her pupils dilated. Her squalid appearance could easily be mistaken for someone under the influence of narcotics. It seemed her dirty, dishevelled look was not gaining her any sympathy with pedestrians.

Around half past eight a mother pushing a pram, toddler in tow, glanced towards her.

'Don't look, Tommy, just keep on walking,' she said as she hurried her brood away from Tina.

Tina tried to raise an arm to get the woman's attention, but her muscles were locked, rigid and unable to move. Every fibre of her being suffered cramping from lactic acid build-up.

A small cry escaped her lips, 'Help me.'

But no one heard her.

***

Camden Market was winding down for the evening as Morton approached from the south. It was 4:56 p.m., over a full hour before closing, but many stallholders were already packing away. The pavements had gained a fresh coat of ice the previous night, and Morton was forced to walk slowly to avoid slipping.

Morton's first ports of call were the two eateries between the point Tina disappeared off CCTV and the next set of cameras at the crossing to the north. One, a fast food joint serving up deep-fried battered chicken, was not to Tina's tastes. There was no way she'd voluntarily consume that many carbohydrates in one sitting.

The second was the Scarlet Lion, a fixture on the local real-ale scene. It was slightly closer to the market, and as well as offering local beers, had a decent food menu. It was by no means a gastro pub, but as the poster outside declared, it was homemade grub at student prices, served from Monday to Sunday. It seemed a better bet than the fast food joint, so Morton made a beeline for the entrance.

As he skipped over the black ice on the pavement, Morton read the bronze plaque above the door, which proclaimed that the publican was Mr H M Barry.

Inside, the Dragon was relatively empty. A pair of elderly gentlemen propped up the bar, supping pints of cider, and eying up a pair of women sharing a bottle of rosé. Morton ignored them as he strode towards the bar. 'Mr Barry?'

The bartender looked up from wiping a pint glass with a rag that was in severe need of a wash. 'Who's asking?' He spoke in a thick Scottish brogue.

'DCI David Morton. Metropolitan Police. I'm looking into the disappearance of a young woman in the area. Were you working on Sunday?'

'Aye, me and the missus. Plus a couple of the waitresses.'

Morton produced a picture of Tina. 'Did you see this woman?'

'Nae. No lass like that. We had a load of students in, plus a few of our regulars.' Barry gestured towards the drunks, who were appraising Morton with sly glances.

'Was it busy?'

'Sundays usually are. We open at midday, serve dinner through 'til five, then close up an hour later.'

'This woman would have been in the area shortly before one,' Morton prompted.

'Like I said, she didn't come in here. Pretty lass like that, these guys would have been drooling all afternoon.'

Morton twisted to face the two elderly drunks. 'Did you see this woman?'

'Might have. What's in it for me?' the nearest replied, resulting in a low chuckle from both of them.

Morton considered threatening them with drunk and disorderly charges, but they were too world-weary to fall for that trick. 'I'll buy you a round,' he conceded.

The nearer drunk nodded, a cruel smile forming on his thin lips. 'She never came in.'

'Marvellous,' Morton said bitterly and threw a ten-pounds note onto the bar. 'Enjoy your drinks.'

Morton turned to go when the drunk grabbed his collar. 'Hey, young 'un. I said she didn't come in. Didn't say we didn't see her, 'cause we did, didn't we, Cecil?'

'That we did, Frank. Walked right past. Pretty lass.'

Morton's heart leapt. He had to be sure they weren't making it up in the hopes of more drinks. 'What was she wearing?'

'Knee-high boots. Those fur-lined things. Matched her overcoat, light brown thing. She wore it open at the front, showing off her... you know. Barely concealed under a black and white top, weren't they, Frank?'

'Oh yes, Cecil. Lovely legs too. And the prettiest eyes.'

'What time did she go by, gentlemen?' Morton asked, recognising the description of the Tina's clothing.

'Must have been before our lunch. We always eat at one. Not long before though,' Frank replied.

'And which way was she going?'

'Heading up the road. Away from the tube.'

'Thank you, gentlemen.' Morton threw another note on the bar, then made his way back to the high street.

Outside, he glanced up the street. There was very little between the pub and the crossing. Tina had to have disappeared somewhere in that short space. There were no side roads for her to have taken, not even an alleyway. She had to have disappeared somewhere between the Scarlet Lion and the intersection.

***

'Ayala!' Kiaran O'Connor's singsong voice called out as he walked into the Incident Room.

'No. Whatever it is, find someone else.' Ayala didn't bother to look up from his laptop.

'I'm not after a favour. Have you seen Vaughn? I need her to sign off on some paperwork from Saturday and she's not answering her phone.'

Ayala bolted upright. 'You haven't heard? She's missing. She disappeared sometime Sunday without telling anyone.'

'I've been in court. I take it that's why I've got missed calls from your chief. You got Missing Persons out looking?' Kiaran perched on the edge of the conference room table.

'Of course. Morton sorted all that on the dot of twenty-four hours. He's out retracing her steps now.'

'What's he found?'

'She disappeared somewhere in Camden Market. At lunchtime Sunday, she went past a pub called the Scarlet Lion on Camden High Street. She never made it to the crossing a hundred feet or so past that point and she didn't come back along Camden High Street either. She's just disappeared into thin air.'

'Camden? She was there on Saturday. She called me in over a fencing bust.'

'What was she doing investigating stolen goods on her day off?'

'No idea. It was supposed to be my day off, too. I wasn't exactly pleased to get roped in. The guy she was investigating was in Camden. Get my case history up on that laptop of yours. It was in that area. Maybe she went back for some reason,' Kiaran suggested.

'Got it. She was at the residence of Craig Linden, right on Camden High Street – between the Scarlet Lion and the intersection of Camden High Street, Hawley Crescent and Jamestown Road. I'll call David.' Ayala reached for his phone and began to dial.

'You do that; I'll get a warrant to search the flat.'

***

By the time an ambulance was finally called, Tina's body had gone into what her doctors would later call a metabolic icebox state. To the untrained eye, she was already dead. Her pulse had slowed to less than half her normal heart rate, and her breathing was so shallow that it created no mist in the cold January air. Biting winds snapped through Brockwell Park Gardens, chilling Tina to the bone.

She was unaware of the hands swaddling her in blankets, layer upon layer until she was cocooned in fabric. She didn't even notice as she was lifted into the ambulance that would speed her to Chelsea and Westminster Hospital's accident and emergency department.

'Sweetheart, stay with me. Can you tell me your name?' The paramedic tried in vain to get her to talk. She had no ID, not that it would pose a problem for the hospital. The NHS treated all patients equally, but if she didn't improve soon then a name would expedite finding a next of kin.

As the ambulance screamed towards the hospital, the only movement Tina could muster was a flickering of the eyelids, which would soon cease.

***

'Craig Linden! Open up.' Morton thumped the inside door with his fist. They had piggybacked a neighbour at the front security door, and Morton now stood in the stairwell. Ayala stepped forward, interposing himself between Morton and the door. In his hand, he held a battering ram, ready to force entry.

'Open it.' Morton nodded at Ayala, and then covered his ears to insulate himself from the noise that would emanate from the impact.

Ayala swung backwards then forwards, throwing his weight into the ram. With an almighty crack, he made contact with the door, scattering splinters and flecks of green paint over the well-worn carpet. He swung again, this time going straight through the weakened door panels. He passed the ram back to Morton, then reached through the newly created gap in the door, and unlatched the door from the inside using a manual release switch. With a click the door opened inwards. Ayala crept forwards cautiously with three uniformed officers in his wake.

One uniformed office dashed towards the kitchenette while the other two dashed towards the tiny bedroom and its en-suite bathroom. It was blindingly oblivious that no one was home, but each uniformed officer dutifully called out 'Clear!' in turn.

'No sign of Linden or his wife. They could be out,' Ayala called towards Morton as Morton ducked into the living room.

'Chief! In here,' one of the officers called from the small bathroom. Morton and Ayala darted into the bedroom, and then shimmied around the bed to the bathroom, where a cast-iron bath on clawed feet stood against the far wall.

'That looks like blood to you?' Ayala pointed at the sinkhole in the bath, which had a slight pink discolouration.

'Could be. We need to get forensics in here.' Morton stepped back to make room, then lifted his radio and thumbed the push-to-talk button.

'This is David Morton, it's all clear. Send forensics up.' Morton's request was immediately acknowledged with a double-beep. Forensics then disembarked from the unmarked van parked on the double-yellow lines outside, and made their way up to the flat.

Stuart Purcell came up the stairs first, panting heavily. He followed the sound of voices into the bedroom. Morton jerked a thumb towards the bath, and Purcell bent over the bath with a cotton swab, dabbed at the plughole, then straightened up. After a quick chemical spray, the swab turned pink.

'Positive for blood,' Purcell declared.

'Get that sample back for DNA, and put a rush on it.' Morton swept Purcell from the room with an arm, then peered around the bathroom. Apart from the tiny splotch of blood, there were no signs of a struggle.

'What do you think, boss?'

'Something went down here. I just don't know what. Tina isn't here. The question is: how did she leave? Was she alone? And more importantly, where is she now?'

Chapter 39: Switched

Morton and Ayala worked in silence with only the barely audible click of fingers on keyboards resounding through the Incident Room. The detectives had two cases to work: the murder of Joe Bloggs Junior, and the disappearance of Tina Vaughn. The latter had stalled when re-examination of the CCTV proved Ayala hadn't missed Tina's departure, so Morton was forced to turn his considerable attention back to the murder investigation.

'I don't get it,' Ayala whispered. 'How can someone have switched a kid, and no one noticed?'

'He's in the system. Sad to say it, but no one pays attention to foster kids. They come and go. We know the real Charlie was with the Grants for years. The neighbours confirmed that. The next foster carers, Adrian and Prudence Lovejoy, allegedly remember the fake Charlie, the one we've interviewed twice,' Morton said.

'Allegedly? You don't seriously think they did it. They've got a houseful of kids. One of them would have noticed.'

'The substitution happened either immediately before Charlie stayed with them, during that time, or immediately after. They're crisis foster carers so only have kids for about a month. With a high turnover, they could easily substitute one child for another.'

'You think the Lovejoys killed Charlie, and then put another kid in his place? How? Why?'

'I don't know. I can't see the Grants killing Charlie, and then dying in a house fire. That's too much of a coincidence. It clearly didn't happen at the Lattimers', as we know the real Charlie was gone before then. That leaves the Lovejoys as the logical suspects.'

Ayala arched a dubious eyebrow. 'What does the substitution gain them?'

'Money? Our faux-Charlie doesn't speak much. We, and the school, thought that was down to autistic tendencies. What if he simply doesn't understand much English? There are plenty of families around the world who would pay to give their kids a chance at the English lifestyle. We moan day in, day out, but we've got it pretty easy compared to some,' Morton said.

'I'll run a check on the Lovejoys, and see if they've been spending beyond their means then.' From his tone, it was easy to tell that Ayala didn't expect to find anything.

'Good. I want to know who this faux-Charlie really is. There's something bigger than one child at stake here, I can feel it.'

***

'David, open the door. I know you're in there.' Sarah stood in a long hallway. The door in front of her, leading to Tina Vaughn's apartment, had the number thirteen marked by large bronze numbers. Sarah was carrying a cheap plastic carrier bag containing a Chinese takeaway.

When the door opened, David Morton appeared in the doorway wearing a t-shirt, and sporting three-day-old stubble.

'Sarah, what are you doing here?'

'I heard about Tina,' his wife replied.

Morton wondered whom she'd heard it from. Sarah was friendly with only a few of his colleagues, and only Ayala would have the nerve to speak to his wife behind his back.

'I'm sorry she's missing. I thought you might need a bite to eat. Maybe we can talk about your case theory, like old times.'

Morton sniffed at the alluring scent of chicken chow mein rising from the bag. 'I don't need any food,' he lied stubbornly. At that moment, his stomach betrayed him and a loud rumble erupted from his belly. Lunch suddenly seemed an eternity ago.

'Come in,' he relented.

Sarah followed her husband, relief flooding her face when she saw blankets smothering the settee.

'How have you been?' she asked.

'Bloody marvellous. Three-course a la carte meals, and the occasional trip to the theatre.' Morton's voice rose an octave, and he gestured theatrically at the instant noodles on a trestle table.

'Me too. I'm sorry I overreacted before. You know I can get a bit tetchy when it comes to money.'

'We'll get it sorted. Want to grab a couple of plates, and some cutlery from the kitchen?' Morton indicated the small galley kitchen at the back of the living room. 'I've just got to grab something from my car.'

Sarah grabbed the cutlery, set the plates on the sideboard and dished up the takeaway. As she waited for Morton to return, she wandered around the small apartment examining the photographs. On the centre of the mantelpiece, a framed ten-by-eight showed Tina with Detective Ayala at a New Year's party in Mansion House. She was wearing a ball gown, in stark contrast to her usual attire, while Ayala was his usual dapper self, dressed to the nines in a plum waistcoat and tails. David and Sarah had been there too, and waltzed the night away after enjoying champagne and canapés with the City of London's aldermen.

While Sarah was lost in her reverie, David returned carrying a parcel wrapped up in brown paper and string. He sat down, and then tucked the parcel underneath a cushion.

They ate without talking. The sound of munching was merged with the twang of cutlery reverberating on china as David demolished his share of the takeaway.

'I spoke to the bank today,' Sarah said.

Morton chewed his noodles quickly, gulped, then asked, 'What did they say?'

'They've cancelled all the unauthorised credit charges.'

'Well, that's a start. We can get by on credit cards for a few weeks while we sort the actual debit payments out.'

Sarah looked down with her hands folded in her lap. 'That's the thing, David, they said they've got no intention of refunding the money; that it is our fault.'

'It'll get sorted. I promise. For God's sake, they can't just empty our bank accounts without our consent,' David declared.

'Apparently they can.' Sarah smiled wryly, then looked up and met her husband's gaze. 'I've missed you, David.'

'I've missed you too. Here. This was for Valentine's, but that's weeks away. I want you to have it as a peace offering.' David proffered the parcel wrapped in brown paper.

'David, I'm not sure. I wouldn't feel right opening it now. We're sat in another woman's apartment, and she's missing.'

'OK. Well then, the moment we find Tina, you open it. Deal?'

'Deal. Now, let's go home.'

***

Doctor Larry Chiswick whistled cheerfully as he strode down the corridor outside Autopsy Room Number Three. While it was nine o'clock on a Monday morning, he had no immediate superior, and the prospect of an entire weekend's worth of dead bodies waiting to be autopsied posed no problem. The dead were a patient bunch.

Larry pushed open the door with one hand, and picked up a clipboard with the details pertaining to the morning's first corpse. It was an unidentified female body, a Jane Bloggs in coroner parlance. The hospital notes reported that she was white, approximately thirty years old and possibly homeless. She had been 'dead on arrival' at the Westminster and Chelsea Hospital. Accident and emergency had noted that she appeared to have suffered catastrophic heart failure caused by an arrhythmia, which would make it an open-and-shut case. If only all Larry's cases were so straightforward.

He lowered the clipboard, and then double-checked the toe tag to confirm he had the right body on the autopsy table, #0113/247. Larry pulled back the sheet, ready to begin his autopsy, then froze. The body on the table was a woman he'd seen in Autopsy Room Number Three many times, Detective Inspector Tina Vaughn.

Larry's skin paled as he reached for the internal phone hung beside the doorway and dialled the extension for Morton's office.

'David, this is Larry Chiswick. You need to come down here, right now. I'm in Autopsy Room Number Three.' Larry's voice quivered as he spoke.

'Larry, is everything OK?'

Larry replied instantly, 'No, it most certainly is not.'

'I'll be down straightaway.'

***

Morton jogged as he took the flight of steps down to the coroner three at a time. It was highly unusual for there to be an urgent development in the coroner's office and for a senior officer to be summonsed at no notice was exceptional.

He made it to the basement where the morgue was situated in just under three minutes. From the stairwell, it took a further two minutes to swipe his access card, and gain entry to the morgue proper. The security door slid open, and Morton sprinted through towards Larry's location, coming to a stop outside Autopsy Room Number Three. His shoes squeaked as the rubber soles found purchase on the floor.

Larry had the door open, and stood over a corpse. The sheet had been pulled back up over Tina, and Larry had closed Tina's eyes lest their vacant stare bore into Morton.

'Larry?' Morton spoke quickly, trying to catch his breath.

'David. Thanks for coming so quickly. Would you like a cup of tea?'

At the offer of a drink, Morton's heart sunk. Hot sweet tea was the quintessential British response to bereavement, and that meant he knew the victim. His mind connected the dots instantly. 'Tina?' His eyes widened as he spoke, and a note of pleading entered his voice. It couldn't be her. She was barely half his age.

'I'm afraid so, David.' Larry raised a hand to Morton's shoulder, unsure if he should be offering comfort in such a familiar way to a superior. 'Do you want to see her?'

Morton nodded, knowing that if he didn't see her, he'd never believe she was gone.

Tears began to roll down Morton's cheek, and a sob escaped him as Larry lowered the sheet to reveal Tina from the neck up. 'Wh-what happened?'

'They found her in Brockwell Park Gardens, down in South London. She was on her own, barely conscious and covered in God knows what.'

'How did she get down there?'

'No idea. It was a freezing cold night. She'd half frozen to death before help was called, and her heart gave up on the way to the hospital. That's our cause of death. I also noted marks around her wrists and ankles.'

'She was bound,' Morton said sharply.

'I'd say so. The paramedics noted that she was badly dehydrated. It could be a ransom attempt gone wrong.'

'Any defensive wounds? DNA under the fingernails?'

'No. They either drugged her, or got the jump on her when they tied her up. We'll test the blood, but if she disappeared on Sunday then it's possible any drug would be out of her system by now.'

'Is there anything to suggest where she went?'

'I'm afraid not, Chief. She was bound, kept somewhere without sufficient water and then either she was dumped or she escaped. Given her physical condition, the former seems more likely.'

'But, she was alive when the paramedics arrived on scene. So either they dumped her alive deliberately, assumed she would die shortly, or they dumped her thinking she was already dead.' Morton balled up his fists as he spoke through clenched teeth.

'She could have lived,' Larry said mournfully. 'The combination of extreme dehydration and exposure did it, but our kidnappers wouldn't have been able to predict a timeline well enough to dump her alive but assume she'd be found dead. Not unless a doctor was involved. It's possible they thought she was already gone. The body goes into what's known as a metabolic icebox stage where it appears dead. She wouldn't have felt much by then,' Chiswick elaborated as if the textbook explanation might provide some comfort. With an effort, Morton pulled himself together and tried to match the coroner's matter-of-fact approach.

'OK, Larry, let's assume they dumped her knowing she was alive. If that's true, then they must have been one-hundred percent confident that she didn't see their faces, or gather any sort of information that could identify them. That makes them careful, and dangerous.'

'But doesn't explain why they'd take her in the first place. Did you track down where she went missing?' Larry asked.

'Somewhere in Camden. We thought she might have gone to see a lowlife called Craig Linden, but his apartment was empty. We found a small amount of blood in the bath, but it wasn't Tina's. No sign of Linden since.'

'So, he could have taken Tina. Why was she involved with him?'

'I'm not sure but I'll find out; Ayala said Tina had called in Kiaran O'Connor on his day off, so it must have been serious,' Morton said.

'OK. I've got nothing else for you, but I'll send her clothes over for trace analysis.'

'Keep me posted.' Morton was already heading for the door.

Chapter 40: Without a Trace

As the clock struck twelve, Morton leant against a wall with a clear view of DiamondJewlz. Ayala stood nearby, yapping into his mobile phone in rapid Spanish.

No one had attempted to enter Craig Linden's flat since they had searched it the previous evening, but a deputy had been posted nearby to see if Linden returned. So far he hadn't, and his stall, DiamondJewlz of Camden, was closed.

Ayala finished his call then turned to Morton: 'Craig Linden is a small-time fence, a nobody. He deals with low-volume art, jewellery and drugs. Nothing special about him.'

'Any idea who he works for?' Morton kept his eyes fixed on Linden's stall. The neighbouring stallholder kept stealing glances towards it as if he expected Linden to show at any moment.

'He's an independent, not part of any one group. He's bound to be involved with a number of gangs though. If he's fencing small-time stuff, he needs volume. He was trying to flog diamonds when Tina busted him.'

'Any identifiers on them?' Morton asked.

'No laser engraving. Forensics did some chemical analysis of the gems. Minor impurities in their chemical composition suggest the diamonds are African in origin, but that doesn't give us much,' Ayala said.

'I've not been in touch with the boys working organised crime for a while, but wasn't there a big diamond bust on the news a few weeks back?'

Ayala nodded. 'One of the high-security warehouses in Antwerp got hit. Interpol are all over it, but SOCA are still seeing cheap gems flood the market. The smart sellers are cutting them to remove the engravings, even though that decimates their profit margins. No one wants tiny diamonds.'

'So we could be looking at gems from that heist.' Morton chewed the end of his fingernails as he spoke, a nervous habit he'd been trying to kick for decades. 'Have Interpol got any leads in that case?'

'None they've shared publicly. If you're right, though, then we already know who stole the gems. Or we know one of the intermediaries anyway.'

'We do?'

'Tina's bust ended in Linden ratting out his supplier. He's in league with the Bakowskis,' Ayala said.

Morton's teeth tore into the quick of his nail, and he winced. 'So the Bakowskis either did the Antwerp job, or bought the diamonds en masse to resell to petty fences like Linden. Now he's in the wind. If Kiaran gave him full immunity, it's unlikely he's scarpered to escape the law. I doubt the Bakowski brothers take kindly to snitches.'

'You think they did him in, boss?'

'Maybe. Either Linden is our bad guy, or someone he's working for is. Either way, I'd bet my badge on Tina being collateral damage,' Morton said, simmering.

***

Sarah Morton tiptoed out of her bedroom, keeping the light off to avoid disturbing David. She crept towards the kitchen, intending to get a glass of water. When Sarah had gone to bed, David had been passed out on the sofa, so she'd laid a blanket over him, then removed his half-empty bottle of whisky from the coffee table.

'Sarah?' Instead of being fast asleep, Morton was sat bolt upright on the sofa with his blanket folded between his arms.

'David. What are you doing still awake? It must be three o'clock in the morning.'

'Can't sleep, too many thoughts running through my head.'

'About Tina?' Sarah asked.

Morton shifted on the sofa, pulling the blanket up around himself.

'Yeah. I've lost officers before in the line of duty, but seeing her like that; it was so unexpected. The last thing I knew, she'd gone out shopping, then she was in the morgue having suffered extreme dehydration, exposure and heart failure. She is... was,' David corrected himself, 'half my age. It's just so unfair. I can't face the funeral on my own.'

'You won't be alone. When is it?'

'Three o'clock tomorrow.'

'I'll be there,' Sarah promised. 'Come to bed.'

***

Morton arrived at the Nag's Head early, and settled down in the back with a non-alcoholic beer poured into a normal glass to give the appearance that he was drinking. He couldn't face any more booze after the hangover he'd been nursing since dawn.

271

The crowd inside the pub was mostly other police officers, but the occasional tourist drifted in after seeing the pub marked on their phone's mapping system. They rarely stayed long.

Right on time, Morton's contact walked through the door. Morton rose, and then waved to get his former colleague's attention. 'Xander. Long time no see.'

'No doubt. You've not been involved with undercover operations in more than a decade now.'

Morton laughed. 'Way to make me feel old.'

'I'm as old as you are.'

'Well, then you're a bastard, 'cause you sure as hell don't look it,' Morton said. He was right; Alexander Thompson had a few flecks of grey in his blue-black hair and the hint of a wrinkle on his brow, but it seemed he had largely escaped the ravages of time.

Xander grabbed a chair, and then set his pint down on the table. 'What's with the monkey suit?'

'Funeral,' Morton said simply.

'So, what's so urgent after all these years?'

'I need to talk to you about the Bakowskis. One of my officers may have tangled with them inadvertently while going after a petty fence. She's now in the morgue.'

'I'm so sorry... Who was it?'

'Tina Vaughn.'

'Pretty Welsh lass? She was so young. What was she, thirty?'

'That's her. She was thirty-two. No age at all,' Morton lamented.

'My condolences.' Xander raised his pint in a toast, and the pair chinked glasses to Tina's memory.

'Anyway, the short of it is a fence named Craig Linden ratted out the Bakowskis as his supplier. In exchange for immunity, of course.'

'Naturally.'

'Linden claims the gems were from the Antwerp heist that went down in October. After he told us that, Tina disappeared. So did he. We think that Linden's paymasters might be involved. You got anything on them?'

'David, I appreciate the heads-up regarding the gems, but the situation with the Bakowski family is exceptionally delicate. They've been a thorn in my side for as long as I can remember.' Alexander Thompson spoke softly, nursing a Guinness in his hands. 'SOCA's on-the-record answer is that we can't comment on any ongoing investigation.'

'And off the record?' Morton prompted.

'I've got a guy inside their drug operations. He's not been under long, but he's heard enough stories to know Dimitri Bakowski, also known as Tiny, is calling the shots. They're running coke in from Colombia via the Middle East. It's a big operation.'

'How does that tie in with the diamond heist?'

'It doesn't. The Bakowskis have their fingers in a lot of pies. Guns, prostitution, drugs, stolen goods. If you can think of a crime, they can think of a way to make money out of it. It's a huge organisation, and it's set up like a terrorist group. Every region and criminal task is a cell, and those running each cell are in the dark about the rest of the business. At the centre of the web are the Bakowskis. They flit in and out of high society, throwing money at good causes to buy themselves a veneer of respectability. Some of their most recent businesses are legitimate, but there's no explanation for the source of the seed money.'

Morton squirmed uncomfortably. It seemed odd that a low-level fence like Craig Linden would be allowed close enough to the Bakowskis to have any real dirt. In their position, Morton would have farmed out that contact to someone else.

Xander took another swig from his glass, and then continued: 'Interpol have wanted a shot at the brothers for years, but they're like Teflon, nothing sticks.' Xander leant in conspiratorially. 'They've got apparently legitimate property holdings all over London, even in Westminster. It's all via holding companies and trusts and the like, but I've got dozens of houses and flats identified that I think are theirs.'

'I bet you'd like to get the brothers on a Proceeds of Crime Act application. The press would be singing your praises for months.'

'I'm sure they would, until someone loses a flash drive or says something ridiculous on the Internet to divert their attention.' Xander smiled ruefully. Both had happened in the past year.

'Can I get a copy of those holdings?'

'I'll see what I can do. You know my first concern has to be my undercover. It's all public record, though, so you could piece it together yourself.'

'Fair enough.' Morton nodded. He could respect protecting an undercover operative.

'If you've got a specific property that you want to ask about now, I could give you the nod either way, off the record.'

'Thanks. I'm not hugely concerned with what land they own, though. I need to know who they've got on the ground in London. They won't have got their hands dirty, not directly. Can you help with that?'

'I'll keep an ear out, and let you know after I check in with my undercover,' Xander promised.

'Give me a call. You've got my number, right?'

'I've got one for you from the turn of the millennium.'

'It hasn't changed,' Morton said.

'Nor have you, old friend.'

***

A sombre procession lined the walkway into St Luke's Anglican Church in Old Street. Behind the crowd, which consisted mostly of colleagues past and present, an obelisk tower loomed on the western edge of the church. Flowers lined the walkways. Many had sent wreaths, but David and Sarah Morton had opted to bring a bouquet of pink and purple orchids, Tina's favourite flower.

Uniformed officers carried Tina's oak casket. They walked straight-backed and proud, seemingly unburdened by the weight. At the doorway to the church, the coffin was received by the minister. The crowd filed in slowly behind, and began to take their seats in the pews. At the front, Catrin sat alone in the family pew, seemingly lost in her own thoughts.

Once they were all seated, the minister cleared his throat. He spoke slowly, blue eyes wandering over the assembled crowd.

'I am the resurrection and the life, says the Lord. Those who believe in me, even though they die, will live, and everyone who lives and believes in me will never die,' the minister quoted from the Book of John.

'We meet in the name of the Lord Jesus Christ, who died and was raised to the glory of God the Father. Grace and mercy be with you. We have come here today to remember Tina Vaughn, to give thanks for her life and to commend her unto the Lord. Let us pray.'

As they rose for the first hymn, Morton realised how many mourners were fellow police officers. Apart from Tina's sister, it seemed every face in the crowd was a police officer. In all, over three hundred people had turned out to pay their respects.

'And now, a reading from Bertram Ayala,' the minister announced.

Ayala appeared from the back of the church. He walked briskly, resolutely focussed on the lectern. When he got there, he set his notes under the lamp, and then looked up.

'The Lord is my shepherd; therefore I lack nothing. He makes me lie down in green pastures and leads me beside still waters.' Ayala's voice croaked as he spoke and then evened out as he fought to control his emotions.

'He shall refresh my soul and guide me in the paths of righteousness for his name's sake. Though I walk through the valley of the shadow of death, I will fear no evil; for you are with me. Surely goodness and loving mercy shall follow me all the days of my life, and I will dwell in the house of the Lord forever.'

Ayala began to cry freely, bowed his head and made for the back pew, trying to hide his sorrow from his colleagues. He needn't have bothered, as there wasn't a dry eye in the house.

***

Even a double espresso couldn't reinvigorate Morton the morning after Tina's wake. A bottle of nineteen forty-eight McCallan had been the culprit. It was technically evidence, but the case it related to had long since been closed, and with no one coming forward to claim it, it hadn't taken long for the bottle to surreptitiously end up in a store cupboard.

After forgoing his morning drive in favour of the tube, Morton spent the morning listlessly shuffling paperwork. He'd read, and reread, Craig Linden's witness statement from the previous weekend without it sinking in.

The rest of the squad were equally worse for wear, and the result was that the staff in the Incident Room wandered around zombie-like, and achieved very little before lunch.

At the strike of noon, a tech dressed in a lab coat entered the room and called out: 'David Morton?'

Morton waved a hand half-heartedly. 'Over here.'

'For you. sir.' He handed Morton an envelope, and disappeared.

Ayala looked over curiously. 'What have you got?'

Morton tore open the envelope, not bothering to use a letter opener. He upended it, and two A4 pages fell out.

'Analysis on the fibres found on Tina's body. Very odd. The fibres were all carpet,' Morton announced.

'Carpet? Why'd they bother telling you about that?'

'It's not just one kind of carpet. They found dozens of different samples.'

Ayala screwed up his face as he fought to process what that meant. 'She was kept in a carpet shop?'

'Don't be daft. You don't keep someone captive in the home ware and furnishings department at John Lewis. I'm thinking sound studio. You know, a home one. Carpet can be used as cheap soundproofing,' Morton said.

'Which makes it ideal to keep someone in, if you need to keep them quiet,' Ayala said.

'I'm not sure this is going to give us much to go on in terms of identifying Tina's abductor. If we could get a warrant, then we could search all properties owned by the Bakowskis... But that's a big ask. If we do get in, then we'll look for the carpet off cuts as solid circumstantial evidence. Ayala, get yourself down to a few big carpet stores. The forensic analysis showed twenty-two different carpet samples, so the shops might remember a bulk buyer of samples.'

'You cannot be serious. Do you have any idea how many carpet shops there are in Greater London? The carpet could be from any one of them or a combination of them, or none at all if our perp bought online,' Ayala said.

'It's a long shot, but we've got to try.'

Chapter 41: Digital Documentation

While Ayala went on a wild goose chase looking for carpets, Morton was free to do some old-fashioned detective work. Morton knew that Charlie was switched either immediately before joining the Lovejoy household or soon after.

Poor Charlie had suffered extensively in his twelve short years. He'd lost his parents as a toddler, and then lost his adopted parents, the Grants, in a house fire shortly before Christmas. After that, he had been murdered by persons unknown.

Charlie's impostor had taken over Charlie's identity around the time of his death, and had moved to the Lattimer residence in Charlie's place during early January. From that, Morton had a fairly firm timeline for the switchover. The body was found in the Marshes on January fifth, and had been in the ground for at least a few weeks, which meant that the real Charlie had been killed in early to mid December, right around the time that Charlie had moved into the custody of the Lovejoys.

Morton decided to pay Children's Services a visit to investigate the children in the Lovejoys' care. Unfortunately, Children's Services was a fractured organisation, so Morton could not simply talk to one contact, but had to investigate with multiple authorities. Instead of being run as a national service, it was federated at the local authority level. They shared a common database, but every London local authority was run autonomously.

Working on the principle that the most recent local authority to have dealt with Charlie would be most likely to yield evidence, Morton headed for the offices of the Lambeth Council department responsible for Children's Services.

An eighties concrete monolith a few blocks south of Waterloo Station accommodated all of Lambeth Council's various departments. After bypassing security Morton was met by a winding labyrinth of narrow corridors. Third left, second right, straight ahead, Morton recalled the instructions from the front desk.

Behind the clean front office, the landscape changed immediately. Filing cabinets appeared to have been flung along the corridors at random. Some were waist-high, others to Morton's chest. A harried secretary knelt nearby, vainly trying to stuff a thick brown folder into an already overstuffed drawer. If that filing cabinet were indicative of the rest, Morton calculated there to be upwards of a million pages locked away in the main corridor alone.

He reached the correct office without hindrance, where a piece of paper was taped to the door with 'Looked After Children Service' written in bold red pen.

At the first knock, a woman's voice invited him in. Inside the room, an elderly lady sat in a wheeled office chair facing away from the door, staring intently at an antique CRT monitor that dominated her desk.

Morton cleared his throat, and the woman spun around on her chair.

'Hi, I'm Detective Chief Inspector Morton. And you are...?'

'Edith Faulkner-Wellington. How can I help you, officer?'

'I hope so. I'm looking into the death of a child who was in your care–'

'Which one?' Edith cut him off mid-sentence.

Morton almost smiled. The old lady wasn't one for chat-chat. 'Charles Anthony Matthews,' he answered.

'Hmm. It doesn't ring a bell. Let me check my notes.' Edith withdrew a ledger from the top drawer of a filing cabinet, a ledger which Morton soon realised was an index to her filing system.

She pursed her lips as she scanned the ledger, running a bony finger down its length, 'Cabinet 22, third drawer. Come on then, young man.'

Morton held the door aside with a grin, trying to remember the last time he'd been called 'young man'. She led him down the corridor, away from the way he had come in, until they reached a corner room which sported another handwritten sign labelling it as 'Document Repository A'.

A thin layer of dust covered the top of most of the cabinets, but cabinet 22 was much cleaner, as if it saw more use than some of the others. After a moment's fishing inside the third drawer down, Edith pulled out a thin file.

'Here we go, Charles Anthony Matthews. Born 23 April 2000 to Jacqueline and Eric Matthews. He went into care at three, and then lost his adoptive parents. Poor lad. Aha, here's how we got him. He's an ex-T.'

'Ex-T?'

'Ex-trauma. London has many small departments like mine, but children touched by severe trauma spend time with one of a very small pool of specialist foster homes. The Lovejoys, who Charlie spent a month with at the end of last year, deal with about a hundred such cases a year.'

'So, how did he come to you?'

'I'd have to check the digital file. This is just a summary sheet. Come on, back down the hall. Chop-chop!' Edith spun on her heel and led the way back to her office once more.

By the time Edith's computer system had been booted up, Morton and Edith were already on first-name terms, and Morton learnt that Edith's late husband had been a policeman.

'So that's when I said to him, "Barty, pull over!" and he says, "No, it's a jumper!" I don't know how he got into the police. I hope standards are higher these days.'

'Edith, I'm sure Barty was a fine cop back in his day. He wouldn't have lasted 'til retirement if he wasn't,' Morton said.

'True enough. It looks like your file has loaded. This look like the right young man?'

On-screen, a picture of the faux-Charlie appeared, along with a copy of all the details from the print file.

'Hmm, that's odd. Can you print that for me?'

'Yep, but you'll have to collect the print yourself. They've gone and stuck all the printers up on the third floor. My back isn't going to make it up those sixty-six stairs without complaining.'

'That's a deal. While you're in the file, can you see the case history?'

She clicked twice, and then spoke again: 'It looks like he started off under the care of Harrow Council. Then he got shunted out to the Lovejoys, who in theory work for the London Borough of Havering Council. Romford is, of course, in Essex so I'm not sure how that is supposed to work but there you are. Then he came to us. He should have gone back to Harrow really, but they do get shunted around to suit what slack capacity we all have. No note as to why. I can dig deeper by looking at our financials; we pay the other councils a fee when they take our charges and vice versa, so we should have had a one-off transfer payment from Harrow Council. I'll have to talk to accounting about that, and it'll take time to match up the payment with the records. Sometimes they used what we call offset accounting.'

'What's that?'

'Well, instead of us paying them, them paying us, us paying another council and it getting complicated, we just add up what we owe each council and what we're owed by them. Then we just pay the difference. It's easier than transferring money back and forth, but it makes it hard to track down the individual charges.'

'Sounds pretty sensible. Last request, and then I'll let you get back to work,' Morton promised. 'Do you have a file on the Lovejoys, and their charges? Any sort of profile?'

'Nope. The shared IT system only covers the children and the administrative details for the foster carers. If you want all of their info, you'd need to talk to their local authority. They're with Havering Council, so you'll need to call them.' Edith saw Morton's disappointment then added, 'Mary Bushey is in charge over there... If you want, I'll call her and get her to fax you through a copy of her files.'

'That would be great.' Morton beamed. 'Thank you, Edith. One more very quick question. How do your social workers fit into the system when it's all split up over councils?'

'They're hired by the councils. We hire them on zero-hours contracts, which gives us the freedom to use them when we need them.'

'So it's possible one social worker might work for multiple councils?'

'Absolutely. One council isn't likely to give them enough work to fill every week, so many will sign on with more than one. They tend to move around a bit as well.'

'Edith, you've been very helpful.' The woman beamed at the compliment, clearly delighted to have had her usually drudgery interrupted.

'Where was that printing room again?'

'Third floor. Right opposite the stairwell. Can't miss it.'

***

Xander had come up trumps, and supplied a thick dossier on the Bakowskis' allegedly legitimate property holdings which now occupied most of the main desk in the Incident Room, forcing Morton to perch his laptop on top of an upended cantilever file. Some parts of the file had been redacted with thick black marker drawn across the text, leaving behind only snippets.

What was clear was the extent to which the Bakowskis had gone to hide their ownership of land. A myriad of trusts and foreign holding companies had been used, but ultimately the Bakowskis were the beneficiaries and shareholders. The sweet-wrapper layers applied by their lawyer needed peeling back, but with enough time it would be possible to uncover their declared holdings.

The vast majority of properties were held by companies registered in the Cayman Islands, the British Virgin Islands and Lichtenstein. Someone at the Serious Organised Crime Agency, possibly Xander Thompson himself, had helpfully added Post-it notes throughout the file. One indicated that it was common for companies to be formed in those jurisdictions to take advantage of generous tax incentives offered to companies. They were so-called hundred-dollar companies, with a nominal shareholding, but the Bakowskis didn't own the companies directly. The shares had been put into trusts which were then managed on behalf of the family, and that insulated the Bakowskis from personally appearing on public documents, such as the UK's Land Registry.

As far as Morton could tell, the total value of the combined holdings was well into eight figures; the Bakowskis had more money than any man could ever earn honestly in one lifetime. He suspected the list he had so far was the tip of the iceberg, but if the Bakowskis were ever convicted of a crime that was used to fund the holdings, then the taxpayer would be in for a substantial windfall thanks to the Proceeds of Crime Act.

'Hmm, that's odd,' Morton mused aloud.

'What is?' Ayala asked, tearing his attention away from his own work.

'These properties are all over the place. It's mostly in-demand properties; they've got houses all over the desirable parts of London.'

'That makes sense. Those areas see the most capital appreciation.'

'Right, but they've also got some big houses in areas like Brent, Hackney, Southwark, Tower Hamlets and Crystal Palace. If you're investing mega money in property like this, it doesn't make sense to buy big houses. The demand these days is for one- and two-bed flats. They make more, and they're easier to manage.'

'If they're growing marijuana or dealing, then it'd be logical to have a base of operations nearby,' Ayala said.

'Yeah, but these aren't small places used to stash drugs. They're too big for that. They could be running cannabis farms... though I reckon the Bakowskis are too smart to grow anything on their own property. Check it out anyway – have an infrared-equipped helicopter go over, and see if there's any extraneous heat being released.'

Ayala jumped up and down excitedly, his eyes lighting up at the prospect. 'Awesome. I've always wanted to go in one of those.'

***

'They've gone and sent me bloody zip files. How the heck do I get these open?' Morton pushed his laptop away, frustrated with the morass of emails from Mary Bushey at Havering Council. She'd sent dozens, each with a few attachments, totalling just under five megabytes in size.

'Give it here, boss. You've got to decompress the files, then load them up into the reader software.' Ayala took the laptop, then swiftly clicked on Morton's screen, and an unzip prompt appeared. 'Here we go. It looks like we've got the files for all the kids that have stayed with the Lovejoys since 2006.'

'Since 2006? Why then?' Morton asked.

'I guess that's how far their records go back. So, what are we looking for?'

'When I was at Lambeth Council, their records showed a picture of the fake Charlie. I need to know when that file got uploaded.'

'I can do you one better than that, boss. The upload is easy – it was done by Mary Bushey in mid December, says so right here.' Ayala pointed to a timestamp in the file signature. 'But the clever bit is this...'

A few more clicks, and a new screen appeared showing a cornucopia of data. 'This is called meta data. We know exactly when the photo was taken – the eighth of December. We also know it was taken with a digital SLR, quite a pricey model. It's got a geotag to it as well.'

'So you know where it was taken?'

'Yep, but in GPS co-ordinates. Let me translate that into real address data. Here we go, somewhere in Little Hatters Wood.'

'That's got to be the Lovejoy residence. That ought to be enough to secure a warrant to search the premises.'

Chapter 42: Search and Seizure

'Mr and Mrs Lovejoy, step outside please.' Morton steeled himself for a violent reaction, but the couple simply grabbed their coats off the rack by the front door, then stepped out into the driveway.

'What's going on?' a rosy-cheeked Mr Lovejoy asked.

'We have a warrant to search the premises,' Morton handed him a copy. 'We'll require you to wait with one of my officers while we do so. Is there anyone else inside the house?'

This time, Mrs Lovejoy replied, 'Of course there is! We've got six children staying with us.'

Morton nodded at Ayala, who immediately went in search of the children. One by one they were brought out, swaddled in blankets and clutching video games and mobile phones. One of the search team would have to check that those exiting the house had not concealed evidence on their persons, but for Morton and Ayala the next step was to sweep the property.

'C'mon, we'll start in the study. I'm sure I saw some filing cabinets and electronics in there,' Morton said.

'Lead on, boss,' Ayala called over his shoulder as he recounted the children to make sure no one had been left inside. A group of uniformed offers stood by to ensure no one left during the search.

In the study, Morton quickly found the Lovejoys' home computer, and a digital camera that appeared to be the same model that had taken the picture of Charlie on file with Children's Services. He turned the digital camera on, and turned it over to look at the LCD screen on the rear. He depressed a green play button, bringing up the photos stored on the camera's SD memory card. They displayed one at a time, in chronological order. Each picture showed a child stood against what Morton recognised as being the wall to the study he now found himself in. He kept flicking back until a picture of the faux-Charlie appeared, dated for the eighth of December 2012.

'Ayala, come look at this. We've got a picture of our fake Charlie,' Morton said.

'Looks like the same one as we saw in Charlie's Children's Services profile. Same date too. I'll get forensics to check the metadata to confirm it's the same picture, but it looks like we've got our smoking gun.'

'I wish,' Morton said wistfully, 'This is all circumstantial. All it shows is the substitution occurred on or before the eighth of December. I'm guessing on the eighth, but the forensic window could be out by a day or two earlier. It's not enough to get a conviction.'

'No, but it's enough to bring the Lovejoys in for a chat.'

'Definitely. Right, seize the lot. We'll comb through it later.'

Morton left Ayala to oversee the evidence being logged, and headed outside to find the Lovejoys sitting on the back step of a police van, wrapped up in police blankets.

'Mr Morton, what's going on?' Adrian Lovejoy asked.

'Mr Lovejoy, Mrs Lovejoy, we have reason to believe that Charles Matthews was murdered on or around the time that a boy falsely bearing his name came into your custody. For that reason, I'd like you to come down to the station with me.'

The Lovejoys exchanged startled glances. Mrs Lovejoy clapped her hands over her mouth, and her eyes went wide with apparent bewilderment. Adrian threw an arm around his wife protectively and said to Morton: 'Of course, of course. Whatever you need from us. As long as we can call our boss to get someone to look after the children while we're gone.'

'One of my officers will take care of that. Can I please take any mobile phones you may be carrying? It's procedure,' Morton said in a tone he hoped came across as sympathetic. In reality, the phones were covered by Kiaran's search warrant, but there was no need to get the Lovejoys' hackles up yet.

***

'This interview is being tape-recorded. It is being conducted at New Scotland Yard, Broadway, London. I'm Detective Chief Inspector David Morton of the Metropolitan Police. With me today are Detective Bertram Ayala, Adrian Lovejoy and Prudence Lovejoy of Little Hatters Wood. Mr and Mrs Lovejoy, could you confirm your dates of birth please?'

'I was born on February twenty-second, 1964. Pru was born on the twenty-sixth of February in the same year,' Mr Lovejoy said.

'The time is now 16:32, and the date is Thursday the twenty-fourth of January 2013. Mr and Mrs Lovejoy, you do not have to say anything, however it may harm your defence if you do not mention when questioned something that you later rely on in court. Anything you do say may be used in evidence against you.'

Mrs Lovejoy leant heavily on her husband, and hid her face behind her hair.

'Mr Lovejoy, can you confirm your occupation please?'

'I'm a trained psychotherapist. I specialise in helping children who have experienced significant trauma. As part of that, I am a short-term foster parent working with a number of local authorities in London and the Home Counties. My wife is similarly qualified, and works with me.'

'Did you take a young man called Charles Matthews into your care on December the eighth, 2012?'

'We did.' Both Lovejoys nodded.

'At that time, did you take a photograph of Charlie?' Morton asked. The camera was with forensics to confirm, but Ayala had already compared the metadata of the file with Children's Services and the same image on Adrian's camera. They were identical.

'Yes.'

'For what purpose?'

'To keep the photographs in the system up-to-date, for one. Some of the children who come to us have never been in the system before, and some haven't had their photograph taken in some time. Charlie's last picture was when he was much younger. Children often change as they age,' Mr Lovejoy explained calmly, then added almost as an afterthought, 'I also display the photos of every child I've cared for on the wall in my office.'

Morton pulled a copy of the photograph from the file on the desk. 'Is this the photograph you took?'

'Yes.'

'Let the tape reflect that Mr Lovejoy has identified Exhibit A to the file as the photograph he took. Mr Lovejoy, who was present when you took Charles Matthews into your care?'

Furrows appeared on Mr Lovejoy's brow as he strained to remember. 'Just me, I guess. It's usually a pretty quick handover. The local authority drop 'em off, I sign a bit of paper, then get the kid settled in. As I recall, Charlie had his photo taken, had a bit of tea, then went straight to bed. He was a quiet lad.'

'Were you there, Mrs Lovejoy?' Morton asked.

It took a while for Prudence Lovejoy to reply, but when she did it was in a slow and measured tone that didn't reflect the glassy-eyed state which she had been in minutes earlier.

'No, not that day. That was the day the cold snap started. I'd gone down to my sister's to visit, and when the snow started to fall, I stayed put.'

'Where was that?'

'Down Stockbridge way.'

'And how did you get there?'

'I took the train. I went up early in the morning so we could go for lunch at one of the fancy new gastro pubs on the High Street; then when the weather took a turn, I stayed over until the Sunday.'

Hampshire, not too far to go then come back if one was minded to fake an alibi, Morton thought.

'Inspector Morton, what do you want from us? We're simple foster parents. We've answered all your questions, and it is quite an inconvenience,' Mr Lovejoy said.

Morton looked at him with an icy stare as he replied coolly, 'What I want, Mr Lovejoy, is to find the person or persons responsible for the murder of a twelve-year-old boy. I'm sorry if that inconveniences you.'

Adrian Lovejoy turned white. 'Not at all; sorry, officer,' he said sheepishly.

'Mr Lovejoy, did you murder Charles Matthews?'

'No! I did not.'

'Mrs Lovejoy, did you murder Charles Matthews?'

'No, of course not.'

'How do you explain the fact that Charles Matthews left the hospital after the fire at the Grant residence, and an impostor was found with you?'

'I... I don't know. There could be a mix-up with the local authority, or at the hospital?' Mrs Lovejoy replied.

'And you just happened to change the photograph in the system that day, knowing full well the old one would be deleted?'

'I told you, we always do that,' Mr Lovejoy said.

'I think you did it,' Morton put it to them. 'It's the perfect set-up. The children you foster go between local authorities so there is no audit trail. You see lots of kids, so no one is going to notice if one disappears. I think you killed Charlie Matthews then sold his identity.'

'Sold it to whom? I have no idea what you're on about. How could I have left all the other children at home, killed Charlie and then dumped the body and come back with a replacement? Do you have any idea how preposterous that sounds? We want that lawyer now, please.'

They had said the magic words.

'Interview terminated at,' Morton glanced at his watch, '17:07.'

Morton turned off the tape recorder, and then turned to the Lovejoys. 'You can have a lawyer. I'm placing you in custody pursuant to section 41 of the Police and Criminal Evidence Act. Ayala, show them to the holding cells.'

***

'Boss?' Ayala said, 'What do you think?"

Morton stared into space, oblivious to Ayala's question. 'Huh?'

'Away with the fairies today, eh boss? I was asking what you think about the Lovejoys.'

'God knows. They're our best suspects. They're our only suspects. She's got an alibi, but it's from her sister and even by train you can get back from Stockbridge in less than ninety minutes.'

'And being away on the day of Charlie's arrival doesn't mean she isn't culpable,' Ayala said, clearly thinking of the so-called 'inchoate offences' of assisting, procuring, or encouraging criminality.

'Kiaran will have a hard time proving that, short of an incriminating email, text or voicemail. I doubt they'd be that stupid.'

'If they were clever, they'd have demanded a lawyer straight off the bat,' Ayala said.

Morton shook his head. 'Not at all. Asking for a lawyer looks guilty. If they wanted to try and hoodwink us into believing in their innocence then they played it perfectly. Their reactions were measured, and convincing.'

'So what do we do now?'

'We need more evidence to charge them with murder. Right now, we've got a little less than twenty-four hours to find something or they can walk.'

Ayala look at his watch. 'But we can get more time.'

'Yes and no. We can get an extension to thirty-six hours from the time they arrived at the station fairly easily. That just needs the Superintendent to sign off on it, and he will – it is a murder investigation.'

'But you don't think we'll get another extension after that?'

'Let's cross that bridge when we come to it. For now, we need something linking the Lovejoys with Charlie's murder. How far is it from Little Hatters Wood to Hackney Marshes?'

Ayala made a quick guesstimate: 'About an hour's drive.'

'Then check any CCTV that exists along the route, and see if Adrian Lovejoy's car was there.'

'Consider it done, boss.'

Chapter 43: Tick Tock

Morton rubbed his eyes blearily as he shuffled the Lovejoy files around his desk. Forensics had confirmed that the photos from Adrian Lovejoy's camera matched Children's Services database. Each of the Lovejoys' pictures had been entered into the database by a system admin account owned by the user 'MBushey', which Morton knew to be Mary Bushey, one of the local authority's employees who oversaw the Lovejoys.

With the clock ticking on the twenty-four hour deadline for detention without charge, and the high probability that the Lovejoys would flee or destroy evidence the moment they were released, Morton was feeling the pressure. In a few short weeks, he'd had a marital breakdown, been the victim of identity theft, lost one of his senior officers and had made less progress than he might have wished for in a murder investigation. It was now 6:44 p.m. precisely; Morton had twenty-two hours before he'd need to get the custody sergeant to formally extend the time limit to thirty-six hours.

The door to Morton's office swung open, and a uniformed officer walked in.

'Chief, the addresses you wanted,' the officer said as he handed Morton a printout, before making a hasty retreat.

The paper showed the current addresses of the Lovejoys' former charges. Morton picked one whose time with the Lovejoys overlapped with Charlie's stay, then picked up the phone to make an urgent appointment to speak to her that evening.

***

Christina Baker, aged sixteen, was out at Bloomsbury Bowling Alley when Morton called to arrange an interview. With the deadline looming, Morton rushed over and parked his BMW on double yellow lines outside the venue. A neon sign was the only indication of a bowling alley on the premises. Underneath the sign, a single doorway led to steps burrowing down into the basement. At the bottom of the steps, the room fanned out in a huge subterranean cavern with twenty-six lanes side by side, divided by racks of bowling balls. An access path ran along the end. At the end of the path Morton could see a combined bar and payment station. A spotty-nosed teenager sat behind the bar flicking through a sports magazine.

'Excuse me; I'm looking for Christina Baker. Which lane is she in?'

The boy looked him up and down, 'Who are you then, her granddad?'

Morton glared. 'Detective Chief Inspector David Morton. I'm not going to ask you again.'

'Hang on.' He consulted the iPad used to allocate bookings. 'She's in lane six, mate.'

'Thanks.'

Morton doubled back to lane number six, near the entranceway. Christina was playing with two older bowlers whom Morton presumed were her current foster parents.

'Christina Baker? Detective David Morton, we spoke on the phone.'

'Hi.' She turned to the couple with her. 'Mum, Dad, I'll be right back.'

She led Morton away from the noise of the lanes towards a couple of high tables surrounded by bar stools.

'God, it feels weird saying that.'

'Saying what?' Morton asked, curiosity getting the better of him.

'Mum and Dad.' Christina jerked her head towards the couple. 'They adopted me, last week. They've insisted I call them Mum and Dad. Still doesn't feel right, yet.'

Morton perched on the edge of a bar stool, and then continued his questioning: 'Had you been in the system long?'

'Yeah. On and off. Mum was an addict, so I got taken into care when I was fourteen. After that, I've been with a few families, and did a stretch in Borstal.'

Morton realised she was watching for a reaction to her revelation that she'd been in a juvenile facility, and decided to ignore it. It wasn't relevant to his line of investigation. Instead he simply carried on with the interview: 'And in December you were with the Lovejoys?'

'Yep. It was a temporary thing while they sorted out the adoption paperwork. I was there from the first until a week before Christmas.'

'Did you meet Charlie Matthews during that time?'

'Yep. Quiet kid. Seemed sweet, I guess.'

'When did you first meet him?'

'Err, I don't know. About a week after I got there. The day he arrived.'

Morton stroked his chin thoughtfully. Charlie had been switched by the time he met the other Lovejoy charges on December the seventh. He'd left the hospital the same day, after doctors were certain he hadn't been physically affected by the fire.

'Right,' Morton changed approach, 'and what did you think of the Lovejoys?'

'Adrian and Pru? They're alright. Always got time if you need a word.'

'Did you ever notice anything strange going on?'

'Like what?'

'Kids being too quiet, strange comings and goings,' Morton said.

'Nothing like that. Oh hang on, now you come to mention it, Charlie didn't reply when I called his name a few times. I thought that was a bit odd. Is he a bit deaf?'

'Maybe. Well, thanks for your time, Miss Baker.'

***

'Are you OK, hon?' Sarah watched her husband intently, concern bleeding into her voice.

'Fine,' Morton lied.

'I know that 'fine'. What's really wrong? Anything I can do to help?'

'Thanks, but no. I feel guilty about Tina. She disappeared looking into my credit card fraud problem. I should have been the one to go to Camden. It should have been me going toe to toe with whoever took her.'

'David, survivor's guilt is totally natural. You've lost enough colleagues to know that. She wouldn't want you moping. She'd want you out there finding her killer.'

'What do you think I've been doing?' Morton snarled. 'I've run down every lead we've had. I've hit dead end after dead end.'

'You'll crack it eventually. You always do,' Sarah soothed.

'Maybe. But right now, I need to focus on finding something definitive to nail the Lovejoys with. If I don't, they'll walk.'

'What you need right now,' Sarah stood behind him and rubbed his shoulders, 'is to take a break, and go to bed.'

Morton shook his head, 'I'm too wired to sleep.'

'Who said anything about sleep?'

***

Two hours before the sun rose Morton pulled into the Met's staff car park, easily finding a space near the entrance. He made his way inside, passing no one apart from John Ritter, New Scotland Yard's head of security, to whom Morton nodded briefly as he headed for the Incident Room.

He flicked the light switch just inside the empty room and the strip lighting stuttered to life with a hum. One of Morton's team, he wasn't sure who, had set up an iPad at the end of one table so that red glowing lights ticked down the time they had left until the Lovejoys would have to be released. The countdown assumed the Custody Sergeant would authorise an extension to thirty-six hours. If that assumption held true, Morton had twenty-two hours left to come up with enough evidence to charge the Lovejoys. Less than half the remaining time would be truly productive, as it was highly unlikely that Morton would stumble across new evidence in the middle of the night.

Morton began pacing the room, his eyes darting up and down the boards, searching for that one breakthrough clue amongst all the pertinent information which had been pinned to the board by his team. Eventually, he was joined by Detective Ayala, who sauntered in holding a breakfast sub.

'Good morning, boss,' Ayala said as he entered, casting off his overcoat and flinging it over the back of a chair.

'What's so good about it?'

'My my, we are a chirpy soul this morning. You and Sarah still at each other's throats?' Ayala swung a chair around, and sat on it back to front with his arms resting on the back.

'We're OK. It's not all better, but she's been an absolute rock since, you know.'

'I know. At the risk of exacerbating your mood, I've got bad news. The CCTV was a bust.'

Morton groaned involuntarily. 'What's wrong this time?'

'Nothing mischievous. The cameras are fine. The bad news is that the tape is only kept for four weeks at a time. I'm told they only record cars that are speeding anyway. If Adrian Lovejoy drove from Little Hatters Wood to Hackney Marshes and back, then he did so without tripping any red lights or going over thirty miles per hour.'

'Then we've got no evidence at all that Adrian Lovejoy drove from Little Hatters Wood to Hackney Marshes and back.'

'What if he killed Charlie on arrival, stashed the body somewhere, then dumped him later?' Ayala said.

'It's a creative theory, I'll give you that. It's not going to cut it in court without some pretty damning evidence.'

'Boss, if you had to store a body, wouldn't you store it in a freezer? That minimises any trace evidence from bugs, blood, et cetera.'

Morton's memory flicked back to his brief tour of the house before the search team had swarmed in. 'The Lovejoys have a big household. They had a chest freezer in the garage.'

'There was. It was empty.'

'Of course it's empty now, Ayala. Get Purcell to swab it for any traces of human blood. '

'Will do. Anything else, boss?'

'Yes – chase up that report on the Lovejoy's finances. I need it on my desk within the next few hours.'

***

'Spray it.' Ayala pointed at the chest freezer in Adrian Lovejoy's garage. It looked spotless, but if blood had been present then it was probable that residue would remain in the crevices.

Stuart Purcell stepped forward with an aerosol in his hand, sprayed, then pulled out an ultraviolet light.

'Hit the lights please, Detective.'

Ayala turned the lights off, and then put on a pair of goggles to see the result for himself. The entire freezer lit up.

'We've got blood,' the tech needlessly announced.

'Hang on, it could just be bleach.' Ayala was mindful of Tina's past experience with false positives using Luminol.

'I doubt it.'

'I bet it is,' Ayala said glumly.

'Twenty quid says it's blood.'

'Stu, you're on.'

'Better get back to the lab to test it then.'

***

'Pay up,' Ayala said.

'Nope,' Purcell replied.

'Why not? You've just proved it's not human blood.'

'I did a basic antigen test, for all blood types, and no human antibodies are present. It isn't human blood... But it is blood.'

'Yeah, right.' Ayala held out his palm for twenty pounds.

'See this?' Stuart passed Ayala a vial labelled 'Pig antigens'.

'This is to test for pig blood?'

'Yep; only pigs produce antibodies in response to the substance in that vial. The human immune system doesn't recognise it as a threat, which definitely shows it isn't human blood. I've already done this once, but just to prove it to you, I'll do it again.'

Purcell daubed a smear of blood onto a gel-coated glass plate and applied the pig antigen to the sample, then put it under the microscope. Ayala leant in, and saw that the two samples had begun to diffuse towards each other, forming a visible band at the point where they met.

'Damn, you're right.'

'Of course I am. Besides, the bet wasn't "Is it human blood?" but "Is it bleach?", so you'd have lost either way.'

Ayala pulled out his wallet. 'Take your blood money.'

'Terrible pun, mate. I can see why you're a cop, not a comedian.'

'You watch it, or I'll have Morton assign you to lab duty for the next three months. No more field work,' Ayala threatened.

'Aye-aye, captain!' Purcell mock-saluted, then ran out of the room before Ayala could punch him.

***

'Superintendent, thanks for seeing me at such short notice,' Morton simpered, hoping he sounded like he meant it. The Superintendent wasn't likely to notice any insincerity. The man genuinely believed he could do no wrong.

'It's no trouble, David. I've just come back from a round of golf. Three under par, would you believe it?'

Morton forced himself to unclench his jaw and paint a goofy smile on his face. 'Excellent news, sir. Who were you playing with?'

'Oh, a couple of the city aldermen, a high court judge and a politician who's a friend of mine. You should come along some time,' the Superintendent said.

I would, but I'm working. Unlike you, Morton thought, but he didn't say it out loud. Instead he said, 'I'm not much of a golfer, I'm afraid. I'm actually here about two detainees I have in the cells. I need you to give s42 PACE authorisation to keep them until thirty-six hours. Just a formality, of course.'

The Superintendent's jovial demeanour changed instantly. 'Why? Surely you've got enough to charge them after a full day.'

'Sir, this is an exceptionally delicate case.'

'The one involving that child?'

'Yes sir. We believe the detainees have been involved with child trafficking. We need to put our best foot forward on this one. We won't get another chance if they flee before we've got our act together.'

The Superintendent shuffled uncomfortably in his seat. 'What do you have on them?'

'The substituted child was first seen in their care. On the day the substitute appeared, they changed the details in the Children's Services database to reflect the substitute by uploading a new photograph, which Adrian Lovejoy has admitted to taking, after being confronted with metadata evidence.'

'So far so good. What about the wife?'

'We're on shakier ground here, sir. We believe she has acted as an accessory. It would be impossible for someone in her position not to notice if her husband was involved in human trafficking, and for that reason we believe she is complicit.'

'OK, I'll give you the time. On one condition.'

'Which is?' Morton asked.

'You really do need to get a new suit, Morton.'

***

'We got the extra twelve hours,' Morton announced to the almost empty Incident Room.

'Like that's going to make a difference,' Ayala said.

'If the Superintendent hadn't agreed, then we'd be releasing them in half an hour.'

'Yeah, but it's four o'clock now. The new time takes us to four in the morning. What are we supposed to be doing between now and then to find something?'

'Have some faith, Bertram.' Morton used Ayala's first name, knowing full well that he hated it. 'First things first, you're going to go make me some coffee. Then I'm going to read the financial report on the Lovejoys that I assume you've finally obtained in my absence. I'm going to need you to head over to Kiaran's office and tell him I need a Warrant of Further Detention. You're right that twelve hours probably won't cut it. What are you waiting for? Off you shuffle.'

Ayala skittered out of the room, and Morton pulled an envelope from Ayala's side of the desk towards him. After upending the envelope, Morton opened the binder, hoping that whoever had compiled the report had the foresight to stick an executive summary at the front rather than expecting him to dig through a dozen appendices.

For once, he wasn't disappointed.

Chapter 44: I Swear

'I swear by the Holy Bible that the evidence I shall give shall be the truth, the whole truth and nothing but the truth,' Morton rested his hand on a bible as he spoke. As the senior investigating office, he was duty-bound to appear in court to assist with the application. The Custody Sergeant, with whom Morton had consulted prior to the court hearing, sat in the public galley awaiting the outcome of the application.

'Detective Chief Inspector, could you summarise the facts of this case for the court?' Kiaran O'Connor spoke directly to Morton, as if having a conversation rather than getting the key facts into a court record.

'We're investigating a murder which appears to have been committed to abet human trafficking. Charles Anthony Matthews, a twelve-year-old boy in the care of Mr and Mrs Lovejoy was murdered, and an impostor took his place on or around the eighth of December 2012.'

The District Judge, perched high above them at the back of the courtroom in a leather swivel chair, scribbled furiously.

'And what evidence do you have so far?'

'It's mostly circumstantial. We have digital records changed at the instigation of the Lovejoys to reflect the impostor, and an affidavit from a nurse that the real Charles Matthews was released into the custody of social services unharmed.'

'And what do you need further time for?'

'Unimpeded investigation. We need to find more concrete evidence prior to releasing the Lovejoys, to avoid any risk of them contaminating the evidence.'

'Thank you, Mr Morton.' Kiaran turned to the bench. 'Your Honour, I believe we have satisfied the requirements of s42 of the Police and Criminal Evidence Act, and I ask that the court extend the duration of the Lovejoys' detention by thirty-six hours.'

'Not so fast, Mr O'Connor. You've dealt with both defendants as a single entity. Is the evidence against them equal? Mr Morton?'

Morton swallowed. 'Your Honour, the evidence is strongest against Mr Lovejoy. At present, we have no reason to believe that Mrs Lovejoy's alibi is flawed; however, we believe that she is acting as an accessory to her husband in this matter.'

'So you've got nothing on Mrs Prudence Lovejoy. In respect of her, your application is denied. I will allow you to detain Mr Lovejoy for a further thirty-six hours, but unless you find something compelling I would not be minded to grant any further applications. Do I make myself clear?'

'Yes, Your Honour, thank you.'

***

'Looks pretty normal to me, boss.' Ayala sifted through a stack of financial documents on the Lovejoys, his foot tapping on the floor.

'Would you stop that? And I'm not so sure normal is right,' Morton's tone was playful, a tone Ayala recognised as his 'I know something you don't know' voice.

'They've got a credit rating of 702. That's almost dead centre, middle of the range.'

'Ah. But they also own a farm in Norfolk with two hundred acres of land.'

'What? That can't be true. I checked the Land Registry myself,' Ayala said.

'It's not registered land.'

'I thought all land had to be registered. Isn't that the whole point?'

'Yes and no. It has to be registered, if you want to sell it. The registration system wasn't a binary switch. Most land is on the register, but it doesn't cover all of England yet. Eventually it will, but this is all off the system. They've had the land since the old paper-based system, and haven't voluntarily registered it yet,' Morton said.

'So, how'd you find out about it?'

'I found recurring payments going into their account from a tenant farmer, got a copy of the lease off him to confirm.'

'So it's legitimate?'

'It's odd. They acquired the property in 1981. They've had been in their early twenties then, at most.'

'My maths says they'd have been seventeen, boss. They're forty-nine now, so unless they age differently to the rest of us...' Ayala's voice trailed off.

'Don't be a pedant, Bertram. No one likes a wise-ass. The point is the same: how did they afford that purchase back then?'

'I'm not buying it, boss. That was decades ago. You think that's linked to criminality now?'

'Once a criminal, always a criminal. You wait and see.'

***

'Interview resumed at 13:21. Present are Bertram Ayala, and David Morton from the Metropolitan Police. The defendant, Adrian Lovejoy, is present together with his solicitor Miss Federica Boseli of Huntingdon Fox and Associates,' Morton said.

Mr Lovejoy squirmed in his seat, looking pallid after his second night in the cells. By contrast his lawyer, dressed in a smartly cut suit jacket and knee-length skirt, could have passed muster in almost any setting.

'Mr Lovejoy, can you explain why Charles Matthews speaks very little English?'

'I believed he was simply suffering from a great deal of stress. He lost his adoptive parents in a fire, and that could have triggered post-traumatic stress disorder.'

'Is that your professional diagnosis?'

'No. I'm a psychotherapist, not a psychologist. It would be inappropriate for me to diagnose any child. I raised Charlie's problems with Mary, Mrs Bushey that is, in mid December.'

'What was the outcome of that?'

'I don't know. I guess, what with it being Christmas, that it wasn't actioned too quickly. Then in January he moved on.'

'Have you had language issues with other charges?' Morton asked.

'Yes. Like I said, children often clam up after a trauma, and we deal exclusively with trauma cases so it isn't uncommon.'

'How often does that happen?'

'I don't know. Perhaps one in twenty will be affected, but that's just a ballpark. It's about extent and degree. Sometimes only Pru will bond with them, or only I will. Between us we tend to catch any major issues even when we've got the maximum of eight children with us.'

'How many charges did you have when Charlie was with you?'

'Seven or eight throughout the four weeks he was with us.'

Morton swiftly changed subject, hoping to catch Adrian out: 'And how much money do you earn per year?'

'You don't have to answer that,' Boseli said.

'It's fine. Last year we made £110,000. About £45,000 of that was from fostering.'

'Where did the rest come from?'

'I own a farm which is let out.'

'How did you acquire that farm?'

'Inheritance. It belonged to my great-aunt. I had to sell off several fields to cover the inheritance tax, but I've managed to keep it in the family. Our tenant farmer produces beef there, and we sometimes use a small cabin that's near the lake for retreats with the kids.'

Morton was thrown off balance, and turned to Ayala to give himself a moment to recover. Ayala, rather unhelpfully, mouthed 'told you so'.

'Did you kill Charles Matthews and put another child in his place?' Morton asked.

'What? No! Why would I do that?'

'Someone did. If it wasn't you, who did it?'

Something flashed in Adrian Lovejoy's eyes, 'I... I don't know. I spend my whole life looking after kids. Ask anyone.'

'Did you kill Charles Matthews on the night of December fourth?'

'No.'

'Did your wife?'

'No!'

'Did you allow someone else to do so?'

'Of course not. How dare you?' Adrian Lovejoy leant forward, as if about to get up and punch Morton. Lovejoy's lawyer, Federica Boseli, put an arm in front of him protectively.

'Mr Morton, if you're going to badger my client then this interview is over.'

'Thank you for your time, Mr Lovejoy. Interview terminated at 13:37.'

***

'No dice. Judge Hearney wasn't kidding when he said he wouldn't be minded to grant another extension,' Kiaran O'Connor announced as he walked into Morton's office, where Morton and Ayala were finishing up a takeaway. As Kiaran had expected, the s44 application was fruitless and the seventy-two hour deadline had become set in stone.

'So at half past four in the morning, Adrian Lovejoy walks,' Morton replied, jabbing at his salad with a plastic fork.

'I'm afraid so.'

'Gents, I've had an undercover keep an eye on Mrs Lovejoy since release. If she isn't innocent, then she's incredibly good at acting it. Apart from a few calls to her sister and lawyer, she's done nothing to suggest she's trying to hide evidence.' Ayala voiced the doubt that had been nagging at him since Mrs Lovejoy's release.

'Could be, or she could just be very good. Sit tight until the trail's cold, then ease back into it. If she's been trafficking children then we know she's a master manipulator. I've jailed more than a few psychopaths in my time, and they can be that cold,' Kiaran said.

'She doesn't read like that to me. I know I don't have David's experience, nor yours, but the only reactions I've seen from her are shock, surprise and righteous anger. She's got a solid alibi.'

'I've had doubts myself, but we can't take chances with this investigation. One false move and whoever is behind it could decide to up sticks and disappear. Worse yet, they could try and disappear the witnesses.'

Disappear the witnesses, the thought resonated in Morton's mind. Could Tina's death, Craig Linden and the diamond smuggling be linked to the child trafficking?

'David. Earth to David.' Ayala waved his hands in front of Morton's glazed-over eyes. 'You with us, boss?'

'Huh? My mind wandered.'

'Where'd it go?'

'I have a hunch that Tina and this trafficking are linked. We've been treating them as two separate investigations,' Morton said.

'For good reason. There's no evidence linking them,' Kiaran said sceptically.

'David's hunches are usually good. Let's see if there's anything linking the Lovejoys with Craig Linden.'

Chapter 45: Media Malaise

In Dacre Street, trouble waited for David Morton. Adrian Lovejoy's lawyer, Federica Boseli, loitered on the narrow pavement with a television crew consisting of a cameraman, sound engineer and a wizened old anchor. They stood on the opposite side of the one-way from New Scotland Yard with a camera pointed towards the secure entrance. At five o'clock, with the sun hanging low in the sky, David Morton emerged from the entrance.

'There he is!' the sound engineer cried, leaping into the road, his dead cat microphone swaying vigorously in the wind.

Morton twisted away, heading towards the safety of The Feathers pub. Before he had even reached Broadway, the film crew had interposed themselves between him and his destination.

'Detective Morton. Donny Travis, Sky News. You've arrested the wrong man, and in doing so allowed a killer to escape. What have you got to say for yourself?'

Morton felt his fingers clench into a fist, and hastily stuffed his hands into his pockets. They were looking to ambush him in the hopes of getting a sound bite or a guilty look.

'Good evening, Mr Travis. I'm afraid I wasn't expecting you. I'd be happy to talk to you tomorrow if you call my office,' Morton repeated his media training verbatim.

'Is it true there's a psychopath killing kids in foster care?'

'As I said, Donny, I'd be happy to talk to you. Tomorrow. Please call our press office, and we'll set something up. Right now, I'm afraid that I have somewhere to be.'

Morton started to back away, deliberately keeping his face turned towards the camera in order to deny Donny Travis the much-coveted walking-away shot.

'Give us something. Why'd you arrest Adrian Lovejoy? He's innocent, isn't he?'

Morton carried on walking. As he was about to turn the corner and escape into the darkness, Travis launched his parting shot, 'Why aren't you going after the real criminals? Afraid you'll get stabbed again?'

It was puerile, and clearly intended to rile Morton. His eyes flashed darkly.

'How bloody dare you! I am no coward.'

Donny Travis grinned; he had him.

'Then why did you arrest a foster parent? And what are you doing to catch the real killer?'

'I can't comment on an ongoing investigation,' Morton said stiffly.

'Then can you comment on why you arrested Mr Lovejoy?'

'We had reason to believe Mr Lovejoy might be involved, and took all reasonable precautions to investigate that assumption. At this time, Mr Lovejoy remains a person of interest so I can give no further comment. Thank you.'

'Mr Morton, why did you release him if you still think he did it?'

This time, Morton turned and strode off without pausing. If they wanted a shot of him walking off that badly, then they could have it. As he went, he could hear the female solicitor begin her spiel to the camera. The phrases 'innocent', 'upstanding', and 'pillar of the community' carried through the night air.

***

The door to the Superintendent's office was ajar. Inside, the Director of Human Resources, Doctor Emma Hart, sat in the Superintendent's chair. Morton had met her only once before, and on that occasion had received only a commendation for bravery and an offer of a place at the Lord Mayor's Garden Party. He wisely declined. This time, Morton would not escape unscathed. Morton steeled himself, knocked once and entered. The Superintendent was stood by the window, his back to Morton.

'Good morning, Superintendent, Director.'

The Director nodded curtly, and Morton took a seat.

'Chief Inspector Morton, we've had a complaint from Mr Adrian Lovejoy, courtesy of his solicitor. What have you got to say for yourself?' Doctor Emma Hart held a gold-plated ballpoint pen between perfectly manicured fingers. Her hand hovered over a yellow legal pad.

Morton blinked mildly, and then stroked his chin as he prepared his response.

'It's a baseless complaint. I had good reason to hold Mr Lovejoy, even if it does turn out that he is entirely innocent. His detention was authorised by no less than three others: the custody sergeant, the Superintendent and a magistrate. Are you suggesting we were all out of bounds? I appear to be the only one being chastised at this meeting.'

The superintendent kept his back to the pair, and stared out of the window, but Morton knew he was listening intently. In contrast, the Director scribbled furiously on her legal pad.

'The others weren't in Dacre Street yesterday evening.'

'I handled that according to protocol. I offered no inflammatory words, no sound bites and no photo opportunities. What would you have had me do?' Morton had watched the news carefully for any sign of the footage and nothing had surfaced.

'You should have given a statement.'

'Not at all. I'm not obliged to give a statement. Any press releases that concern my investigation are entirely within my purview. I invited Mr Travis to call at a proper hour for comment. I will not reward ambush tactics lest I encourage them.'

'We're just looking for you to be reasonable here, Mr Morton. A simple statement would have sufficed.'

'No, you're looking for a scapegoat. And I'm having none of it. Besides, you said this was about Adrian Lovejoy, not Dacre Street, or did I misunderstand you?'

'No, but...'

'Then I think we're done here. I will find the man or woman responsible for the death of Charlie Matthews. I would appreciate it if you left me to get on with that. If you want to talk about this again, you can speak to my union rep.'

With that, Morton left the Superintendent and Doctor Hart. Hart was still scribbling furiously as he left.

***

According to the weather service, it had been raining until six in the morning on the day that Tina had been found in Brockwell Park Gardens. She was found on a Saturday, giving her a full five days unaccounted-for. The glow from Morton's laptop illuminated his home office. The door was shut, and he had headphones on at full volume. Sarah knew better than to disturb him when he was like this.

The golden rule for survival echoed around Morton's mind as he sat stock-still and stared at the screen. Three minutes without air. Three days without water. Three weeks without food. If she was gone for five days, then her captors must have given her water. Why?

Tina had been rushed to hospital at shortly after eight, and pronounced dead on arrival. The weather had certainly contributed to her death; Chiswick's autopsy report had confirmed as much.

Morton's gut feel was that the early risers hit the park from around five o'clock, which would be typical of the type-A personalities that jogged before dawn. That gave a fairly narrow window for Tina to have been dumped without someone noticing.

Morton glanced at the handsome carriage clock on the left-hand side of his desk. It was fast closing on nine o'clock, well past working hours. He shut his laptop down, and headed for an early night. By the time his head hit the pillow, he was out cold.

***

Fresh from his early night, Morton had made it to Brockwell Park Gardens shortly after half past four. No jogger had yet made it out onto the path, but a few of London's transients were huddled together near a clump of trees.

'£20 for a quickie, mister?' A girl, wrapped in a tattered assortment of wraps, approached Morton. Her eyes were bloodshot, and train tracks were clearly visible on her arms.

'How old are you?' Morton asked.

'Nineteen,' she replied. To Morton's eye, she looked more like thirty.

'So you want a go or not? I'll go to fifteen.'

'No.' The girl turned to walk away, but Morton called her back.

'Have you seen this woman?' Once again, he produced the photo. He turned his phone screen towards it as a makeshift torch.

'I think so. Last week. She was over there.' The girl gestured towards the fencing where Morton knew Tina had been found.

'Are you sure?'

'Yeah. I tried to offer her a blanket, but she ignored me.'

Morton marvelled at the kindness of someone down on her luck. It had been minus two degrees Celsius, yet she was willing to share the meagre rags she had.

'Was she conscious?' Morton asked.

'Dunno.'

'Well, what time was it?'

'What do I look like, the talking clock?'

'Was before or after the bells at the church chimed?' St Giles' Church was located less than three hundred feet away. From his research, Morton had found out that the pastor rang the bells until ten p.m., then stopped until six in the morning out of respect for the local residents.

'After the night ones, but before the morning. Maybe halfway between.'

'And did you see who she was with?'

'Nah, I heard an engine purring, real soft-like, followed by a boot clicking shut. Then the sobbing started. At first I thought it was a fox, but eventually I decided I had to check. The foxes are more scared of me than I am of them.'

'And that's when you found her?'

'Yep. Left a blanket over her, and went back to sleep.'

'Thanks. Are you always around here?' Morton wondered how he'd find her again if he needed to.

'Naw, but I've got a mobile.'

'A mobile?' Morton was incredulous. Evidently even homeless people need to keep in touch.

'Yeah, we all do. We let each other know where there's space to sleep, or a hot meal going.'

She scribbled her number onto a scrap of paper that Morton hastily dug out of his pocket. It was only when she had gone that Morton glanced at it, and immediately felt his eyes begin to water. Her name was Tina too.

***

Hank Williams scattered £20 notes all over his double bed. Tiny had sent over a bundle of notes as a bonus. It wasn't the first time he'd given Hank a bonus. The first bonus he'd handed over was Hank's Mercedes. Ostensibly it was a hand-me-down from his big sister, Tiny's wife. Hank had thought it flashy, but the provenance meant it should pass muster if Hank ever caught any heat from the police.

Unlike this money. A second-hand car was an over-the-top gift. A bundle of twenties was downright dirty, especially a bundle this large. Hank guessed that there was over twenty thousand pounds on the bed. Hank frowned. It was an odd amount. Too much to simply pretend it had been saved legitimately, but too little to be worth laundering excessively.

Hank leant over the bed, and began the tedious process of bundling back up his ill-gotten gains. For now, the loose floorboard in the lounge would do.

***

The morning flew by as Morton searched through speed camera records for the night of Tina's disappearance. The good news was that South London's camera system was state of the art. Rather than simple film cameras, the cameras were all digital and sent their photos back to a central database, which made Morton's task pretty easy.

The bad news was that the cameras only triggered if a passing car went over the speed limit. A few cameras had been triggered during the night, but none of the speeding cars looked suspicious. A couple of boy racers had been speeding up the Norwood Road, and then caught again racing around Holborn in midtown. A little after midnight an elderly gentleman had sped through Tulse Hill to the west of Brockwell Park Gardens, but there were no realistic suspects between two and four a.m.

Morton was looking for a medium-to-large car. The boot had to be big enough to contain a human, and the purring mentioned by the witness suggested a diesel engine. Morton's gut told him that he was looking for a midsize estate of some kind, which only narrowed it down to the many thousands registered in London and the Home Counties.

The obvious next step was to pull the registration details of every car owned by anyone that either the real Charlie, or the impostor, had come into contact with, and then see if any of those cars fit Morton's diesel estate theory.

As if Morton was going to do that drudge work himself. He headed out of his office towards the Incident Room in search of Bertram Ayala.

Chapter 46: New Beginnings

In a bustling school hall, Martin Neil consoled, cajoled and cursed the endless stream of parents who had booked appointments with him for parents' evening. He had two groups of parents. The larger group were those whose children he taught maths. Mostly, these were a two-minute exercise in repeating the comments he had contributed to the child in question's school report. Parents nodded appreciatively at compliments, and tutted gravely when given the news that their child wasn't working hard enough.

But Martin's main concern was his tutorial group. He had thirty tutees, and twenty-nine sets of parents had booked in to see him. At ten minutes per appointment, Martin was expected to sit at a desk in the school hall for five hours in order to see them all.

The one child who didn't have a parent or guardian in attendance was the one Martin was most concerned about. It was often the way: that parents being absent told more about a student's academic chances than any ten-minute discussion ever could. No one spoke for Charlie Matthews. No one cared to learn that he was top of the year in maths, and bottom in English. Martin Neil had never told anyone, not even his wife Ingrid, but he was in fact adopted. His real parents had him out of wedlock, and could not bear the shame. His very name was taken from the home in which he had been unceremoniously dumped, St Neil's. Martin was far too young to remember the home but the knowledge of his own pedigree honed his sense of responsibility to those in the system.

If Mrs Lattimer had cared enough to attend then she would have learned that Charlie's school report recommended weekly sessions with the school's special needs department. But in Mr Neil's opinion what Charlie needed wasn't homework help. It was a father.

***

As he was about to leave for lunch, Morton received an email summons from the Superintendent's personal assistant demanding his immediate attendance. With a heave, he rose from his desk. In years gone by, he might have pleaded ignorance of the message or pretended to be out of the building, but Scotland Yard's state of the art 'swipe in, swipe out' security system put paid to any such notion. The Superintendent knew full well that Morton was in the building.

On arrival, Morton heard two men talking inside the office. One voice belonged to the Superintendent. The other was that of Alfred McNamara, the Met's resident celebrity. McNamara was the eldest child of legendary Irish cage fighter Paddy 'Iron Fist' McNamara. According to station gossip, the death of his younger sister under mysterious circumstances, and McNamara's exceptional work in solving that crime, had catapulted him from young upstart to the position he now enjoyed. Morton had the feeling that McNamara was being groomed to become a future Superintendent.

McNamara certainly cut a dashing figure. At six foot four, he topped Morton by a clear two inches and was all the leaner for it. The younger man had a mane of blue-black hair, a chiselled jaw and blindingly blue eyes. Morton was a man's man, but even he could tell that McNamara was, as Tina used to put it, 'man candy'. Worse still, he clearly knew it.

Morton knew he'd hate him before he even spoke.

'David, I'd like to introduce Detective Alfie McNamara. He'll be joining your Murder Investigation Team.' The Superintendent puffed out his chest, as though bracing himself for Morton's response.

'Superintendent, I didn't ask for an assignee.' Morton glared.

'You have one all the same. Someone has to replace Detective Inspector Tina Vaughn.'

'It's been less than two weeks, sir.'

'And in those two weeks, you've made next to no progress. If anything, you've harassed an innocent couple and offered a red rag to the media. Your team is understaffed, Morton, and McNamara is the best junior officer we have available. I trust you'll impart your usual wisdom.'

Morton ground his teeth together. 'Yes sir.'

The Superintendent nodded, then turned towards his laptop and began to click away in earnest. It was clear that Morton and his new protégé had been dismissed.

'After you,' Morton said.

They stepped into the lift, and Morton hit the button for the fourth floor, where the Joe Bloggs Junior Incident Room awaited.

'No offense, Alfie, but this is a temporary reassignment. I'm one officer light so need someone on hand, and you're it. But come the end of this investigation, you'll be back in the pool for reassignment. Do I make myself clear?'

'If that's the craic, so be it,' Detective Alfie McNamara said. He didn't quite shrug his shoulders, but it was obvious Morton's grudging acceptance didn't trouble him.

This time Morton made eye contact with the brash youngster and said firmly: 'It is. This is our floor.'

Morton led the way through the winding corridors, then paused outside the Incident Room.

'Detective, I've heard you like to go solo, but this unit operates as a team. You're coming in at a stressful time. The group is in mourning over the loss of your predecessor, and we're mid-investigation, so you'll be playing catch-up. Can you handle that?'

McNamara stared intently for a moment, and then nodded.

'Let's go introduce you to the team then.'

***

McNamara, Morton and Ayala occupied the large table in the Incident Room. Three mugs of tea sat on the table. McNamara had yet to bring his own mug, and so he used Tina's, a faux pas which caused both Morton and Ayala to wince.

McNamara was oblivious. He'd read all the details, and the Superintendent had given him Tina's notes. He'd even listened to her Dictaphone. But McNamara was the only detective who could be truly dispassionate about Tina's death. He had never met her.

'Let me get this straight. The kid's dead, and is the biological son of the Matthews. But the kid living as Charlie Matthews isn't related to the dead boy or either of the Matthews?' Alfie McNamara knotted his eyebrows in consternation. In his left hand he held a notebook with tiny writing scribbled into every available space.

'Not quite,' Morton admonished. 'We know the kid isn't related to the father. But that doesn't rule out the mother cheating.'

'Then wouldn't there be a lesser DNA match between Charlie and Joe if they share a mother?'

Morton fidgeted in his seat as he considered his response. 'They share no mitochondrial DNA, so we know they have different mothers. Y-chromosome testing using Eric Matthews' DNA proves he fathered only Charlie, not the boy who took his identity.'

'So you're going with the 'impostor theory'?' Alfie injected a note of scepticism into his tone, but privately he had come to the same conclusion.

'It's the best we've got. Faux-Charlie isn't related to the Matthews or their son. He has no knowledge of a priceless heirloom, and no memory of anything to confirm his identity.'

'But t'at beggars belief! How would no one notice? Hospital staff, a doctor, a teacher, a support worker. Someone must have seen the switch happen.'

Morton scratched his nose thoughtfully. 'If they did, we haven't found them. We're working on the theory that the faux-Charlie assumed the identity of Charlie Matthews on arrival at the Lovejoy residence. Before that, we know that the real Charlie lived with the Grants. Neighbours confirmed it, with photographic proof.'

'And you've looked into the Lovejoys themselves?'

'If they did it, there isn't any tangible proof.'

'When did this all happen?' McNamara still looked confused.

'It had to be the seventh of December. After that, the impostor was with the Lovejoys, and social services updated their photos. Before that, the real Charlie was in hospital after the fire. Right, Ayala?'

Ayala nodded. 'That's it.'

McNamara looked slowly from Ayala to Morton, and then set his pen down before he spoke again: 'No, it's not.'

'Excuse me?' Morton asked incredulously.

'He wasn't in hospital overnight.'

'How do you know that?'

McNamara delved into a bag under the table, and pulled out Tina's Dictaphone.

'Listen to Vaughn's interview with the fire investigator.' He hit play, and Lucien Darville's dulcet tones played back through the Dictaphone's built-in speakers.

'He got taken to the hospital for a once-over that afternoon as I recall, but he wouldn't have suffered any permanent physical damage from the fire.'

'See. He had a check-up, that's all. No overnight stay,' McNamara said.

Morton thumped the table. 'Then our whole bloody timeline is off!'

Ayala shuffled his chair back. The overnight stay had been information he'd supplied. Ayala's cheeks flushed red, but the others didn't notice.

'If this is true, we've got a one-day window for Charlie to have disappeared in. The fire at the Grants was on the sixth, early in the evening. Adrian Lovejoy's photo wasn't taken until the next evening, and he said he'd taken it as soon as Charlie arrived. Ayala, where did you get the idea Charlie had stayed overnight?'

'Err...' Ayala hesitated, and scrolled through his own notes to check. 'It was during my interview with the social worker, Hank Williams.'

'Well, that's just grand. He'd have had plenty of chances to swap the boys,' McNamara said.

Morton nodded. It seemed the most logical conclusion if the Lovejoys were innocent. He dunked a custard cream into his coffee to buy himself a moment to think. If this proved to be another false lead, the Superintendent would be sure to kick the case over to the Cold Case Team. 'Ayala, what did he seem like when you interviewed him?'

'Friendly. We met at shared offices. They use a hot desk system, so I can't imagine there'd be many secrets in their office.'

'Secrets? I think I have an idea how Charlie's photo was altered in the Looked After Children database,' McNamara said.

'So?' Ayala said.

'We've been assuming this was a routine update. The Lovejoys admitted to taking new photos every time they had a new ward, right?'

'You think someone knew the Lovejoy routine,' Morton interjected. He tried to ignore the sudden up-swell in his respect for the Irishman.

'I think passwords would be easy to steal in a shared office space. Hank could have glanced over Bushey's shoulder, or used a computer that she'd left herself logged onto. Mrs Bushey might even have given Hank her password. If he had those details, he could easily remove any data that would contradict the substitution, and slip in Adrian Lovejoy's new photo.'

Morton snapped his fingers, 'Ayala, run down McNamara's idea. Phone Adrian Lovejoy, and ask how he sent the photo to be updated. Do it now.'

Ayala scurried out of the Incident Room to find the right number.

Morton turned to his new officer. 'McNamara, this is a good lead. But we need to be totally on the ball here. Several times we've been convinced we had the right idea, and it's turned out to be totally off-base. We need to get all our ducks in a row before we bring Hank Williams in for a chat. Is that clear?'

'Whatever you say, boss.'

***

The offices of the 'Looked After Children's Services' at Lambeth Council hadn't changed a jot since Morton's last visit. The corridors were still littered with boxes, and Edith Faulkner-Wellington was once again in her office pottering around purposefully.

The door was open, but Morton still knocked out of politeness.

'Ah, Detective! Nice to see you again. Come in, come in. Have a seat.' Edith gestured at a pile of upturned boxes.

'Hello again, Edith. This is Detective McNamara, who has recently joined my department.'

Edith Faulkner-Wellington beckoned them both to sit, before offering them refreshment.

'No, thank you. We can't stop too long,' Morton said. Edith's smile fell ever so slightly as she realised that it was a flying visit.

'Well then, what can I do for you today?'

'Tell me about Hank Williams. We know he works for you.'

'Oh no, he doesn't. He works for the council. I don't pick 'em. Like I'd want that feller near children. The man's a giant. Any little kid would be terrified.'

'So why didn't you sack him?' McNamara asked.

'Can't, as much as I might want to. His work is faultless. I've never had a complaint from one of his kids. Don't expect I ever will.'

It's hard to make a complaint if you don't speak English, Morton thought.

'So why don't you like him? Surely you've got other tall staff.' McNamara asked.

'That one's no gentle giant. He comes around here, hitting on the girls in reception. Nasty man. He throws money around like candy, as if it would make up for his personality.'

'Money?' It was the first time Morton had heard any suggestion that Hank Williams was rich.

'Yep. Said he had family money. If I had some inheritance, I'd be out of this line of work like a shot. He's got a flashy Mercedes, last year's plates! Who in their right mind parks that all over London when visiting kids?'

'Do you have a licence plate for that car?'

'Should have. It'll be in our insurance documents. You sit tight, and I'll get them from the storeroom.' Edith shimmied past Morton, and went out of her office.

'What do you think, boss?'

'I think it's hard to keep up a Mercedes on a social worker's salary. Let's see where it got registered, and how he paid for it.'

'Want me to go look that up?' McNamara rose, and stretched.

'No. I'll have Ayala do it. You're staying here. I think Edith's rather fond of you.' Morton laughed at his junior officer's discomfort. McNamara valued his hard-man image too much to like the idea of an old lady doting on him.

Edith reappeared holding a folder full of insurance documents. 'Here you are, officers.'

McNamara took the folder, and then copied the licence plate number down carefully.

'Miss Faulkner-Wellington, how are social workers supervised?'

'Supervised? We don't exactly spy on our staff. They're all CRB checked. They've got appropriate degrees. Beyond that, we leave them to it unless we have any issues. There isn't a long line of qualified staff wanting to become social workers.'

McNamara focussed on her intently, and twiddled his thumbs.

'Don't you look at me like that, young man. Our system might have a few cracks – it's not perfect I'm sure – but we're hard-working folk. You can't tar us all with the same brush, just because of one bad apple.'

Morton held up a hand. 'Edith, my colleague didn't mean anything by his questions. Thank you ever so much for your time today.'

Edith huffed. 'You're welcome,' she said reluctantly.

***

'Boss, I've checked with Adrian Lovejoy. He provided the photos to Hank Williams via email. He's forwarded the email on, and it looks legit. I've sent it down to be checked by cybercrimes.' Ayala clicked away at his laptop. It was plugged into an HDMI socket on the conference table to connect it to the projector on the ceiling, which allowed Morton and McNamara to watch in real time.

'And, here's the registration information on his Mercedes,' Ayala continued. The car was less than a year old, and had been bought without finance at a South London dealership who registered it on Hank's behalf.

'Nice one, Ayala. Get down to the dealership, and see how he paid.' Morton felt the hairs on his arms rise. They were finally getting somewhere.

'I can do better than that, boss. You said your witness believed he'd inherited money?'

Morton nodded.

'Totally untrue. I checked probate, and got Kiaran to sort out the paperwork to look through Hank's bank account. Hank's balance breaks the four-figure mark once a month, on the sixth, when the various councils pay him. His income has been erratic, which is down to the zero hours contract, but he's never had real money. If he's splashing cash around, it isn't from his current account.'

'That ought to be enough for an arrest warrant. You go talk to the dealer this morning. We'll get Kiaran on board for the search warrant.'

***

The lawyer was out of his office when Morton and McNamara strolled into the Crown Prosecution Services offices. It wasn't uncommon, as Kiaran was a brawler famed for his thirst for court work. They waited in the antechamber, under the watchful eye of Kiaran's legal secretary.

'What made you accept the assignment to my team?' Morton tried to make small talk as the clock ticked by.

'I'm a detective. I do what I'm told.'

'I'm not buying that, Alfie. There are dozens of Murder Investigation Teams. Why mine?' Morton watched his unwelcome protégé.

McNamara met his gaze. 'You're up for retirement in the next few years. If I want to go to the top, I need a way to get there.'

Morton grinned. So that was what the Superintendent had planned: the old fool wanted to slip McNamara into a highly rated team, and then promote his hand-picked successor from within.

'I'm afraid they'll be carrying me out of my office in a coffin. I'm not your ticket to the Superintendent's office.' Morton pursed his lips, amused at McNamara's forthright declaration.

'We'll see.'

Morton was about to reply when Kiaran walked in, and Morton found himself caught in the middle of the men. Kiaran, who was from Dublin, nodded curtly at the Belfast-born detective.

'Gentlemen. To what do I owe the pleasure today?' Kiaran beckoned them to follow him as he spoke. Once they were inside Kiaran's office, Alfie shut the door with a thud.

'We've had progress in the Joe Bloggs case. The photo taken by Adrian Lovejoy was sent to Hank Matthews, Charlie's social worker. Hank told us he picked Charlie up from the hospital on December seventh, the day after the Grant fire, and dropped him off at the Lovejoys. He didn't. Charlie was released on the sixth; hospital records confirm it. Further, he's living well beyond his means: he owns a brand new Mercedes, but has a pitiful bank balance.'

'What do you need from me?

'Get us a search warrant for his house. If he's involved, we need to check for any pertinent evidence,' Morton stated simply. It was standard procedure to search a murder suspect's home.

'Right. What time did Charlie leave the hospital?'

'According to Lucien Darville, an hour after he left the scene,' Morton said, and then pre-empted the prosecutor's next question: 'That was at 6:12 p.m.'

McNamara looked at Morton astounded that Morton could remember such specific detail off the cuff.

'And he arrived at the Lovejoy home when?'

'Half past seven the next day, December seventh.'

'And there's no reasonable explanation for the missing twenty-four hours?'

'None.'

'I'll have a search warrant without the hour. I assume you'll execute it at dawn?' Kiaran asked. It was the most likely time of the day for Hank to be home but unaware of the police amassing outside for the raid.

'Actually, I have a better idea...'

Chapter 47: Tricky Questions

A thick envelope waited on the kitchen table when Morton arrived home. He practically danced through the doorway, excited about the impending arrest of Hank Williams.

'Sarah!' He grabbed his wife excitedly as he walked in, and planted a kiss on her cheek.

'David. What's got into you? Good day?' Sarah asked.

'Definitely. I'm millimetres from closing the Joe Bloggs case.'

'Good. At the risk of dampening your high spirits, an official-looking letter arrived for you today.' Sarah gestured at pile of envelopes on the counter. A large stack had gathered since the start of the year, including many unpaid bills. If the identity theft issue wasn't resolved soon, it wouldn't be long before angry red final reminders began to appear on the doormat.

On top of the pile was the brown official envelope Sarah had indicated. Morton grabbed it and tore the top off with his teeth. Inside, the twin lion crest of Her Majesty's Courts and Tribunals Service glared up at him.

He decanted the envelope's contents, and scanned through the paperwork.

'We've got a date for our identity theft case. It's next week.'

'Whoa. Don't they usually take months to schedule civil cases?'

'I guess not.' Morton tossed the envelope aside. It wasn't important.

***

Morton loitered in the security suite just inside New Scotland Yard, sharing a doughnut with John Ritter, New Scotland Yard's burly chief of security. On the main security screen before them, Hank Williams could be seen sitting in the waiting room. He was there at Morton's request, having agreed to attend after Morton implied that Hank might be a witness in the case against Adrian Lovejoy.

Williams appeared to believe that subterfuge. He was calmly scrolling through something on his mobile phone, totally at ease in the police station.

'Thanks for the doughnut, John. Let him wait for half an hour, then show him through. I'll conduct the interview in my office.'

Ritter screwed up his face. 'Not in the interview suite, boss?'

'No. At the moment, he thinks he's a witness. Let's not disabuse him of that notion too soon. Can you have one of your team nearby, just in case he tries to make trouble when he realises he's been played?' Morton asked.

'Will do, boss,' Ritter said with a smile.

***

The residence of Hank Williams was above a former workshop in Bryanston Mews, a few minutes' walk from Marble Arch. The property included a ground-level garage, and a small apartment above it. Ayala knew that the car wasn't there, as Morton had given Hank a pass to park in the subterranean New Scotland Yard car park.

Ayala didn't have to wait long for the all-clear from Morton. Ayala's phone flashed as a simple message came through: 'Go!'.

'We're on, lads.' Ayala waited for one of the search team to break open the front door, then pulled out a certified copy of the search warrant and dropped it neatly inside. He stepped over it, and then called out in case Hank had any house guests. When no one answered, he led the way inside.

***

Once he had set Ayala's team to work, Morton joined his guest and McNamara in his office. They sat either side of his desk, chatting away over a Styrofoam cup of coffee. Once McNamara saw Morton walking in, he jumped to his feet, nodded curtly, and vacated Morton's favourite chair.

'Morning, Chief,' McNamara greeted him. 'I take it you already know Mr Williams?'

'Only in passing,' Morton said.

'Good morning, Chief.' Hank rose to offer a hand. Morton took it, then eased into his seat, shuffled forward and glanced at the recorder on the edge of the desk to make sure it was on.

'Mr Williams, thanks for coming down. I see you've already got a drink, so I'll get down to business. As you have no doubt read in the press, we arrested Adrian Lovejoy for murder earlier this week. How well do you know Mr Lovejoy?' Morton was careful to stick to the facts, but eager to create the impression that Adrian Lovejoy was still front and foremost on his suspect list.

'I've known him for years, but we only meet fleetingly and never ever socially. I drop kids off, pick them up and stop by to check on them occasionally,' Hank replied.

'How would you characterise him?'

'Breathless. He's a constant whirlwind of activity. He needs to be to keep up with the kids. I suppose he appears overeager in a bid to come across as jovial. I wish I'd known better.' Hank glanced down momentarily with his eyes downcast, and Morton almost laughed at how quickly he'd taken the bait.

'Did you ever suspect he might be more than just a foster parent?'

'I always thought he was odd. But no, I never thought he'd kill a child. Who was it?'

'Charles Matthews.'

'No!' Hank cried, and clapped his hands over his mouth in horror before frowning in consternation. 'That can't be. I've seen Charlie since then.'

Since then? Morton thought. I haven't said when yet.

'I'm afraid so. Charles Matthews died in December.'

Hank flushed angrily. 'You're wrong! You interviewed Charlie two weeks ago.'

Morton raised an eyebrow, and waited for Hank to carry on speaking. When Hank remained silence, Morton asked: 'How long have you been in charge of Charlie?'

'Since December sixth, when his long-term foster parents died.'

'And when did you last see him?'

'Two weeks ago, with you. Like I said, he isn't dead.'

'I'm afraid he is. We believe that Charles Matthews was murdered on or around the seventh of December, and that an impostor took his place.' Morton watched Hank carefully.

He's showing all the right emotions, but they're coming a little too late to be authentic.

Hank stammered: 'H-How can this be? I would have noticed. I should have noticed.'

'Are you saying you didn't?'

'Of course not!' Hank declared. As he spoke, he pushed himself away from the desk, physically separating himself from the detectives.

'Tell us about the seventh.'

'What about it? I wasn't there.'

'You weren't? Can you tell us how Charlie got to the Lovejoys?'

Hank chewed on his upper lip for a second, then shrugged.

'Would they have picked him up from the hospital?' Morton asked.

'Yes, yes. That would make sense.' Hank nodded vigorously.

'For the record, can you tell us where you were on the seventh?'

Hank paused again to gather his thoughts, then said: 'I honestly can't remember.'

'So you haven't got an alibi?'

'I suppose I haven't.' Hank's eyes narrowed. 'Do I need one? Should I be asking for a lawyer?'

'No innocent man needs a lawyer, Mr Williams.' Morton's eyes twinkled.

Hank tugged at his collar, then gulped, but said nothing.

'When did you first meet Charlie?'

'Sometime in December. I'd have to check my calendar for the exact date. It would have been a routine trip to see how Charlie was settling in.'

'But you were emailed a photo before then?'

Hank's eyes widened in surprise, but he composed himself quickly, and nodded.

'For the benefit of the tape, Mr Williams is nodding. Hank, what did you do with that photo?'

'I would have passed it on to be added to Charlie's file, I guess.'

'You didn't change it yourself?'

'No, I'm not given that sort of access.'

'And you didn't see Charlie before mid December?'

'No.'

'Then why does the discharge nurse at the hospital remember seeing you?' Morton bluffed.

Hank's nostrils flared. 'I think I'll have that lawyer now.'

***

Morton and McNamara watched Hank through the one-way mirror. The lawyer hadn't arrived yet, but Hank looked more bored than anxious. He tapped his foot against the floor, with his eyes closed, as if he might drop off at any moment.

'Smug git,' McNamara declared.

'Not for long. He clearly picked Charlie up on December sixth, which makes his failure to report the faux-Charlie inexplicable. He's in on it.'

'Don't look now, boss, but there's a sharp-looking lawyer walking this way.'

The skeletal frame of Elliot Morgan-Bryant, wearing yet another Saville Row suit, strode down the corridor towards the detectives.

'Gentlemen.' Elliot Morgan-Bryant nodded. 'Would you mind terribly if I closed the privacy blinds? I need to consult with my client.'

Morton flicked a switch, and the red light for the interview suite's speaker went out. The lawyer shut the door behind him with a quiet click, and then pulled curtains across the one-way mirror.

Morton stared at the spot where the lawyer had just been, sure that there was something important about him.

'What is it, Chief?' McNamara asked.

'That lawyer. He represented Craig Linden, the guy Tina busted.'

'So?'

'So, we've got two criminals with no legitimate funds hiring the most expensive criminal lawyer in the country.'

'You think Hank's connected to the Bakowskis?'

'I do. It's too much of a coincidence otherwise. Tina disappears investigating the Bakowskis, and then the Bakowskis' pet barrister appears to defend a scumbag like Hank Williams. Everything is connected. I need you to find out how, and put Kiaran on notice we might need him.'

'I'm on it.' McNamara turned and marched towards the lift, leaving Morton to wait for Hank to finish chatting with his lawyer.

Morton grabbed his mobile, and dialled Ayala.

'Bertram. How's the search going?'

'Not too bad. I've been through the house. We found a stack of cash, about ten grand. All of it in unmarked twenties.'

Morton punched the air. 'Good work. That ought to be enough to hold him. When you're done there, I need you to do me a favour and check out Mary Bushey.'

'The old lady at Havering Council? Why?'

'She uploaded the photo, so she could be working with Hank.'

'Or she could just be an admin. She must deal with a lot of photos.'

'Just check it out,' Morton ordered.

Chapter 48: Ambush

When Morton returned to the interview suite, Hank's demeanour was subtly different. He seemed to have paled in the short time Morton had been out of the room, and he slumped in his chair. Hank's lawyer was the polar opposite, with perfect posture and an aura of calm confidence about him.

Morton unpaused the audio recorder, and enunciated: 'Interview resumed at 11:15. Now present are DCI David Morton, Mr Hank Matthews and his lawyer, Elliot Morgan-Bryant.'

The lawyer placed his elbows on the desk and leant forward. 'Mr Morton. My client agreed to talk to you of his own volition. Make your move.'

'This isn't a game, Elliot. Your client was the last known person to see a child before his body was found in Hackney Marshes. Start talking.'

'There's nothing to explain. Until you've arranged a line-up, we won't be commenting on your accusations. Otherwise, I think we're done here.'

Morton flicked his wrist dismissively. 'Hold your horses. We're not done yet. Tell me about the money.'

The lawyer turned to his client. Hank's eyes were now wide with fear. The lawyer leant in, and whispered something too quietly for Morton to hear. Hank shook his head slightly, and looked at his lawyer with narrowed eyes.

'Tell me about the money,' Morton repeated firmly.

'To what money do you refer?' Morgan-Bryant asked.

'The ten thousand pounds underneath a loose floorboard in your client's living room.'

Hank leant forward, sneered and said: 'No comment.'

'Mr Morgan-Bryant, you might wish to remind your client that a court may draw adverse inferences from his refusal to comment.'

'No comment,' Hank repeated.

'How did you afford a brand new Mercedes last year?' Morton asked. After Edith had suggested Hank owned a plush car, Morton had looked up the car in the DVLA's database. Hank owned a Mercedes C class executive estate that had been purchased without the aid of any finance.

Hank sagged in his seat. There was no way to deny he owned the car; the paper trail would eventually lead them to how he got it. He didn't even look at his lawyer as he said: 'It was a gift.'

Morton laughed derisively, 'A gift? It must be worth nearly thirty grand. I need me some new friends.'

'It was from my sister,' Hank said.

'Wow. What does she do for a living to be slinging cars around?' Morton asked.

'You don't have to answer that,' Elliot Morgan-Bryant said quickly to his client.

Morton looked at the lawyer through narrowed eyes. He let his client tell me about the car, but shut me down when I asked about the sister. Very strange. 'No, he doesn't. I assume your client will have paid tax on the car? Gifts over three grand aren't tax-free.' As Morton spoke, the interview room door slid open and Ayala stepped in. He wordlessly placed an envelope in front of Morton, and then winked before retreating quickly.

Hank's eyes shot from the detective to his lawyer. He clearly hadn't thought of that when answering so confidently. Morton was about to smile, then scowled as the lawyer interjected on Hank's behalf: 'Of course not, not yet anyway. He was given the car in August. The tax year doesn't end until April. He has no duty to discuss any future tax payments as they do not pertain to this investigation.'

The lawyer looked so smug that Morton wanted to punch him. Instead, he picked up Ayala's envelope and held it away from the suspect before skimming it. The printout inside was from a Mercedes dealer in Hammersmith showing the VAT invoice for Hank's car. There was a note at the top in Ayala's spidery handwriting: 'Someone outside to see you.' Morton was about to put it down when he spotted the name highlighted in the 'payee' section: 'Bipa Bakowski'. No wonder the lawyer closed us down when we started to talk about the sister.

'Hank, what's your sister's name?'

This time, Hank began to shake visibly.

'C'mon, Hank, it's not a secret is it?'

'Faith. My sister's name is Faith.'

'Not 'Bipa'?'

Hank hung his head. 'It's over, isn't it? Yes. My sister is Bipa Bakowski. Bipa is the Ukrainian equivalent of Faith. She changed it when she got married.'

'She's married to Dimitri Bakowski, isn't she?'

'Yes, she's married to Tiny,' Hank confirmed. His eyes began to water as he wondered what was going to happen to him.

Morton was about to press him, when someone rapped on the door once more.

'I'll be right back.'

***

Once he was out of the interview suite, Morton found a small group waiting for him, including his two detectives, as well as Xander Thompson and Kiaran O'Connor.

'Xander. I don't see you for a decade, then twice in a week. What's going on? Why did you pull me out?' Morton asked.

Xander refused to meet Morton's gaze. 'David, the Superintendent has authorised me to take over with Hank Williams.' Xander handed over signed authorisation from the Superintendent, which Morton read while the others waited with bated breath.

'Why the hell would he do that?' Morton cursed.

Kiaran put a hand on Morton's shoulder, which Morton promptly threw off. 'David, the decision has been made to cut Hank a deal.'

'A deal? We don't even know the extent of his crimes yet. I've barely started questioning him! The bastard could have killed a child. I'm convinced he's involved with Tina's death too: both he and Linden use the same lawyer.'

'There are only so many lawyers in London. Even if he did kill Tina, the deal stands: the Superintendent was adamant that we cut this deal. Xander needs Hank's testimony to get the Bakowski brothers. Do you want to catch the minnow or the whale here?'

'I want both. The Attorney General signed off on this?' Morton glared.

Kiaran nodded. 'The decision has been made. If Hank can give us Interpol's most wanted criminals, he walks.'

'You do what you have to do. I'll do what I have to,' Morton said gruffly. He stormed off down the corridor towards the Superintendent's office, with Ayala and McNamara in tow.

Chapter 49: Said and Done

The interview suite became claustrophobic once Kiaran and Xander sat opposite Hank and his lawyer. Kiaran felt a sense of déjà vu as he slid an immunity notice across the desk for Elliot Morgan-Bryant to peruse.

Kiaran took the lead, while Xander sat back to watch his newest witness. 'Hank, while your lawyer peruses the document I'll summarise it for you and then your lawyer can ask any questions you want. This document, once signed, grants you full immunity from prosecution for all summary offences committed on behalf of the Bakowski brothers. Further, it immunises you against any and all crimes conducted at the behest of Dimitri Bakowski. You will be required to give us your full co-operation, including testifying at trial. Once the prosecution is concluded, we'll make you disappear. New identity, new life.'

'And I get to keep my money?' Hank asked hesitantly.

Kiaran shuddered with repulsion. Two dead bodies, and Hank was most interested in his bank balance. 'Yes. Once you're immune, we can no longer issue any confiscation orders.'

Hank looked to his lawyer, who had finished reading through the immunity notice. 'The paperwork looks pretty standard,' Morgan-Bryant said, as if he dealt with immunity notices every day. He held out a fountain pen to his client and said: 'Sign at the bottom.' It was a fantastic deal, even by Morgan-Bryant's exacting standards. Hank had been looking at thirty years for his part in the death of Tina Vaughn alone.

Hank took the pen, and then in a loopy cursive etched his name onto the bottom of the immunity notice. Xander countersigned at the bottom of the page as a witness, and the deal was done.

Kiaran grimaced, 'You're a free man. Now start talking.'

'It all started last spring. I suppose you'd call it a crime of opportunity.' Hank was back to the arrogant man they'd first met. Now that he was immune, his nerves and tears were long gone.

'As you might expect, foster kids get into trouble, a lot. Some are abused, but nearly all of them have some demons in their past. They get into drugs, fall in with the wrong crowd, or they simply run away. I realised long ago that no one seemed to notice. When you've got twenty kids screaming for attention, the quiet ones slip through the cracks. I know first-hand the consequences of that. One of my charges, a girl called Emily, ran away. I spent months looking for her. The foster parents didn't care, and nor did the police. All you lot did was put her on the missing persons list, but when you heard that she was a recreational drug user you soon lost interest.'

At the use of 'you', Kiaran was affronted. He wanted to defend the system, but there was some truth in Hank's accusation. He nodded encouragingly, desperate to hear the rest of the story.

'I found her eventually. She was in this slum that belonged to her dealer, lying on the floor among a bunch of other addicts. She was dead, and they hadn't even noticed. It was a heroin overdose. I was distraught. I panicked, and instead of calling the police, I tried to call my sister on her landline for a shoulder to cry on. Her husband, Dimitri Bakowski, answered. Where I saw tragedy, he saw an opportunity. He told me all about this girl he knew, Alina. He told me Alina was living in a slum back in Kiev. She was the same age as Emily, and the same height. Tiny told me she was half starving, had been beaten by her stepfather, and that she deserved better. Looking back, I'm sure it was all a lie, but I believed it.'

'So I told Emily's foster carers that we'd found her, and moved her on as she was clearly in need of closer supervision than they could provide. I told Children's Services a similar story. That's when Alina took Emily's place. I coached her in English for a while, helped her to adjust. A few months later, she was adopted. I saw just her before Christmas. She's grown up into an amazing young woman.'

'But it didn't stop with Alina?' Kiaran asked.

Hank shook his head sadly, 'No. Kids kept going missing. Not enough to arouse any interest from Children's Services, but it wasn't long before I suspected Tiny might be involved. For a while, I stuck my head in the sand and tried to pretend I was helping. The gifts Tiny bestowed on me helped. My sister adores him, and he was good to me. He bought me my car, albeit in my sister's name. He gave me the money you found.'

Kiaran leant forward, enthralled. 'What happened when you realised what was going on?'

'I couldn't look myself in the mirror. I tried to end it all. Pills. Obviously, it didn't work. I consoled myself that I was helping some children have the lives they deserve. Tried to convince myself I was doing good. But in the end, I was as guilty as Tiny. Whenever I had a kid changing foster homes that looked like one of Tiny's kids, he made my charge disappear and brought me a kid fresh from the Ukraine. I simply took them to the next foster family, and looked the other way. I also edited the computer records for my charges, using a password I watched my boss type in. She's too stupid to use a proper password, and I added a disposable email address to the recovery details on her account. Even when she changed it, I simply sent myself a reminder then carried on using her account.'

'And what about Charlie?'

'He was like the rest. After a while, Tiny perfected the con. He primed the kids back in Kiev, to make sure they learnt enough English to pass muster. I don't know how he found Kolia.'

'Kolia?'

'That's the boy's real name. The one living as Charles Matthews. No one was looking out for the real Charlie. His parents are gone, and so are the Grants. He had nothing and no one. So when I had to drive him to the Lovejoys, I gave him a cola laced with a sedative. One of Tiny's lackeys did the rest. I met them in an empty car park, swapped the kids, and then dropped Kolia off in Charlie's place.'

'You said one of Tiny's lackeys. Who was that?'

'It was usually one of his brothers. Nicodemus and Pavel do all the dirty work, or supervise it at least. The time with Charlie, both of them showed up.'

Hank's voice was becoming hoarse, so he gestured for his cup of water to be refilled. When he'd had a sip, he continued: 'The next thing I know, you're looking at Kolia and questioning him about Charlie's past. I tried to coach him, but I didn't know enough about the real Charlie to give Kolia the right backstory, so I told him to keep his answers short and pretend to forget if he couldn't think of something good. I thought your detective – Vaughn, wasn't it? – I thought she might be onto me when I ended the interview prematurely.

'So, when we thought the net was closing in, I had one of Tiny's goons distract you. I don't know the name of the hacker we used but from what I gather the guy emailed in one of your anonymous tips, and managed to put a key logger on your network. Detective Chief Inspector Morton didn't even notice when we emptied all of his accounts. What Tiny didn't expect to happen was for Detective Vaughn to investigate some low-level credit card fraud. The woman's a bloodhound. She came in when I was carving up the Linden couple. I hit her, knocked her out cold. I called Tiny, and thought he'd take care of it. He said no, that he didn't kill cops unless he had to, and told me to grow a pair and sort out my own problems.'

'What did you do then?'

'I locked her up. Tiny has many houses, and one of them has a soundproofed basement. It was originally a wine cellar. I stashed your detective in there. Eventually, I decided she'd never seen me, and so I dumped her in Brockwell Park Gardens. No harm, no foul,' Hank said dispassionately, as if he were recounting someone else's actions. Kiaran shuddered at his callousness.

'That's where you're wrong. She's dead,' Kiaran said.

'She's dead? But she was still breathing just fine when I left her.' Hank turned to his lawyer. 'They can't pin this on me. Can they?'

'Nope, you're covered by the Immunity Notice,' Elliot Morgan-Bryant said.

'But you were behind the credit fraud perpetrated against Detective Morton?'

'Yes. I had one of Tiny's goons do it. Tiny didn't even know about it. I wanted to distract Morton from looking too closely at us.'

Elliot Morgan-Bryant looked like he wanted to slap his client. 'Shut up! Now.'

'What? It worked, didn't it?' Hank smiled.

'Oh, it worked all right. But you just shot yourself in the foot,' Morgan-Bryant fumed.

It was Kiaran's turn to smile. 'Your lawyer is right. Your immunity covers crimes committed at the behest of the Bakowskis. The identity theft was your own initiative.'

Hank looked like someone had slapped him, his eyes going wide in shock. Kiaran pressed a security buzzer under the desk, summoning an officer. A minute later, Morton came running in.

'David, Hank here has just confessed to being behind all your identity theft problems. Would you care to arrest him?'

Morton glared at Hank, and then his eyes began to dance. 'With pleasure.'

'Wait, wait!' Elliot Morgan-Bryan tried a last ditch attempt to save his client.

'You've forgotten one thing.'

'Which is?'

'If you prosecute my client, then it becomes public knowledge that those kids are here illegally. That means every one of them will have to be deported.'

Morton paled, but Kiaran replied firmly, 'That's not my problem.'

'Legally, maybe not, but I hope it doesn't weigh too heavily on your conscience, detective,' Elliot Morgan-Bryant said.

***

'David, I need to know: are you with me on this?' Kiaran O'Connor asked, as he and Morton walked out of the interview suite.

'I thought it was out of my hands anyway.' Morton tried to avoid the question, facing straight ahead as they walked down the corridor. *As if you care. You've already gone over my head on this,* Morton thought angrily.

'I saw your face in that interview. Elliot Morgan-Bryant is an ass. But he's right. Those children are here illegally. The UK Border Agency may well decide to deport them if only to make a political statement about human trafficking. If they let the children stay then they'll look weak.'

McNamara's eyes flared angrily. He knew first-hand that the law was fallible. But he stayed silent as they walked towards the elevator.

Kiaran took a deep breath, then said: 'We've got a choice: prosecute the Bakowskis for the trafficking racket and harm the children, or turn a blind eye.'

They reached the end of the corridor, where Morton hit the up button to call a lift. The nearest lift pinged open immediately and they stepped inside.

'Kiaran, they're not the victims. The victim is Charles Matthews, and he's on ice down in the morgue. Prosecuting Hank won't bring him back, but it will give him some justice.'

'I know that, but... he's dead. Like you said, anything we achieve in court isn't going to bring him back. The other kids, they're still alive. If we deport them, we will be sending them back to poverty. It was bad enough that their parents paid to have them brought here. The right thing to do here is to protect the living.'

The lift pinged as the doors opened for Kiaran's door. As he stepped out, Morton said: 'Kiaran, it's your call. I know what I think we should do. Think it over. Charles Matthews deserves justice.'

***

'Move,' McNamara barked. He stood behind Hank Williams as they headed for the holding cells. Hank had yet to be charged, but with every step they took, McNamara felt himself grow angrier. Adrenaline flowed through him as he pushed and prodded Hank onwards.

Hank had been allocated a cell to himself, a luxury McNamara didn't believe he deserved. Shove him in with the drunks and the rapists, McNamara thought harshly.

It didn't help that Hank had taken to mimicking McNamara's singsong lilt: 'I'll be free tomorrow. Top of the morning, I'm telling ya. You think you've got me, but you need me too much. Your prosecutor will never charge me.'

'I'm telling you for the last time, shut the hell up,' McNamara yelled.

'What you going to do, big man? I killed one of your own, and you can't even touch me,' Hank spat as they made it to his cell.

With one enormous hand, McNamara grabbed Hank by the throat and slammed him against the cell wall, then kicked the cell door shut with one foot as Hank tried to cry out for help. As McNamara let go, Hank slid down to the floor sobbing loudly. 'Never. Speak. To. Me. Again.'

With each word, McNamara rained down a flurry of punches on Hank. A security guard came running, but in the time it took to unhook a key and thrust it into the cell door, the damage was done. Hank was a bloody pulp.

'We need a doctor down here!' The security guard pulled McNamara away from Hank, up and out of the cell before returning to tend to the suspect's wounds.

The next few minutes were a flurry of activity as medical help arrived, shunting past McNamara to get to Hank. McNamara was in a daydream, barely aware of the nurse who bandaged up his hands.

It was only when Morton arrived on scene, angrier than he had ever been, that McNamara began to come out of his stupor.

'Detective McNamara, you're on suspension, effective immediately. Give me your badge, now.'

***

Sarah was waiting when David Morton made it home. As usual, he took off his shoes and coat, then marched towards the lounge and plonked himself down in the largest armchair.

'Long day?' Sarah asked, tightening the fabric belt around her dressing gown. Coq au vin and a bottle of champagne on ice waited in the kitchen.

'The longest. Xander Thompson screwed my case.'

Sarah sighed, then reached for the kettle, and poured out two cups of tea. Her romantic evening was over before it had begun. She snatched a custard cream and headed for the sofa before replying. 'The lead detective at the Serious Organised Crime Agency? What did he do?'

'He offered my suspect immunity to flip on his paymasters. It was an ambush: both the Superintendent and the Attorney General had signed off on the deal before they let me know. After that, the suspect confessed to two counts of murder, and I can't do a damn thing about that. Worse still, my new guy Alfie McNamara beat the shit out of him.'

'Why? He should know better.'

'I wish I could have, to be honest. Hank Williams is scum. He's also the scum behind our identity theft problems.' Morton gestured at the growing pile of 'final demands' on the counter dividing the living room from the kitchen.

'You're kidding? The same guy? Does this mean the bank will refund us now?'

'I suppose so. Can you phone Teddy tomorrow and ask him? I'll email a transcript of Hank's confession over for you to pass on.'

Sarah nodded, 'Of course.'

'The thing that's really bugging me is the kid. The Bakowskis have been trafficking children from the Ukraine. Once we start prosecuting, that becomes public. They could be deported.'

'I'm sorry, but there's nothing you can do about that. The law is the law. You can't take responsibility for everyone all the time.'

'I know, but...'

'No excuses, David,' Sarah interrupted. 'Do you even know what day it is?'

Morton squinted through at the calendar pinned to the kitchen wall, February fourteenth. 'Oh God. Sarah, I'm sorry.'

'It's OK. At least you already gave me my present.' Sarah smiled.

'Have you opened it?' Morton asked.

'No, I thought we could exchange gifts together.' She bounded out of the room to go fetch the parcel Morton had tried to give her back at Tina's apartment. It was very flat, about a foot long and half as wide.

'What is it? It's really heavy.'

'Just open it, woman.'

Sarah grabbed at the ends of the bow with which the parcel had been tied, and gently pulled them in opposite directions. The ribbon came loose, and Sarah pried off the lid. Inside, wrapped in tissue paper, was a blank granite slate. Confusion spread across her features, and Morton laughed.

'Flip it over.'

She did, and on the other side of the slate she found a poem engraved in grey, shining against black stone.

What is love?
It can strike at a moment's notice.
It can build to a crescendo.
It can make your heart pump faster,
It can set your tummy all aflutter.
A yearning, a connection beyond all others.
True love is not false. It is not based on looks, pretences or things.

True love is being comfortable in your own skin, warts and all.

Love is there through thick and thin, supporting you through the bad and redoubling the joy in the good.

Love is putting the other person's happiness before your own. It is a sort of delirium, but one you want to endure. It is the pain you feel when they aren't there, the sparkle in your eye and the spring in your step.

Love is the song in your heart, the rhythm that shapes and nurtures. Love is based on trust, honesty and a connection.

You click from the start, and it builds from there. Every trial and tribulation you go through together is a building block, a tower towards the heavens.

But you have no need of such a tower, for love is heaven on Earth.

Sarah looked up, locking eyes with her husband. He said, 'It's made of granite. I thought it was poetic. It's fragile, but if you treat it right, it'll last forever.'

'David...' Sarah was speechless.

'So where's my gift?'

'Right here.' Sarah tugged at the fabric belt, and her dressing gown fell to the floor.

Chapter 50: Rule of Law

It was barely nine o'clock when Morton knocked on the door of Alfie McNamara. The Irishman took almost ten minutes to answer, and when he did so, it quickly became apparent that he had endured a fitful night.

'What the feck do you want?' McNamara squinted at Morton's outline shadowed in the morning sunlight.

'I want to talk to you. Can I come in?' Morton stepped forward as Alfie bowed mockingly to welcome him.

'You here to charge me?'

'No. I don't think it'd be too wise for Hank Williams to make any complaint against you. It was still stupid, but I understand why you did it.'

'He killed a child and a cop, and he laughed about it. That scum deserved it.'

'No comment. I'm afraid you will remain on suspension, unpaid, until a hearing next month.'

'It's still worth it.'

'You've got the right to have a union rep or a lawyer present, and the details will come in the post soon enough, but I wanted to tell you in person.'

'What will happen to Williams?'

'Nothing. The deal stands. He will help bring down the Bakowskis, and then disappear into the moonlight.'

'That's crap, and you know it. He deserves jail. No more, no less.'

'I agree. But it's out of my hands. O'Connor gets that decision. If he prosecutes Hank for identity theft, Hank could tank our case against the Bakowskis. He's got to testify, but even the slightest slip could be reasonable doubt. And if we do prosecute, the kids who are here illegally don't have the right to remain.'

'The kids'll be deported?'

'Yep. And if we don't prosecute, then the Bakowskis will find another Hank, and start up all over again.'

'Then we've got no choice.'

'I agree. We owe more to the future victims than we do to those trafficked. Justice demands that we prosecute. All we have to do is convince Kiaran. You want to come along?'

'What else have I got to do?'

***

Once Kiaran made the decision to prosecute, and to bring Hank up on the charge of identity theft, the paperwork began to fly. In short order, arrest warrants were issued for the Bakowski brothers, and Hank was formally charged. In what seemed like no time at all, Kiaran found himself once more inside a magistrate's courtroom, this time for Hank Williams' bail hearing.

Hank sat in the dock, his hands folded forlornly as if he were the victim. His left eye was black and purple, with lacerations clearly visible on his face and neck. Kiaran winced as he looked over: Alfie McNamara had really done a number on Hank, and in turn had made Kiaran's job much more difficult.

'All rise!' the court's clerk called as the magistrates filed in.

Kiaran stood slowly, being careful not to disturb his wig, which had the awkward habit of leaning lopsidedly at the slightest movement. He had a folder on the desk with all the facts, but no intention of referring to it. Bail hearings were always simple, and this would be no exception. Hank enjoyed the presumption that bail would be given. It would be up to Kiaran to make the case for remand, and Elliot Morgan-Bryant, who was standing to Kiaran's side, to make the case for bail.

The magistrate gestured impatiently, and Kiaran began his argument: 'Hank Williams is charged with the identity theft of a police officer. He has relatives abroad, and represents a flight risk. Further, we believe his personal security is best assured by keeping him on remand.'

Kiaran paused. He was limited by the rules on bad character evidence, which constricted what he was able to say. He glanced at the public gallery where Morton, Ayala and McNamara waited, then grimaced almost imperceptibly. It wasn't likely Hank would run, not if doing so meant he got convicted for murder.

The magistrate sat in the centre of the bench waved for Kiaran to sit down. Elliot Morgan-Bryant rose to make Hank's case.

'Hank Williams is a hard-working public servant. For twelve years, he has worked as a social worker in London helping the most disadvantaged. As well as having a stable job, he is a home-owner who has lived at his current address for almost twenty years. Mr Williams has strong family ties in the area, and is an active participant in his local community. He has volunteered at his local church for almost his entire adult life.' Elliot Morgan-Bryant paused to look between the three magistrates to gauge how hostile they were.

'My client is accused of a white-collar crime, and has no prior criminal record. Hank Williams is not a flight risk, and there has been no suggestion that he would go on to commit further crimes whilst on bail. However, as a gesture of goodwill, he would like to offer to surrender his passport to the court.'

The magistrate sniffed derisively. 'We will decide the conditions of bail, Mr Morgan-Bryant. Would you care to address the point the prosecution made about security?'

'My client is, as you can see, over six feet tall. He is a second Dan black belt, and has military training. He is willing to assume any risk to his person.'

'Then bail is granted. Mr Williams is hereby released upon his own recognisance.'

Hank smiled as he was led out. Morton stepped forward to offer protection, but Hank sneered at the offer. Hank Williams was a free man.

***

Sarah bounced on her heels as she skipped down High Holborn towards the fancy restaurant she had texted David to meet her at. When she arrived, he was waiting outside by a doorman dressed in top hat and tails.

'Sarah, what are we doing here? This place is seriously pricey.'

'Having lunch,' she chirped.

'Does this mean...?' Morton gulped nervously.

'Yes. Teddy's done it. The witness statement was enough to get the banks to agree it wasn't our fault. Teddy threatened them with the bad press of being associated with child trafficking, and they caved. We've got all our money back!' Sarah smiled, and Morton felt the tension of the last few weeks melt away.

He threw his arms around his wife. 'That's wonderful!'

'Isn't it? I have another surprise for you too.'

'What is it? You know I hate surprises.'

'I booked it.'

'Booked what?'

'The holiday. I saw your emails cancelling everything, but I want to go on a second honeymoon too. It's a wonderful idea. We leave on the twenty-eighth!'

'Our fake wedding anniversary? We should just tell everyone.'

'Never, it's our little secret. Let's go inside, it's freezing out here.'

Chapter 51: Unexpected

Three days after he was granted bail, Hank was found hanging in the stairwell of his apartment. A thick rope was tied in a noose around his neck, tied in the classic hangman's style with thirteen coils.

'They say thirteen is unlucky,' Dr Larry Chiswick said when he saw Morton staring.

'It certainly was for him. Are you going to cut him down, Larry?'

'Give an old man a moment. We've only just photographed him.' Chiswick nonetheless went to the top of the stairs, walked around the banister and began to saw at the nylon rope. Each layer began to fray in turn, and when there were only two or three left, he called down to Morton: 'You got him? I don't want any post-mortem injuries to assess.'

Morton grabbed Hank's corpse around the waist, and Larry cut the last strands of rope.

As he staggered under Hank's weight, Morton cursed the dead social worker: 'Stupid bastard. He should have taken our offer of protection.'

Morton laid the corpse down at the base of the stairs, then backed away to let Chiswick examine the body.

'Protection? You can't protect him from himself,' Chiswick said as he jabbed a metal probe into Hank's corpse. He held it in place for a few moments, then pulled it out and read the temperature from the top.

'It's pretty warm in here, so he's probably been dead about seven hours, putting time of death at nine o'clock this morning. Odd time for a suicide, just when the sun is coming up.'

'You can't seriously think this is a suicide? He's the key witness against the Bakowski brothers. Without him, we haven't a leg to stand on.'

'Looks like it to me. The noose is tied over the correct shoulder for a right-handed man, and it looks like a classic suspension drop to me. You see any signs of a struggle?'

'Nope.' Morton looked around. The flat was spotless, almost too tidy.

'There you are then. Find me something suspicious, and I'll take it into account. The whole inquest will take months at the least. Our department is still dealing with the Christmas backlog.' Chiswick finished photographing the body, and straightened up. His spine clicked, and Chiswick rubbed at his back in anguish.

'You alright, Doc?'

'Getting old, that's all.'

***

'You can't go in there. Mr O'Connor is busy,' a secretary protested. Morton ignored them, stopping for only a second to knock once before he opened the door to Kiaran's office.

'What the hell do you think you're doing?' Kiaran yelled. He was staring into the full-length mirror on the wall, wearing only his boxers and a shirt while rehearsing a closing speech. At the sight of Morton, he dived behind his desk.

'Wow, the CPS really takes dress-down Friday seriously,' Morton quipped.

'My trousers are being ironed: I spilt a coffee down them and I need them clean for court. Besides, I thought that door was locked.'

'Right,' Morton said, choosing not to ask why the lawyer didn't keep a spare pair in his office. It wasn't as if there was a lack of room.

'So?'

'I assume you've heard.'

'That Hank Williams is dead? Yeah, I know.'

'You don't seem overly concerned.'

'It's no big deal. A dead witness might be good for us. You can't cross-examine a witness statement. I'll just apply for his confession to stand as his evidence.'

'The Bakowskis killed him.'

Kiaran folded his lower lip over his upper lip, and shrugged. 'Like I care. My case is solid, and that guy wasn't the most pleasant chap in the world. We're better off without him.'

'If the Bakowskis are knocking off witnesses, won't that make a conviction impossible?'

'Naw. From Hank's list of names, we've got a cornucopia of circumstantial evidence. Jurors are unsympathetic with child killers. Once you catch the Bakowskis, I'll get the conviction.'

Morton sat down suddenly, the exhaustion of the investigation finally hitting him. He placed his head in his hands, and smiled.

Kiaran continued, 'And I've got even better news. You know I said we had a danger of the kids being deported?'

Morton looked up. 'Yes.'

'The Home Secretary has agreed to a blanket grant of leave to remain. We won't even need emergency legislation, as he's got the power to do it if he thinks they might be re-trafficked. Any kids who have parents to go back to, we'll send them back – if that's what they want. If not, we'll find every one of them a home here. A good one.'

'That's fantastic news. You know I'm no fan of lawyers, Kiaran, but you're one of the good ones. I'm glad you're on our side.'

Chapter 52: Flee

Mere hours after the death of Hank Williams, Nicodemus and Pavel Bakowski emptied their bank accounts. Neither had amassed the fortune of their brother, but it still amounted to over £3,000,000 in cash.

Unfortunately for them, modern banking had proved much too clever for them. In order to withdraw such a large amount, they had to provide Coutts with twenty-four hours' notice that they needed the money. The bank immediately alerted the authorities, as the Bakowskis' accounts had been flagged by the police.

When Nicodemus and Pavel parked outside Coutts in Chandler's Ford, near Southampton's international ferry port, Morton and Ayala were waiting on the opposite side of the road.

Morton watched as the brothers walked into the bank.

'Aren't we going to nick them now, Chief?' Ayala reached for the door handle, ready for a confrontation.

'Bertram, what have I said about your lack of subtlety? If we grab them now, all we've got them on is going into a bank. That means an expensive trial for the taxpayer, and lots of time in court for us. We're smarter than that. We'll use this.' Morton held up a GPS tracker, which he'd already paired with an app on his BlackBerry.

Morton stepped out of the car, crossed the busy main road to where the Bakowskis had parked their car and tucked the tracker above the back left tyre where it wouldn't be seen. He checked his phone to make sure the tracker's location appeared properly, then slinked back across the road through a gap in traffic.

'Now what?' Ayala demanded.

'Now we wait, and see where they go. My money says they'll flee the country. They've chosen this branch for a reason. It isn't near home, so either they're heading to Southampton Airport, or they're heading to the docks. If we catch them red-handed fleeing the country, Kiaran's going to have an easy time getting a conviction.'

'Won't their passports get flagged?'

'I doubt they're travelling under their real names. They've not survived this long without going to prison by being that thick. Hang on, they're coming out. Don't look.'

Morton pulled a map out of the glove compartment, and made a fuss as if he was checking it. Once he heard the motor of the Bakowskis' car purr, he dropped the act and watched them drive off into the distance.

'Now we follow them.'

***

Pavel and Nico Bakowski pulled into the car park by the Southampton City ferry terminal. They'd taken their brother's advice, and booked onto a cruise ship rather than a simple ferry. The Queen Boudicca would carry them to Barcelona. From there, it was an easy train ride to meet up with Tiny at the rendezvous point. Nico glanced sadly behind him at his car, which was now parked under a Pay & Display sign declaring that the maximum parking time was thirty minutes. A traffic warden would be along in no time to slap a ticket on it, and eventually have the car towed, but there was no way Nico could take it with him.

Pavel carried a duffle bag containing their savings, and led the way towards the double doors into the terminal. A row of taxis was parked outside, and Pavel barely noticed the black saloon parked behind at the back.

Nico paused to pat his inside jacket pocket, checking that he had the fake papers Tiny had supplied. Once he was satisfied they were still there, he followed his brother into the terminal.

***

'There they go. Let them try and board, then they've got nowhere to run. Go grab an official now, let them know we're here,' Morton ordered. Ayala sauntered off towards the ticket office to stop the boat's leaving without them. There was plenty of time; it wasn't due to leave for twenty minutes yet.

Morton waited outside, peering through the glass at the queue. When the Bakowski brothers were a few places from the front, and ready to have their passports checked by the sole UK Boarder Agency staff member on duty, he followed Ayala inside.

It was a small waiting hall, designed to deal with the traffic for only two cruise ships at a time, but it was still filled with hundreds of gaudily dressed tourists. The crowd was predominantly white, and mostly middle-aged, so Morton had no doubt he'd be able to spot the Bakowskis with ease, but there was potential for civilian casualties if it turned out the Bakowskis were armed.

Morton slipped into the queue, briefly flashing his badge at an elderly woman as he did so. He was now less than ten feet from the brothers. Ayala nodded from the other side of the security gate. The brothers were allowed through, and didn't set off the metal detector. Morton followed them through customs: Ayala had been thorough, and the border official waved him through without hindrance.

Morton closed in as the brothers headed for the boarding ramp, and Ayala cut them off.

'Nicodemus and Pavel Bakowski, you're both under arrest for travelling on a false passport.' Morton pulled out his handcuffs, spun Nicodemus around and slapped the cuffs down on his wrists, tightening them until they became uncomfortable. Ayala did the same to Pavel.

'You do not have to say anything, but it may harm your defence if you do not mention, when questioned, something you later rely on in court. Anything you do say may be given in evidence.'

'We want a lawyer,' Nico declared immediately.

'Sure, but first: where's your brother?'

'He's long gone.'

'Where?'

'Abroad,' Nico said with a wicked grin.

'Don't know what you're smiling about. Two out of three isn't bad. Let's go.'

Morton and Ayala frog marched the pair back towards customs. It was over: with the brothers caught red-handed, conviction would be a slam dunk.

Chapter 53: Fegato Alla Veneziana

Morton kicked back in his armchair, being careful to keep quiet to avoid disturbing Sarah. She had fallen asleep after dining at a family-owned restaurant on nearby Torcello Island. It had been too cold to eat al fresco, but the delicious *fegato alla veneziana* made the trip to the windswept isle worthwhile. To his side, his wife slept soundly on the king-size bed that would be theirs for the three nights they had left in Venice. Her chest rose and fell gently under Egyptian cotton sheets.

After Sarah had begun to snore, Morton had snuck down to the hotel shop to pick up a British newspaper, and had come away with his wallet almost three pounds lighter for the privilege. He flicked to page four, which contained the follow-up to the headline that had caught his eye.

'Ukranian gang leaders Pavel and Nicodemus Bakowski have been convicted following a high-profile child trafficking trial this week. The number two and three on Interpol's Most Wanted List were arrested trying to board a cruise ship out of Southampton docks, bound for Bilbao. They had almost £3 million in cash hidden inside the lining of a roll-on suitcase, money the police believe came from their criminal activities which included trafficking and high-level drug smuggling. The brothers were sought by Scotland Yard in connection with a child trafficking investigation, and are accused of murdering British, French and Spanish children then selling their identities to Ukrainian parents, whose children would be substituted for their European counterparts during routine changes of foster parents. The prosecuting authorities have agreed to waive the right to deport the affected children, and have put in place plans to allow the children to be put up for adoption if it proves impossible to reunite them with their birth parents. A British suspect, Hank Williams of Greenwich, was found hanged in his apartment last month. The coroner has ruled the death a suicide, bringing the British leg of the investigation to a close.

'However, the true ringleader of the scam, Dimitri 'Tiny' Bakowski is still at large. While his brothers led the police towards Southampton, he escaped under an assumed name on the Eurostar, where the trail ends. He is currently believed to be in Romania. His assets have been seized, and Dimitri Bakowski is no longer the kingpin of a criminal empire, but members of the public are urged not to approach him. Instead anyone with information should call Crimestoppers on 08008 555 111. A reward of £50,000 for information leading to his arrest and conviction has been posted by the Organisation to Combat Human Trafficking.'

A sense of contentment spread through Morton. He was in his wife's good books. The identity theft was behind him, and even Rick Houton had turned up safe and sound. The single fly in the ointment was that Alfie McNamara's disciplinary hearing was due to happen while Morton was away. The Superintendent would probably fire him, which was a shame as Morton was beginning to like the junior officer.

The trafficked children would be safe, and those responsible were largely behind bars. Morton's gut told him that it would be down to him to hunt down Tiny Bakowski one day. But not today. He had one more week travelling with his wife. Work could wait.

Chapter 54: Family

Kolia held his small bag in his left hand, and clutched his teddy to his chest with his other hand. The name tag attached to the bag had been scribbled out in black felt tip. He no longer had to pretend any more.

For months now, he'd lived a lie. He'd pretended to be called Charlie, and to be English. It was usually scary to be moving on, but as Kolia stood on the doorstep of 36B Cleaver Square, the harsh chill of winter seemed somehow inviting. The Lattimers hadn't bothered to see him out. As soon as the door was shut, they turned away. Only the face of James Lattimer in an upstairs window hinted at the life Kolia was leaving behind.

'Come on, son, it's freezing out here,' Mr Neil said, holding the door to his Land Rover open. Mrs Neil sat in the driver seat, beaming at Kolia.

Kolia ran forward, and jumped into the back of the car. Mr Neil checked the boy's seatbelt, then shut the door to the back and climbed into the passenger seat.

'You want some music on?' Mr Neil gestured at the radio.

Kolia nodded, and a shiver ran down his spine as he realised he was finally going home.